PYLON

BOOKS BY WILLIAM FAULKNER

The Marble Faun (1924)

Soldier's Pay (1926)

Mosquitoes (1927)

Sartoris (1929) [*Flags in the Dust* (1973)]

The Sound and the Fury (1929)

As I Lay Dying (1930)

Sanctuary (1931)

These 13 (1931)

Light in August (1932)

A Green Bough (1933)

Doctor Martino and Other Stories (1934)

Pylon (1935)

Absalom, Absalom! (1936)

The Unvanquished (1938)

The Wild Palms [*If I Forget Thee, Jerusalem*] (1939)

The Hamlet (1940)

Go Down, Moses (1942)

Intruder in the Dust (1948)

Knight's Gambit (1949)

Collected Stories of William Faulkner (1950)

Notes on a Horsethief (1951)

Requiem for a Nun (1954)

A Fable (1954)

Big Woods (1955)

The Town (1957)

The Mansion (1959)

The Reivers (1962)

Uncollected Stories of William Faulkner (1979, Posthumous)

William Faulkner

PYLON

The Corrected Text

VINTAGE INTERNATIONAL

Vintage Books

A Division of Random House, Inc.

New York

FIRST VINTAGE INTERNATIONAL EDITION, OCTOBER 2011

Library of Congress Cataloging-in-Publication Data
Faulkner, William.
Pylon / William Faulkner.
p. cm.
I. Title.
PS3511.A86P9 1987 813'.52 86-40166

Vintage ISBN: 978-0-307-94678-2

www.vintagebooks.com

Printed in the United States of America

CONTENTS

PUBLISHER'S NOTE

The copy-text for this edition is Faulkner's typescript setting copy, which—under the direction of Noel Polk and
Joseph Blotner—has been compared with the incomplete holograph manuscript and the corrected galleys.
An editors' note on the corrections by Noel Polk follows
the text; the line and page notes have been prepared by
Joseph Blotner.

PYLON

Dedication of an Airport

F or a full minute Jiggs stood before the window in a light spatter of last night's confetti lying against the windowbase like spent dirty foam, lightpoised on the balls of his grease-stained tennis shoes, looking at the boots. Slantshimmered by the intervening plate they sat upon their wooden pedestal in unblemished and inviolate implication of horse and spur, of the posed countrylife photographs in the magazine adver-tisements, beside the easelwise cardboard placard with which the town had bloomed overnight as it had with the purple-and-gold tissue bunting and the trodden confetti and broken serpentine—the same lettering, the same photo-graphs of the trim vicious fragile aeroplanes and the pilots leaning upon them in gargantuan irrelation as if the aero-planes were a species of esoteric and fatal animals not trained or tamed but just for the instant inert, above the neat brief legend of name and accomplishment or perhaps just hope.

He entered the store, his rubber soles falling in quick

hissing thuds on pavement and iron sill and then upon the tile floor of that museum of glass cases lighted suave and sourceless by an unearthly daycolored substance in which the hats and ties and shirts, the beltbuckles and cufflinks and handkerchiefs, the pipes shaped like golfclubs and the drinking tools shaped like boots and barnyard fowls and the minute impedimenta for wear on ties and vestchains shaped like bits and spurs, resembled biologic specimens put into the inviolate preservative before they had ever been breathed into. "Boots?" the clerk said. "The pair in the window?"

"Yair," Jiggs said. "How much?" But the clerk did not even move. He leaned back on the counter, looking down at the hard tough shortchinned face, blueshaven, with a long threadlike and recently-stanched razorcut on it and in which the hot brown eyes seemed to snap and glare like a boy's approaching for the first time the aerial wheels and stars and serpents of a nighttime carnival; at the filthy raked swaggering peaked cap, the short thick musclebound body like the photographs of the one who two years before was lightmiddleweight champion of the army or Marine Corps or navy; the cheap breeches overcut to begin with and now skintight like both they and their wearer had been recently and hopelessly rained on and enclosing a pair of short stocky thick fast legs like a polo pony's, which descended into the tops of a pair of boots footless now and secured by two rivetted straps beneath the insteps of the tennis shoes.

"They are twenty-two and a half," the clerk said.

"All right. I'll take them. How late do you keep open at night?"

"Until six."

"Hell. I'll be out at the airport then. I wont get back to

town until seven. How about getting them then?" Another clerk came up: the manager, the floorwalker.

"You mean you dont want them now?" the first said.

"No," Jiggs said. "How about getting them at seven?"

"What is it?" the second clerk said.

"Says he wants a pair of boots. Says he cant get back from the airport before seven oclock."

The second looked at Jiggs. "You a flyer?"

"Yair," Jiggs said. "Listen. Leave a guy here. I'll be back by seven. I'll need them tonight."

The second also looked down at Jiggs' feet. "Why not take them now?"

Jiggs didn't answer at all. He just said, "So I'll have to wait until tomorrow."

"Unless you can get back before six," the second said.

"O.K.," Jiggs said. "All right, mister. How much do you want down?" Now they both looked at him: at the face, the hot eyes: the appearance entire articulate and complete, badge regalia and passport, of an oblivious and incorrigible insolvency. "To keep them for me. That pair in the window."

The second looked at the first. "Do you know his size?"

"That's all right about that," Jiggs said. "How much?"

The second looked at Jiggs. "You pay ten dollars and we will hold them for you until tomorrow."

"Ten dollars? Jesus, mister. You mean ten percent. I could pay ten percent. down and buy an airplane."

"You want to pay ten percent. down?"

"Yair. Ten percent. Call for them this afternoon if I can get back from the airport in time."

"That will be two and a quarter," the second said. When Jiggs put his hand into his pocket they could follow it, fingernail and knuckle, the entire length of the pocket like watching the ostrich in the movie cartoon swallow the alarm clock. It emerged a fist and opened upon a wadded dollar bill and coins of all sizes. He put the bill into the first clerk's hand and began to count the coins onto the bill.

"There's fifty," he said. "Seventy-five. And fifteen's ninety, and twenty-five is. . . . . . ." His voice stopped; he became motionless, with the twenty-five cent piece in his left hand and a half dollar and four nickels on his right palm. The clerks watched him put the quarter back into his right hand and take up the four nickels. "Let's see," he said. "We had ninety, and twenty will be——"

"Two dollars and ten cents," the second said. "Take back two nickels and give him the quarter."

"Two and a dime," Jiggs said. "How about taking that down?"

"You were the one who suggested ten percent."

"I cant help that. How about two and a dime?"

"Take it," the second said. The first took the money and went away. Again the second watched Jiggs' hand move downward along his leg, and then he could even see the two coins at the end of the pocket, through the soiled cloth.

"Where do you get this bus to the airport?" Jiggs said. The other told him. Now the first returned, with the cryptic scribbled duplicate of the sale; and now they both looked into the hot interrogation of the eyes.

"They will be ready for you when you call," the second said.

"Yair; sure," Jiggs said. "But get them out of the window."

"You want to examine them?"

"No. I just want to see them come out of that window."

So again outside the window, his rubber soles resting upon that light confettispatter more forlorn than spattered paint since it had neither inherent weight nor cohesiveness to hold it anywhere, which even during the time that Jiggs was in the store had decreased, thinned, vanishing particle by particle into nothing like foam does, he stood until the hand came into the window and drew the boots out. Then he went on, walking fast with his short bouncing curiously stiffkneed gait. When he turned into Grandlieu Street he could see a clock, though he was already hurrying or rather walking at his fast stiff hard gait like a mechanical toy that has but one speed and though the clock's face was still in the shadow of the opposite streetside and what sunlight there was was still high, diffused, suspended in soft refraction by the heavy damp bayou-and-swamp-suspired air. There was confetti here too, and broken serpentine, in neat narrow swept windrows against wallangles and lightly vulcanised along the gutter-rims by the flushing fireplugs of the past dawn, while, up-caught and pinned by the cryptic significant shields to doorfront and lamppost, the purple-and-gold bunting looped unbroken as a trolley wire above his head as he walked, turning at last at right angles to cross the street itself and meet that one on the opposite side making its angle too, to join over the center of the street as though to form an aerial and bottomless regalcolored cattlechute suspended at first floor level above the earth, and suspending beneath itself in turn, the outwardfacing cheeseclothlettered interdiction which Jiggs, passing, slowed looking back to read: *Grandlieu Street CLOSED To Traffic 8:00 P.M.–Midnight*

Now he could see the bus at the curb, where they had told him it would be, with its cloth banner fastened by the four corners across its broad stern to ripple and flap in motion, and the wooden sandwich board at the curb too: *Bluehound to Feinman Airport. 75¢* The driver stood beside the open door; he too watched Jiggs' knuckles travel the length of the pocket. "Airport?" Jiggs said.

"Yes," the driver said. "You got a ticket?"

"I got seventy-five cents. Wont that do?"

"A ticket into the airport. Or a workman's pass. The passenger busses dont begin to run until noon." Jiggs looked at the driver with that hot pleasant interrogation, holding his breeches by one hand while he drew the other out of the pocket. "Are you working out there?" the driver said.

"Oh," Jiggs said. "Sure. I'm Roger Shumann's mechanic. You want to see my license?"

"That'll be all right," the driver said. "Get aboard." In the driver's seat there lay folded a paper: one of the colored ones, the pink or the green editions of the diurnal dogwatches, with a thick heavy typesplattered front page filled with ejaculations and pictures. Jiggs paused, stooped, turning.

"Have a look at your paper, cap," he said. But the driver did not answer. Jiggs took up the paper and sat in the next seat and took from his shirt pocket a crumpled cigarette pack and upended and shook into his other palm from it two cigarette stubs and put the longer one back into the crumpled paper and into his shirt again and lit the shorter one, pursing it away from his face and slanting his head aside to keep the matchflame from his nose. Three more men entered the bus, two of them in overalls and the third in a kind of porter's cap made of or covered by purple-and-gold cloth in alternate stripes, and then the driver came and sat sideways in his seat.

"You got a ship in the race today, have you?" he said.

"Yair," Jiggs said. "In the three-seventy-five cubic inch."

"How does it look to you? Do you think you will have a chance?"

"We might if they would let us fly it in the two hundred cubic inch," Jiggs said. He took three quick draws from the cigarette stub like darting a stick at a snake and snapped it through the stillopen door as though it were the snake, or maybe a spider, and opened the paper. "Ship's obsolete. It was fast two years ago, but that's two years ago. We'd be O.K. now if they had just quit building racers when they finished the one we got. There aint another pilot out there except Shumann that could have even qualified it."

"Shumann's good, is he?"

"They're all good," Jiggs said, looking at the paper. It spread its pale green surface: heavy, blacksplotched, staccato: *Airport Dedication Special*; in the exact middle the photograph of a plump, bland, innocently sensual Levantine face beneath a raked fedora hat; the upper part of a thick body buttoned tight and soft into a peaked lightcolored double-breasted suit with a carnation in the lapel: the photograph inletted like a medallion into a drawing full of scrolled wings and propeller symbols which enclosed a shieldshaped pen-and-ink reproduction of something apparently cast in metal and obviously in existence somewhere and lettered in gothic relief:

FEINMAN AIRPORT
NEW VALOIS, FRANCIANA
DEDICATED TO
THE AVIATORS OF AMERICA
AND

COLONEL H. I. FEINMAN, CHAIRMAN,
SEWAGE BOARD
THROUGH WHOSE UNDEVIATING VISION AND
UNFLAGGING EFFORT THIS AIRPORT WAS RAISED UP
AND CREATED OUT OF THE WASTE LAND AT THE
BOTTOM OF LAKE RAMBAUD AT A COST OF
ONE MILLION DOLLARS

"This Feinman," Jiggs said. "He must be a big son of a bitch."

"He's a son of a bitch all right," the driver said. "I guess you'd call him big too."

"He gave you guys a nice airport, anyway," Jiggs said.

"Yair," the driver said. "Somebody did."

"Yair," Jiggs said. "It must have been him. I notice he's got his name on it here and there."

"Here and there; yair," the driver said. "In electric lights on both hangars and on the floor and the ceiling of the lobby and four times on each lamppost and a guy told me the beacon spells it too but I dont know about that because I dont know the Morse code."

"For Christ's sake," Jiggs said. Now a fair crowd of men, in the overalls or the purple-and-gold caps, appeared suddenly and began to enter the bus, so that for the time the scene began to resemble that comic stage one where the entire army enters one taxicab and drives away. But there was room for all of them and then the door swung in and the bus moved away and Jiggs sat back, looking out; the bus swung immediately away from Grandlieu Street and Jiggs watched himself plunging between iron balconies, catching fleeting glimpses of dirty paved courts as the bus seemed to rush with tremendous clatter and speed through cobbled streets which did not look wide enough to admit it, between low brick walls which seemed to sweat a rich slow overfecund smell of fish and coffee and sugar, and another odor profound faint and distinctive as a musty priest's robe: of some spartan effluvium of mediaeval convents.

Then the bus ran out of this and began to run, faster still, through a long avenue between palmbordered bearded liveoak groves and then suddenly Jiggs saw that the liveoaks stood not in earth but in water so motionless and thick as to make no reflection, as if it had been poured about the trunks and allowed to set; the bus ran suddenly past a row of flimsy cabins whose fronts rested upon the shell foundation of the road itself and whose rears rested upon stilts to which rowboats were tied and between which nets hung drying, and he saw that the roofs were thatched with the smokecolored growth which hung from the trees, before they flicked away and the bus ran again overarched by the oak boughs from which the moss hung straight and windless as the beards of old men sitting in the sun. "Jesus," Jiggs said. "If a man dont own a boat here he cant even go to the can, can he?"

"Your first visit down here?" the driver said. "Where you from?"

"Anywhere," Jiggs said. "The place I'm staying away from right now is Kansas."

"Family there, huh?"

"Yair. I got two kids there; I guess I still got the wife too."

"So you pulled out."

"Yair. Jesus, I couldn't even keep back enough to have my shoes halfsoled. Everytime I did a job her or the sheriff would catch the guy and get the money before I could tell

him I was through; I would make a parachute jump and one
of them would have the jack and be on the way back to town
before I even pulled the ripcord."

"For Christ's sake," the driver said.

"Yair," Jiggs said, looking out at the backrushing trees.
"This guy Feinman could spend some more of the money
giving these trees a haircut, couldn't he?" Now the bus, the
road, ran out of the swamp though without mounting, with
no hill to elevate it; it ran now upon a flat plain of sawgrass
and of cypress and oak stumps—a pocked desolation of some
terrific and apparently purposeless reclamation across which
the shell road ran ribbonblanched toward something low
and dead ahead of it—something low, unnatural: a chimaera
quality which for the moment prevented one from compre-
hending that it had been built by man and for a purpose.
The thick heavy air was full now of a smell thicker, heavier,
though there was yet no water in sight: there was only the soft
pale sharp chimaerashape above which pennons floated
against a further drowsy immensity which the mind knew
must be water, apparently separated from the flat earth by a
mirageline so that, taking shape now as a doublewinged
building, it seemed to float lightly like the apocryphal tur-
reted and battlemented cities in the colored Sunday sections, where beneath sillless and floorless arches people with
yellow and blue flesh pass and repass: myriad, purposeless,
and free from gravity. Now the bus, swinging, presented in
broadside the low broad main building with its two hangar-
wings, modernistic, crenelated, with its façade faintly Moor-
ish or Californian beneath the gold-and-purple pennons
whipping in a breeze definitely from water and giving to it an
air both aerial and aquatic like a mammoth terminal for

some species of machine of a yet unvisioned tomorrow, to
which air earth and water will be as one: and viewed from
the bus across a plaza of beautiful and incredible grass
labyrinthed by concrete driveways which Jiggs will not for
two or three days yet recognise to be miniature replicas of the
concrete runways on the field itself—a mathematic mono-
gram of two capital Fs laid by compass to all the winds. The
bus ran into one of these, slowing between the bloodless
grapes of lampglobes on bronze poles; as Jiggs got out he
stopped to look at the four Fs cast into the quadrants of the
base before going on.

He went around the main building and followed a narrow alley like a gutter, ending in a blank and knobless door;
he put his hand too among the handprints in oil or grease on
the door and pushed through it and into a narrow alcove
walled by neatly ranked and numbered tools from a sound,
a faint and cavernous murmur. The alcove contained a
lavatory, a row of hooks from which depended garments—
civilian shirts and coats, one pair of trousers with dangling
braces, the rest greasy dungarees, one of which Jiggs took
down and stepped into and bounced them lightly up and
around his shoulders all in one motion, already moving
toward a second door built mostly of chickenwire and
through which he could now see the hangar itself, the glass-
and-steel cavern, the aeroplanes, the racers. Waspwaisted,
wasplight, still, trim, vicious, small and immobile, they
seemed to poise without weight, as though made of paper
for the sole purpose of resting upon the shoulders of the
dungareeclad men about them. With their soft bright paint
tempered somewhat by the steelfiltered light of the hangar
they rested for the most part complete and intact, with what-

ever it was that the mechanics were doing to them of such a subtle and technical nature as to be invisible to the lay eye, save for one. Unbonneted, its spare entrails revealed as serrated top-and-bottomlines of delicate rockerarms and rods inferential in their very myriad delicacy of a weightless and terrific speed any momentary faltering of which would be the irreparable difference between motion and mere matter, it appeared more profoundly derelict than the halfeaten carcass of a deer come suddenly upon in a forest. Jiggs paused, still fastening the coverall's throat, and looked across the hangar at the three people busy about it—two of a size and one taller, all in dungarees although one of the two shorter ones was topped by a blob of savage mealcolored hair which even from here did not look like man's hair. He did not approach at once; still fastening the coverall he looked on and saw, in another clump of dungarees beside another aeroplane, a small towheaded boy in khaki miniature of the men, even to the grease. "Jesus Christ," Jiggs thought. "He's done smeared oil on them already. Laverne will give him hell." He approached on his short bouncing legs; already he could hear the boy talking in the loud assured carrying voice of a spoiled middlewestern child. He came up and put out his blunt hard greasegrained hand and scoured the boy's head.

"Look out," the boy said. Then he said, "Where you been? Laverne and Roger——" Jiggs scoured the boy's head again and then crouched, his fists up, his head drawn down into his shoulders in burlesque pantomime. But the boy just looked at him. "Laverne and Roger——" he said again.

"Who's your old man today, kid?" Jiggs said. Now the boy moved. With absolutely no change of expression he lowered his head and rushed at Jiggs, his fists flailing at the man.

Jiggs ducked, taking the blows while the boy hammered at him with puny and deadly purpose; now the other men had all turned to watch, with wrenches and tools and engineparts in their suspended hands. "Who's your old man, huh?" Jiggs said, holding the boy off and then lifting and holding him away while he still hammered at Jiggs' head with that grim and puny purpose. "All right!" Jiggs cried. He set the boy down and held him off, still ducking and dodging and now blind since the peaked cap was jammed over his face and the boy's hard light little fists hammering upon the cap. "Oke! Oke!" Jiggs cried. "I quit! I take it back!" He stood back and tugged the cap off his face and then he found why the boy had ceased: that he and the men too with their arrested tools and safety wire and engineparts were now looking at something which had apparently crept from a doctor's cupboard and, in the snatched garments of an etherised patient in a charity ward, escaped into the living world. He saw a creature which, erect, would be better than six feet tall and which would weigh about ninetyfive pounds, in a suit of no age nor color, as though made of air and doped like an aeroplane wing with the incrusted excretion of all articulate life's contact with the passing earth, which ballooned light and impedimentless about a skeleton frame as though suit and wearer both hung from a flapping clothesline;—a creature with the leashed, eager loosejointed air of a halfgrown highbred setter puppy, crouched facing the boy with its hands up too in more profound burlesque than Jiggs' because it was obviously not intended to be burlesque.

"Come on, Dempsey," the man said. "How about taking me on for an icecream cone? Hey?" The boy did not move. He was not more than six, yet he looked at the apparition before him with the amazed quiet immobility of the grown men. "How about it, huh?" the man said.

Still the boy did not move. "Ask him who's his old man," Jiggs said.

The man looked at Jiggs. "So's his old man?"

"No. Who's his old man."

Now it was the apparition who looked at Jiggs in a kind of shocked immobility. "Who's his old man?" he repeated. He was still looking at Jiggs when the boy rushed upon him with his fists flailing again and his small face grimly and soberly homicidal; the man was still stooping, looking at Jiggs; it seemed to Jiggs and the other men that the boy's fists made a light woodensounding tattoo as though the man's skin and the suit too hung on a chair while the man ducked and dodged too, trying to guard his face while still glaring at Jiggs with that skulllike amazement, repeating, "Who's his old man? *Who's his old man?*"

When Jiggs at last reached the unbonneted aeroplane the two men had the supercharger already off and dismantled. "Been to your grandmother's funeral or something?" the taller one said.

"I been over there playing with Jack," Jiggs said. "You just never saw me because there aint any women around here to be looking at yet."

"Yair?" the other said.

"Yair," Jiggs said. "Where's that crescent wrench we bought in Kansas City?" The woman had it in her hand; she gave it to him and drew the back of her hand across her forehead, leaving a smudge of grease up and into the meal-colored, the strong pallid Iowacorncolored, hair. So he was busy then, though he looked back once and saw the apparition with the boy now riding on his shoulder, leaning into the heads and greasy backs busy again about the other aeroplane, and when he and Shumann lifted the supercharger back onto the engine he looked again and saw them, the boy still riding on the man's shoulder, going out the hangar door and toward the apron. Then they put the cowling back on and Shumann set the propeller horizontal and Jiggs raised the aeroplane's tail, easily, already swinging it to pass through the door, the woman stepping back to let the wing pass her, looking back herself into the hangar now.

"Where did Jack go?" she said.

"Out toward the apron," Jiggs said. "With that guy."

"With what guy?"

"Tall guy. Says he is a reporter. That looks like they locked the graveyard up before he got in last night." The aeroplane passed her, swinging again into the thin sunshine, the tail high and apparently without weight on Jiggs' shoulder, his thick legs beneath it moving with tense stout piston-like thrusts, Shumann and the taller man pushing the wings.

"Wait a minute," the woman said. But they did not pause and she overtook and passed the moving tailgroup and reached down past the uptilted cockpit hatch and stepped clear, holding a bundle wrapped tightly in a dark sweater. The aeroplane went on; already the guards in the purple-and-gold porter caps were lowering the barrier cable onto the apron; and now the band had begun to play, heard twice: once the faint light almost airy thump-thump-thump from where the sun glinted on the actual hornmouths on the platform facing the reserved section of the stands, and once where the disembodied noise blared brazen, metallic, and loud from the amplifyer which faced the barrier. She turned

and reentered the hangar, stepping aside to let another aeroplane and its crew pass; she spoke to one of the men: "Who
was that Jack went out with, Art?"

"The skeleton?" the man said. "They went to get an icecream cone. He says he is a reporter." She went on, across
the hangar and through the chickenwire door and into the
toolroom with its row of hooks from which depended the
coats and shirts and now one stiff linen collar and tie such as
might be seen on a barbershop hook where a preacher was
being shaved and which she recognised as belonging to the
circuitriderlooking man in steel spectacles who won the
Graves Trophy race at Miami two months ago. There was
neither lock nor hook on this door, and the other, the one
through which Jiggs had entered, hung perfectly blank too
save for the greaseprints of hands; for less than a second she
stood perfectly still, looking at the second door while her
hand made a single quick stroking movement about the
doorjamb where hook or lock would have been. It was less
than a second, then she went on to the corner where the
lavatory was—the greasestreaked bowl, the cake of what
looked like lava, the metal case for paper towels—and laid
the bundle carefully on the floor next the wall where the
floor was cleanest and rose and looked at the door again for a
pause that was less than a second—a woman not tall and not
thin, looking almost like a man in the greasy coverall, with
the pale strong rough ragged hair actually darker where it
was sunburned, a tanned heavyjawed face in which the eyes
looked like pieces of china. It was hardly a pause; she rolled
her sleeves back, shaking the folds free and loose, and
opened the coverall at the throat and freed it about her
shoulders too like she had the sleeves, obviously and appar-

ently arranging it so she would not need to touch the foul garment any more than necessary again. Then she scrubbed face neck and forearms with the harsh soap and rinsed and dried herself and, stooping, keeping her arms well away from the coverall, she opened the rolled sweater on the floor. It contained a comb, a cheap metal vanity and a pair of stockings rolled in turn into a man's clean white shirt and a worn wool skirt. She used the comb and the vanity's mirror, stopping to scrub again at the greasesmudge on her forehead. Then she unbuttoned the shirt and shook out the skirt and spread paper towels on the lavatory and laid the garments on them, openings upward and facing her and, holding the open edges of the coverall's front between two more paper towels, she paused and looked again at the door: a single still cold glance empty of either hesitation, concern, or regret while even here the faint beat of the band came in mute thuds and blares. Then she turned her back slightly toward the door and in the same motion with which she reached for the skirt she stepped out of the coverall in a pair of brown walking shoes not new now and which had not cost very much when they had been, and a man's thin cotton undershorts and nothing else.

Now the first starting bomb went—a jarring thud followed by a vicious light repercussion as if the bomb had set off another smaller one in the now empty hangar and in the rotundra too. Within the domed steel vacuum the single report became myriad, high and everywhere about the concave ceiling like invisible unearthly winged creatures of that yet unvisioned tomorrow, mechanical instead of blood bone and meat, speaking to one another in vicious highpitched ejaculations as though concerting an attack on something below. There was an amplifyer in the rotundra too and through it the sound of the aeroplanes turning the field pylon on each lap filled the rotundra and the restaurant where the woman and the reporter sat while the little boy finished the second dish of icecream. The amplifyer filled rotundra and restaurant even above the sound of feet as the crowd moiled and milled and trickled through the gates onto the field, with the announcer's voice harsh masculine and disembodied; then at the end of each lap would come the mounting and then fading snarl and snore of engines as the aeroplanes came up and zoomed and banked away, leaving once more the scuffle and murmur of feet on tile and the voice of the announcer reverberant and sonorous within the domed shell of glass and steel in a running commentation to which apparently none listened, as if the voice were merely some unavoidable and inexplicable phenomenon of nature like the sound of wind or of erosion. Then the band would begin to play again, though faint and almost trivial behind and below the voice, as if the voice actually were that natural phenomenon against which all manmade sounds and noises blew and vanished like leaves. Then the bomb again, the faint fierce thwack-thwack-thwack, and the sound of engines again too and trivial and meaningless as the band, as though like the band mere insignificant properties which the voice used for emphasis as the magician uses his wand or handker-chief: "——ending the second event, the two hundred cubic inch class dash, the correct time of the winner of which will be given you as soon as the judges report. Meanwhile while we are waiting for it to come in I will run briefly over the af-ternoon's program of events for the benefit of those who have come in late or have not purchased a program which by the way may be purchased for twenty-five cents from any of the attendants in the purple-and-gold Mardi Gras caps——"

"I got one here," the reporter said. He produced it, along with a mass of blank yellow copy and a folded newspaper of the morning, from the same pocket of his disreputable coat—a pamphlet already opened and creased back upon the faint mimeographed letters of the first page:

Thursday (Dedication Day)

2:30 P.M.	Spot Parachute Jump. Purse $25.00
3:00 P.M.	200 cu. in. Dash. Qualifying Speed 100 mph. Purse $150.00 (1) 45%. (2) 30%. (3) 15% (4) 10%
3:30 P.M.	Aerial Acrobatics. Jules Despleins, France. Lieut. Frank Burnham, United States
4:30 P.M.	Scull Dash. 375 cu. in. Qualifying Speed 160 m.p.h. (1, 2, 3, 4)
5:00 P.M.	Delayed Parachute Drop
8:00 P.M.	Special Mardi Gras Evening Event. Rocket Plane. Lieut. Frank Burnham

"Keep it," the reporter said. "I dont need it."

"Thanks," the woman said. "I know the setup." She looked at the boy. "Hurry and finish it," she said. "You have already eaten more than you can hold." The reporter looked at the boy too, with that expression leashed, eager, cadaverous; sitting forward on the flimsy chair in that attitude at once inert yet precarious and lightpoised as though for violent and complete departure like a scarecrow in a winter field. "All I can do for him is buy him something to eat," he said. "To take him to see an air race would be like taking a colt out to Washington Park for the day. You are from Iowa and Shumann was born in Ohio and he was born in California and he has been across the United States four times, let alone Canada and Mexico. Jesus. He could take me and show me, couldn't he?" But the woman was looking at the boy; she did not seem to have heard at all.

"Go on," she said. "Finish it or leave it."

"And then we'll eat some candy," the reporter said. "Hey, Dempsey?"

"No," the woman said. "He's had enough."

"But maybe for later?" the reporter said. She looked at him now: the pale stare without curiosity, perfectly grave, perfectly blank, as he rose, moved, dry loose weightless and sudden and longer than a lath, the disreputable suit ballooning even in this windless conditioned air as he went toward the candy counter. Above the shuffle and murmur of feet in the lobby and above the clash and clatter of crockery in the restaurant the amplified voice still spoke, profound and effortless, as though it were the voice of the steel-and-chromium mausoleum itself talking of creatures imbued with motion though not with life and incomprehensible to the puny crawling painwebbed globe, incapable of suffering, wombed and born complete and instantaneous, cunning intricate and deadly, from out some blind iron batcave of the earth's prime foundation:

"——dedication meet, Feinman million dollar airport, New Valois, Franciana, held under the official auspices of the American Aeronautical Association. And here is the official clocking of the winners of the two hundred cubic inch

race which you just witnessed——" Now they had to breast
the slow current; the gatemen (these wore tunics of purple-
and-gold as well as caps) would not let them pass because the
woman and the child had no tickets. So they had to go back
and out and around through the hangar to reach the apron.
And here the voice met them again—or rather it had never
ceased; they had merely walked in it without hearing or feeling it like in the sunshine; the voice too almost as sourceless
as light. Now, on the apron, the third bomb went and looking up the apron from where he stood among the other mechanics about the aeroplanes waiting for the next race, Jiggs
saw the three of them—the woman in an attitude of inattentive hearing without listening, the scarecrow man who even
from here Jiggs could discern to be talking steadily and even
now and then gesticulating, the small khaki spot of the little
boy's dungarees riding high on his shoulder and the small
hand holding a scarcetasted chocolate bar in a kind of static
surfeit. They went on, though Jiggs saw them twice more, the
second time the shadow of the man's and the little boy's
heads falling for an incredible distance eastward along the
apron. Then the taller man began to beckon him and already the five aeroplanes entered for the race were moving,
the tails high on the shoulders of their crews, out toward the
starting line.

When he and the taller man returned to the apron the
band was still playing. Faced by the bright stands with their
whipping skyline of purple-and-gold pennons the amplifyers
at regular intervals along the apronedge erupted snatched
blares of ghostlike and ubiquitous sound which, as Jiggs and
the other passed them, died each into the next without loss of
beat or particular gain in sense or tune. Beyond the amplify-

ers and the apron lay the flat triangle of reclaimed and tortured earth dragged with slow mechanical violence into air and alterations of light—the oyster-and-shrimpfossil bed notched into the ceaseless surface of the outraged lake and upon which the immaculate concrete runways lay in the attitude of two stiffly embracing capital Fs, on one of which the six aeroplanes rested like six motionless wasps, the slanting sun glinting on their soft bright paint and on the faint propellerblurs. Now the band ceased; the bomb bloomed again on the pale sky and had already begun to fade even before the jarring thud, the thin vicious crack of reverberation; and now the voice again, amplified and ubiquitous, louder even than the spatter and snarl of the engines as the six aeroplanes rose raggedly and dissolved, converging, coveying, toward the scattering pylon out in the lake: "—fourth event, Scull Speed Dash, three hundred and seventy-five cubic inch, twenty-five miles, five times around, purse three hundred and twenty-five dollars. I'll give you the names of the contestants as the boys, the other pilots on the apron here, figure they will come in. First and second will be Al Myers and Bob Bullitt, in number thirty-two and number five. You can take your choice, your guess is as good as ours; they are both good pilots—Bullitt won the Graves Trophy against a hot field in Miami in December—and they are both flying Chance Specials. It will be the pilot, and I'm not going to make anybody mad by making a guess——Vas you dere, Sharlie? I mean Mrs Bullitt. The other boys are good too, but Myers and Bullitt have the ships. So I'll say third will be Jimmy Ott, and Roger Shumann and Joe Grant last, because as I said, the other boys have the ships——There they are, coming in from the scattering pylon, and it's——Yes, it's

Myers or Bullitt out front and Ott close behind, and Shumann and Grant pretty well back. And here they are coming
in for the first pylon." The voice was firm, pleasant, assured;
it had an American reputation for announcing air meets as
other voices had for football or music or prizefights. A pilot
himself, the announcer stood hiphigh among the caps and
horns of the bandstand below the reserved seats, bareheaded,
in a tweed jacket even a little oversmart, reminiscent a trifle
more of Hollywood Avenue than of Madison, with the modest winged badge of a good solid pilots' fraternity in the lapel
and turned a little to face the box seats while he spoke into
the microphone as the aeroplanes roared up and banked
around the field pylon and faded again in irregular order.

"There's Feinman," Jiggs said. "In the yellow-and-blue
pulpit. The one in the gray suit and the flower. The one with
the women. Yair; he'd make lard, now."

"Yes," the taller man said. "Look yonder. Roger is going
to take that guy on this next pylon." Although Jiggs did not
look at once, the voice did, almost before the taller man
spoke, as if it possessed some quality of omniscience beyond
even vision:

"Well, well, folks, here's a race that wasn't advertised. It
looks like Roger Shumann is going to try to upset the boys'
dope. That's him that went up into third place on that pylon
then; he has just taken Ott on the lake pylon. Let's watch
him now; Mrs Shumann's here in the crowd somewhere:
maybe she knows what Roger's got up his sleeve today. A
poor fourth on the first pylon and now coming in third on
the third lap——oh oh oh, look at him take that pylon! If we
were all back on the farm now I would say somebody has put
a cockleburr under Roger's—well, you know where: maybe

it was Mrs Shumann did it. Good boy, Roger! If you can just hold Ott now because Ott's got the ship on him, folks; I wouldn't try to fool you about that—No; wait, w-a-i-t—— Folks, he's trying to catch Bullitt oh oh did he take that pylon! Folks, he gained three hundred feet on Bullitt on that turn—Watch now, he's going to try to take Bullitt on the next pylon—there there there—watch him WATCH him. He's beating them on the pylons, folks, because he knows that on the straightaway he hasn't got a chance oh oh oh watch him now, up there from fourth place in four and a half laps and now he is going to pass Bullitt unless he pulls his wings off on this next——Here they come in now oh oh oh, Mrs Shumann's somewhere in the crowd here; maybe she told Roger if he dont come in on the money he needn't come in at all——There it is, folks; here it is: Myers gets the flag *and* now it's Shumann or Bullitt, Shumann or——It's Shumann, folks, in as pretty a flown race as you ever watched——"

"There it is," Jiggs said. "Jesus, he better had come in on somebody's money or we'd a all set up in the depot tonight with our bellies thinking our throats was cut. Come on. I'll help you put the 'chutes on." But the taller man was looking up the apron. Jiggs paused too and saw the boy's khaki garment riding high above the heads below the bandstand, though he could not actually see the woman. The six aeroplanes which for six minutes had followed one another around the course at one altitude and in almost undeviating order like so many beads on a string, were now scattered about the adjacent sky for a radius of two or three miles as if the last pylon had exploded them like so many scraps of paper, jockeying in to land.

"Who's that guy?" the taller man said. "Hanging around Laverne?"

"Lazarus?" Jiggs said. "Jesus, if I was him I would be afraid to use myself. I would be even afraid to take myself out of bed, like I was a cutglass monkeywrench or something. Come on. Your guy is already warmed up and waiting for you."

For a moment longer the taller man looked up the apron, bleakly. Then he turned. "Go and get the 'chutes and find somebody to bring the sack; I will meet——"

"They are already at the ship," Jiggs said. "I done already carried them over. Come on."

The other, moving, stopped dead still. He looked down at Jiggs with a bleak handsome face whose features were regular, brutally courageous, the expression quick if not particularly intelligent, not particularly strong. Under his eyes the faint smudges of dissipation appeared to have been put there by a makeup expert. He wore a narrow moustache above a mouth much more delicate and even feminine than that of the woman whom he and Jiggs called Laverne. "What?" he said. "*You* carried the 'chutes and that sack of flour over to the ship? *You* did?"

Jiggs did not stop. "You're next, aint you? You're ready to go, aint you? And it's getting late, aint it? What are you waiting on? for them to turn on the boundary lights and maybe the floods? or maybe to have the beacon to come in on to land?"

The other walked again, following Jiggs along the apron toward where an aeroplane, a commercial type, stood just without the barrier, its engine running. "I guess you have been to the office and collected my twenty-five bucks and saved me some more time too," he said.

"All right; I'll attend to that too," Jiggs said. "Come on. The guy's burning gas; he'll be trying to charge you six bucks instead of five if you dont snap it up." They went on to where the aeroplane waited, the pilot already in his cockpit, the already low sun, refracted by the invisible propeller blades, shimmering about the nose of it in a faint coppercolored nimbus. The two parachutes and the sack of flour lay on the ground beside it. Jiggs held them up one at a time while the other backed into the harness, then he stooped and darted about the straps and buckles like a squirrel, still talking. "Yair, he come in on the money. I guess I will get my hooks on a little jack myself tonight. Jesus, I wont know how to count higher than two bucks."

"But dont try to learn again on my twenty-five," the other said. "Just get it and hold it until I get back."

"What would I want with your twenty-five?" Jiggs said. "With Roger just won thirty percent. of three hundred and twenty-five, whatever that is. How do you think twenty-five bucks will look beside that?"

"I can tell you a bigger difference still," the other said. "The money Roger won aint mine but this twenty-five is. Maybe you better not even collect it. I'll attend to that, too."

"Yair," Jiggs said, busy, bouncing on his short strong legs, snapping the buckles of the emergency parachute. "Yair, we're jake now. We can eat and sleep again tonight. . . . . . . O.K." He stood back and the other waddled stiffly toward the aeroplane. The checker came up with his pad and took their names and the aeroplane's number and went away.

"Where you want to land?" the pilot said.

"I dont care," the jumper said. "Anywhere in the United States except that lake."

"If you see you're going to hit the lake," Jiggs said, "turn around and go back up and jump again."

They paid no attention to him. They were both looking back and upward toward where in the high drowsy azure there was already a definite alteration toward night. "Should be about dead up there now," the pilot said. "What say I spot you for the hangar roofs and you can slip either way you want."

"All right," the jumper said. "Let's get away from here." With Jiggs shoving at him he climbed onto the wing and into the front cockpit and Jiggs handed up the sack of flour and the jumper took it onto his lap like it was a child; with his bleak humorless handsome face he looked exactly like the comely young bachelor caught by his girl while holding a strange infant on a street corner. The aeroplane began to move; Jiggs stepped back as the jumper leaned out, shouting: "Leave that money alone, you hear?"

"Okey doke," Jiggs said. The aeroplane waddled out and onto the runway and turned and stopped; again the bomb, the soft slow bulb of cotton batting flowered against the soft indefinite lakehaze where for a little while still evening seemed to wait before moving in; again the report, the thud and jar twice reverberant against the stands as if the report bounced once before becoming echo: and now Jiggs turned as if he had waited for that signal too and almost parallel he and the aeroplane began to move—the stocky purposeful man, and the machine already changing angle and then lifting, banking in a long climbing turn. It was two thousand feet high when Jiggs shoved past the purple-and-gold guards at the main gate and through the throng huddled in the narrow underpass beneath the reserved seats, one of whom plucked at his sleeve:

"When's the guy going to jump out of the parachute?"

"Not until he gets back down here," Jiggs said, butting on past the other purple-and-gold guards and so into the rotundra itself and likewise not into the amplified voice again for the reason that he had never moved out of it:

"—still gaining altitude now; the ship has a long way to go yet. And then you will see a living man, a man like yourselves—a man like half of yourselves and that the other half of yourselves like, I should say—hurl himself into space and fall for almost four miles before pulling the ripcord of the parachute; by ripcord we mean the trigger that——" Once inside, Jiggs paused, looking swiftly about, breasting now with very immobility the now comparatively thin tide which still set toward the apron and talking to itself with one another in voices forlorn, baffled, and amazed:

"What is it now? What are they doing out there now?"

"Fella going to jump ten miles out of a parachute."

"Better hurry too," Jiggs said. "It may open before he can jump out of it." The rotundra, filled with dusk, was lighted now, with a soft sourceless wash of no earthly color or substance and which cast no shadow: spacious, suave, sonorous and monastic, wherein relief or murallimning or bronze and chromium skilfully shadowlurked presented the furious, still, and legendary tale of what man has come to call his conquering of the infinite and impervious air. High overhead the dome of azure glass repeated the mosaiced twin Fsymbols of the runways to the brass twin Fs let into the tile floor and which, brightpolished, gleaming, seemed to reflect

and find soundless and fading echo in turn monogrammed
into the bronze grilling above the ticket-and-information
windows and inletted friezelike into baseboard and cornice
of the synthetic stone. "Yair," Jiggs said. "It must have set
them back that million.—Say, mister, where's the office?"
The guard told him; he went to the small discreet door almost hidden in an alcove and entered it and for a time he
walked out of the voice though it was waiting for him when,
a minute later, he emerged:

"—still gaining altitude. The boys down here cant tell
just how high he is but he looks about right. It might be any
time now; you'll see the flour first and then you will know
there is a living man falling at the end of it, a living man
falling through space at the rate of four hundred feet a second—" When Jiggs reached the apron again (he too had no
ticket and so though he could pass from the apron into
the rotundra as often as he pleased, he could not pass from
the rotundra to the apron save by going around through the
hangar) the aeroplane was no more than a trivial and insignificant blemish against the sky which was now definitely
that of evening, seeming to hang there without sound or motion. But Jiggs did not look at it. He thrust on among the
upgazing motionless bodies and reached the barrier just as
one of the racers was being wheeled in from the field. He
stopped one of the crew; the bill was already in his hand.
"Monk, give this to Jackson, will you? For flying that parachute jump. He'll know."

He went back into the hangar, walking fast now and already unfastening his coverall before he pushed through
the chickenwire door. He removed the coverall and hung it
up and only for a second glanced at his hands. "I'll wash

them when I get to town," he said. Now the first port lights came on; he crossed the plaza, passing the bloomed bloodless grapes on their cast stalks on the quadrate bases of which the four Fs were discernible even in twilight. The bus was lighted too. It had its quota of passengers though they were not inside. Including the driver they stood beside it, looking up, while the voice of the amplifyer, apocryphal, sourceless, inhuman, ubiquitous and beyond weariness or fatigue, went on:

"——in position now; it will be any time now—There. There. There goes the wing down; he has throttled back now now Now——There he is, folks; the flour, the flour——" The flour was a faint stain unrolling ribbonlike, light, lazy, against the sky, and then they could see the falling dot at the head of it which, puny, increasing, became the tiny figure of a man plunging without movement toward a single long suspiration of human breath, until at last the parachute bloomed. It unfolded swaying against the accomplished and ineradicable evening; beneath it the jumper oscillated slowly, settling slowly now toward the field. The boundary and obstruction lights were on too now; he floated down as though out of a soundless and breathless void, toward the bright necklace of field lights and the electrified name on each hangarroof; at the moment the green light above the beacon on the signal tower began to wink and flash too: dot-dot-dash-dot. dot-dot-dash-dot. dot-dot-dash-dot. across the nightbound lake. Jiggs touched the driver's arm.

"Come on, Jack," he said. "I got to be at Grandlieu Street before six oclock."

An Evening in New Valois

T he downfunnelled light from the desklamp struck the
reporter across the hips; to the city editor sitting behind the
desk the reporter loomed from the hips upward for an incredible distance to where the cadaverface hung against the
dusty gloom of the city room's upper spaces, in a green
corpseglare as appropriate as water to fish—the raked disreputable hat, the suit that looked as if someone else had just
finished sleeping in it and with one coat pocket sagging with
yellow copy paper and from the other protruding, folded, the
cold violent stilldamp black

ALITY OF
BURNED

—the entire air and appearance of a last and cheerful stage
of what old people call galloping consumption—the man
whom the editor believed (certainly hoped) to be unmar-
ried, though not through any knowledge or report but be-

cause of something which the man's living being emanated—a creature who apparently never had any parents either and who will not be old and never was a child, who apparently sprang fullgrown and irrevocably mature out of some violent and instantaneous transition like the stories of dead steamboatmen and mules: if it were learned that he had a brother for instance it would create neither warmth nor surprise anymore than finding the mate to a discarded shoe in a trashbin—of whom the editor had heard how a girl in a Barricade Street crib said that it would be like assessing the invoked spirit at a seance held in a rented restaurant room with a covercharge.

Upon the desk, in the full target of the lamp's glare, it lay too: the black bold stilldamp **FIRST FATALITY OF AIR MEET. PILOT BURNED ALIVE.** beyond it, backflung, shirtsleeved, his bald head above the green eyeshade corpseglared too, the city editor looked at the reporter fretfully. "You have an instinct for events," he said. "If you were turned into a room with a hundred people you never saw before and two of them were destined to enact a homicide, you would go straight to them as crow to carrion; you would be there from the very first: you would be the one to run out and borrow a pistol from the nearest policeman for them to use. Yet you never seem to bring back anything but information. Oh you have that, all right, because we seem to get everything that the other papers do and we haven't been sued yet and so doubtless it's all that anyone should expect for five cents and doubtless more than they deserve. But it's not the living breath of news. It's just information. It's dead before you even get back here with it." Immobile beyond the lamp's hard radius the reporter stood, watching the editor with an air leashed, attentive, and alert. "It's like trying to read something in a foreign language. You know it ought to be there; maybe you know by God it is there. But that's all. Can it be by some horrible mischance that without knowing it you listen and see in one language and then do what you call writing in another? How does it sound to you when you read it yourself?"

"When I read what?" the reporter said. Then he sat down in the opposite chair while the editor cursed him. He collapsed upon the chair with a loose dry scarecrowlike clatter as though of his own skeleton and the wooden chair's in contact, and leaned forward across the desk, eager, apparently not only on the verge of the grave itself but in actual sight of the other side of Styx: of the saloons which have never sounded with cashregister or till; of that golden District where gleam with frankincense and scented oils the celestial anonymous bosoms of eternal and subsidised delight. "Why didn't you tell me this before?" he cried. "Why didn't you tell me before that this is what you want? Here I have been running my ass ragged eight days a week trying to find something worth telling and then telling it so it wont make eight thousand different advertisers and subscribers. . . . . . . But no matter now. Because listen." He jerked off his hat and flung it onto the desk; as quickly the editor snatched it up as if it had been a crust of antladen bread on a picnic tablecloth and jerked it back into the reporter's lap. "Listen," the reporter said. "She's out there at the airport. She's got a little boy, only it's two of them, that fly those little ships that look like mosquitoes. No: just one of them flies the ship; the other makes the delayed parachute jump—you know, with the fifty pound sack of flour and coming down like the haunt of Yule-

tide or something. Yair; they've got a little boy, about the size
of this telephone, in dungarees like they w——"

"What?" the editor cried. "Who have a little boy?"

"Yair. They dont know.——in dungarees like they wear;
when I come into the hangar this morning they were clean,
maybe because the first day of a meet is the one they call
Monday, and he had a stick and he was swabbing grease up
off the floor and smearing it onto himself so he would look
like they look.——Yair, two of them: this guy Shumann that
took second money this afternoon, that come up from fourth
in a crate that all the guys out there that are supposed to
know said couldn't even show. She's his wife, that is her
name's Shumann and the kid's is Shumann too: out there in
the hangar this morning in dungarees like the rest of them,
with her hands full of wrenches and machinery and a gob of
cotter keys in her mouth like they tell how women used to do
with the pins and needles before General Motors begun to
make their clothes for them, with this Harlowcolored hair
that they would pay her money for it in Hollywood and a
smear of grease where she had swiped it back with her wrist;
she's his wife: they have been married almost ever since the
kid was born six years ago in a hangar in California; yair, this
day Shumann comes down at whatever town it was in Iowa
or Indiana or wherever it was that she was a sophomore in
the highschool back before they had the airmail for farmers
to quit plowing and look up at; in the highschool at recess,
and so maybe that was why she come out without a hat
even and got into the front seat of one of those Jennies the
army used to sell them for cancelled stamps or whatever it
was. And maybe she sent a postcard back from the next cow-
pasture to the aunt or whoever it was that was expecting her

to come home to dinner, granted that they have kinfolks or are descended from human beings, and he taught her to jump parachutes. Because they aint human like us; they couldn't turn those pylons like they do if they had human blood and senses and they wouldn't want to or dare to if they just had human brains. Burn them like this one tonight and they dont even holler in the fire; crash one and it aint even blood when you haul him out: it's cylinder oil the same as in the crankcase. And listen: it's both of them; this morning I walk into the hangar where they are getting the ships ready and I see the kid and a guy that looks like a little horse squared off with their fists up and the rest of them watching with wrenches and things in their hands and the kid rushes in flailing his arms and the guy holding him off and the others watching and the guy put the kid down and I come up and square off too with my fists up too and I says 'Come on, Dempsey; how about taking me on next' and the kid dont move, he just looks at me and then the guy says 'Ask him who's his old man' only I thought he said 'So's his old man' and I said 'So's his old man?' and the guy says 'No. *Who's* his old man' and I said it, and here the kid comes with his fists flailing, and if he had just been half as big as he wanted to be right then he would have beat hell out of me. And so I asked them and they told me." He stopped; he ran out of speech or perhaps out of breath not as a vessel runs empty but with the instantaneous cessation of some weightless winddriven toy, say a celluloid pinwheel. Behind the desk, still backflung, clutching the chairarms, the editor glared at him with outraged amazement.

"What?" he cried. "Two men, with one wife and child between them?"

"Yair. The third guy, the horse one, is just the mechanic; he aint even a husband, let alone a flyer. Yair. Shumann and the airplane landing at Iowa or Indiana or wherever it is, and her coming out of the schoolhouse without even arranging to have her books took home, and they went off maybe with a canopener and a blanket to sleep on under the wing of the airplane when it rained hard, and then the other guy, the parachute guy, dropping in, falling the couple or three miles with his sack of flour before pulling the ripcord. They aint human, you see. No ties; no place where you were born and have to go back to it now and then even if it's just only to hate the damn place good and comfortable for a day or two. From coast to coast and Canada in summer and Mexico in winter, with one suitcase and the same canopener because three can live on one canopener as easy as one or twelve,—wherever they can find enough folks in one place to advance them enough money to get there and pay for the gasoline afterward. Because they dont need money; it aint money they are after anymore than it's glory because the glory cant only last until the next race and so maybe it aint even until tomorrow. And they dont need money except only now and then when they come in contact with the human race like in a hotel to sleep or eat now and then or maybe to buy a pair of pants or a skirt to keep the police off of them. Because money aint that hard to make: it aint up there fourteen and a half feet off the ground in a vertical bank around a steel post at two or three hundred miles an hour in a damn gnat built like a Swiss watch that the top speed of it aint a number on a little dial but it's where you burn the engine up or fly out from between the wings and the undercarriage. Around the home pylon on one wingtip and the fabric trembling like a bride and the crate cost four thousand dollars and good for maybe fifty hours if one ever lasted that long and five of them in the race and the top money at least two-hundred-thirtyeight-fiftytwo less fines fees commissions and gratuities. And the rest of them, the wives and children and mechanics, standing on the apron and watching like they might have been stole out of a department store window and dressed in greasy khaki coveralls and not even thinking about the hotel bill over in town or where we are going to eat if we dont win and how we are going to get to the next meet if the engine melts and runs backward out of the exhaust pipe. And Shumann dont even own a ship; she told me about how they want Vic Chance to build one for them and how Vic Chance wants to build one for Shumann to fly only neither Vic Chance nor them have managed to save up enough jack yet. So he just flies whatever he can get that they will qualify. This one he copped with today he is flying on a commission; it was next to the slowest one in the race and they all said he never had a chance with it and he beat them on the pylons. So when he dont cop they eat on the parachute guy, which is O.K. because the parachute guy makes almost as much as the guy at the microphone does, besides the mike guy having to work all afternoon for his while it dont only take the parachute guy a few seconds to fall the ten or twelve thousand feet with the flour blowing back in his face before pulling the ripcord. And so the kid was born on an unrolled parachute in a hangar in California; he got dropped already running like a colt or a calf from the fuselage of an airplane, onto something because it happened to be big enough to land on and then takeoff again. And I thought about him having ancestors and hell and heaven like we have, and birthpangs to rise up out of and walk the earth with your arm crooked over your head to dodge until you finally get the old blackjack at last and can lay back down again;—all of a sudden I thought about him with a couple or three sets of grandparents and uncles and aunts and cousins somewhere, and I like to died. I had to stop and lean against the hangarwall and laugh. Talk about your immaculate conceptions: born on a unrolled parachute in a California hangar and the doc went to the door and called Shumann and the parachute guy. And the parachute guy got out the dice and says to her 'Do you want to catch these?' and she said 'Roll them' and the dice come out and Shumann rolled high, and that afternoon they fetched the J.P. out on the gasoline truck and so hers and the kid's name is Shumann. And they told me how it wasn't them that started saying Who's your old man? to the kid; it was her, and the kid flailing away at her and her stooping that hard boy's face that looks like any one of the four of them might cut her hair for her with a pocket knife when it needs it, down to where he can reach it and saying 'Hit me. Hit me hard. Harder. Harder.' And what do you think of that?" He stopped again. The editor sat back in the swivel chair and drew a deep, full, deliberate breath while the reporter leaned above the desk like a dissolute and eager skeleton, with that air of worn and dreamy fury which Don Quixote must have had.

"I think you ought to write it," the editor said. The reporter looked at him for almost half a minute without moving.

"Ought to write. . . . . . ." He murmured. "Ought to write. . . . . . ." His voice died away in ecstasy; he glared down at the editor in bonelight exultation while the editor watched him in turn with cold and vindictive waiting.

"Yes. Go home and write it."

"Go home and. . . . . . . Home, where I wont be dis—where I can——O pal o pal o pal! Chief, where have I been all your life or where have you been all mine?"

"Yes," the editor said. He had not moved. "Go home and lock yourself in and throw the key out the window and write it." He watched the gaunt ecstatic face before him in the dim corpseglare of the green shade. "And then set fire to the room." The reporter's face sank slowly back, like a Halloween mask on a boy's stick being slowly withdrawn. Then for a long time he too did not move save for a faint working of the lips as if he were tasting something either very good or very bad. Then he rose slowly, the editor watching him; he seemed to collect and visibly reassemble himself bone by bone and socket by socket. On the desk lay a pack of cigarettes. He reached his hand toward it; as quickly as when he had flung back the hat and without removing his gaze from the reporter's face, the editor snatched the pack away. The reporter lifted from the floor his disreputable hat and stood gazing into it with musing attention, as though about to draw a lot from it. "Listen," the editor said; he spoke patiently, almost kindly: "The people who own this paper or who direct its policies or anyway who pay the salaries, fortunately or unfortunately I shant attempt to say, have no Lewises or Hemingways or even Tchekovs on the staff: one very good reason doubtless being that they do not want them, since what they want is not fiction, not even Nobel Prize fiction, but news."

"You mean you dont believe this?" the reporter said. "About h—these guys?"

"I'll go you better than that: I dont even care. Why

should I find news in this woman's supposed bedhabits as long as her legal (so you tell me) husband does not?"

"I thought that women's bedhabits were always news," the reporter said.

"You thought? You thought? You listen to me a minute. If one of them takes his airplane or his parachute and murders her and the child in front of the grandstand, then it will be news. But until they do, what I am paying you to bring back here is not what you think about somebody out there nor what you heard about somebody out there nor even what you saw: I expect you to come in here tomorrow night with an accurate account of everything that occurs out there tomorrow that creates any reaction excitement or irritation on any human retina; if you have to be twins or triplets or even a regiment to do this, be so. Now you go on home and go to bed. And remember. Remember. There will be someone out there to report to me personally at my home the exact moment at which you enter the gates. And if that report comes to me one minute after ten oclock, you will need a racing airplane to catch your job Monday morning. Go home. Do you hear me?" The reporter looked at him, without heat, perfectly blank, as if he had ceased several moments ago not alone to listen but even to hear, as though he were now watching the editor's lips courteously to tell when he had finished.

"O.K., chief," he said. "If that's the way you feel about it."

"That's exactly the way I feel about it. Do you understand?"

"Yair; sure. Good night."

"Good night," the editor said. The reporter turned away; he turned away quietly, putting the hat on his head exactly as he had laid it on the editor's desk before the editor flung it off, and took from the pocket containing the folded newspaper a crumpled cigarettepack; the editor watched him put the cigarette into his mouth and then tug the incredible hat to a raked dissolute angle as he passed out the door, raking the match across the frame as he disappeared. But the first match broke; the second one he struck on the bellplate while the elevator was rising. The door opened and clashed behind him; already his hand was reaching into his pocket while with the other he lifted the top paper from the shallow stack on the second stool beside the one on which the elevator man sat, sliding the facedown dollar watch which weighted it onto the next one, the same, the identical: black harsh and restrained:

FIRST FATALITY OF AIR
MEET: PILOT BURNED ALIVE
Lieut. Frank Burnham in
Crash of Rocket Plane

He held the paper off, his face tilted aside, his eyes squinted against the smoke. " 'Shumann surprises spectators by beating Bullitt for second place'," he read. "What do you think of that, now?"

"I think they are all crazy," the elevator man said. He had not looked at the reporter again. He received the coin into the same hand which clutched a dead stained cob pipe, not looking at the other. "Them that do it and them that pay money to see it." Neither did the reporter look at him.

"Yair; surprised," the reporter said, looking at the paper. Then he folded it and tried to thrust it into the pocket with the other folded one just like it. "Yair. And in one more lap he would have surprised them still more by beating Myers for first place." The cage stopped. "Yair; surprised. . . . . . . What time is it?" With the hand which now held both the coin and the pipe the elevator man lifted the facedown watch and held it out. He said nothing, he didn't even look at the reporter; he just sat there, waiting, holding the watch out with a kind of weary patience like a houseguest showing his watch to the last of several children. "Two minutes past ten?" the reporter said. "Just two minutes past ten? Hell."

"Get out of the door," the elevator man said. "There's a draft in here." It clashed behind the reporter again; as he crossed the lobby he tried again to thrust the paper into the pocket with the other one; antic, repetitive, his reflection in the glass street doors glared and flicked away. The street was empty, though even here, fourteen minutes afoot from Grandlieu Street, the February darkness was murmurous with faint uproar, with faint and ordered pandemonium; overhead, beyond the palmtufts, the overcast sky reflected that interdict and lightglared canyon now adrift with serpentine and confetti, through which the floats, bearing grimacing and antic mimes dwarfed chalkwhite and forlorn and contemplated by static curbmass of amazed confettifaces, passed as though through steady rain. He walked, not fast exactly but with a kind of loose and purposeless celerity, as though it were not exactly faces that he sought but solitude that he was escaping, or even as if he actually were going home like the editor had told him, thinking already of Grandlieu Street which he would have to cross somehow in order to do so. "Yah," he thought, "he should have sent me home by airmail." As he passed from light to light his shadow in midstride resolved, pacing him, on pavement and wall. In a dark plate window, sidelooking, he walked beside himself; stopping and turning so that for the moment shadow and reflection superposed he stared full at himself as though he still saw the actual shoulder sagging beneath the dead afternoon's phantom burden, and saw reflected beside him yet the sweater and the skirt and the harsh pallid hair as, bearing upon his shoulder the archfathered, he walked beside the oblivious and archadultress.

"Yah," he thought, "the damn little yellowheaded bastard. . . . . . . Yair, going to bed now, to sleep; the three of them in one bed or maybe they take it night about or maybe you just put your hat down on it first like in a barbershop." He faced himself in the dark glass, long and light and untidy as a bundle of laths dressed in human garments. "Yah," he thought, "the poor little towheaded son of a bitch." When he moved it was to recoil from an old man almost overwalked— a face, a stick, a suit filthier even than his own. He extended the two folded papers along with the coin. "Here, pop," he said. "Maybe you can get another dime for these. You can buy a big beer then."

When he reached Grandlieu Street he discovered that by air would be the only way he could cross it, though even now he had not actually paused to decide whether he were really going home or not. And this not alone because of police regulations but because of the physical curbmass of heads and shoulders in moiling silhouette against the lightglare, the serpentine and confettidrift, the antic passing floats. But even before he reached the corner he was assailed by a gust of screaming newsboys apparently as oblivious to the moment's significance as birds are aware yet oblivious to

the human doings which their wings brush and their drop-
pings fall upon. They swirled about him, screaming: in the
reflected light of the passing torches the familiar black thick
type and the raucous cries seemed to glare and merge faster
than the mind could distinguish the sense through which
each had been received: "Boinum boins!" **FIRST FATALITY
OF AIR** "Read about it! Foist Moidigror foitality!" **LIEUT.
BURNHAM KILLED IN AIR CRASH** "Boinum boins!"

"Naw!" the reporter cried. "Beat it! Should I throw away
a nickel like it was into the ocean because another lunatic
has fried himself?—Yah," he thought, vicious, savage, "even
they will have to sleep some of the time just to pass that
much of the dark half of being alive. Not to rest because they
have to race again tomorrow, but because like now air and
space aint passing them fast enough and time is passing
them too fast to rest in except during the six and a half minutes it takes to go the twenty-five miles, and the rest of them
standing there on the apron like that many window dum-
mies because the rest of them aint even there, like in the
girls' school where one of them is gone off first with all the
fine clothes. Yair, alive only for six and a half minutes a day
in one aeroplane. And so every night they sleep in one bed
and why shouldn't the either of them or the both of them at
once come drowsing unawake in one womandrowsing and
none of the three of them know which one nor care?—Yah,"
he thought, "maybe I was going home, after all." Then he
saw Jiggs, the pony man, the manpony of the afternoon, recoiled now into the center of a small violent backwater of
motionless backturned faces.

"Why dont you use your own feet to walk on?" Jiggs
snarled.

"Excuse me," one of the faces said. "I didn't mean——"

"Well, watch yourself," Jiggs cried. "Mine have got to last me to the end of my life. And likely even then I will have to walk a ways before I can catch a ride." The reporter watched him stand on alternate legs and scrub at his feet in turn with his cap, presenting to the smoky glare of the passing torches a bald spot neat as a tonsure and the color of saddleleather. As they stood side by side and looked at one another they resembled the tall and the short man of the orthodox and unfailing comic team—the one looking like a cadaver out of a medical school vat and dressed for the moment in garments out of a floodrefugee warehouse; the other filling his clothing without any fraction of surplus cloth which might be pinched between two fingers, with that trim vicious economy of wrestlers' tights; again Jiggs thought, since it had been good the first time, "Jesus. Dont they open the graveyards until midnight either?" About the two of them now the newsboys hovered and screamed:

"Globe Stoytsman! Boinum boins!"

"Yair," Jiggs said. "Burn to death on Thursday night or starve to death on Friday morning. So this is Moddy Graw. Why aint I where I have been all my life." But the reporter continued to glare down at him in bright amazement.

"At the Terrebonne?" he said. "She told me this afternoon you all had some rooms down in French town. You mean to tell me that just because he won a little money this afternoon he has got to pick up and move over to the hotel this time of night when he ought to been in bed an hour ago so he can fly tomorrow?"

"I dont mean nothing, mister," Jiggs said. "I just said I saw Roger and Laverne go into that hotel up the street a minute ago. I never asked them what for.—How about that cigarette?" The reporter gave it to him from the crumpled pack. Beyond the barricade of heads and shoulders, in the ceaseless rain of confetti, the floats moved past with an air esoteric, almost apocryphal, without inference of motion, like an inhabited archipelago putting out to sea on a floodtide. And now another newsboy, a new face, young, ageless, the teeth gaped raggedly as though he had found them one by one over a period of years about the streets, shrieked at them a new sentence like a kind of desperate ace:

"Laughing Boy in fit at Woishndon Poik!"

"Yair!" the reporter cried, glaring down at Jiggs. "Because you guys dont need to sleep. You aint human. I reckon the way he trains for a meet is to stay out on the town all the night before. Besides that—what was it?—thirty percent. of three hundred and twenty-five dollars he won this afternoon.—Come on," he said. "We wont have to cross the street."

"I thought you were going home so fast," Jiggs said.

"Yair," the reporter cried back over his shoulder, seeming not to penetrate the static human mass but to filter through it like a phantom, without alteration or diminution of bulk; now, turned sideways to cry back at Jiggs, passing between the individual bodies like a playingcard, he cried, "I have to sleep at night. I aint a racing pilot; I aint got an airplane to sleep in; I cant concentrate twenty-five miles of space at three miles an hour into six and a half minutes. Come on." The hotel was not far and the side, the carriage, entrance was comparatively clear in the outfalling of light beneath a suave canopy with its lettered frieze: Hotel Terrebonne. Above this from a jackstaff hung an oilcloth painted tabard: Headquarters, American Aeronautical Association. Dedication Meet, Feinman Airport. "Yair," the reporter cried, "they'll be here. Here's where to find guys that dont aim to sleep at the hotel. Yair; tiered identical cubicles of one thousand rented sleepings. And if you just got jack enough to last out the night you dont even have to go to bed."

"Did what?" Jiggs said, already working over toward the wall beside the entrance. "Oh. Teared Q pickles. Yair; teared Q pickles of one thousand rented cunts if you got the jack too. I got the Q pickle all right. I got enough Q pickle for one thousand. And if I just had the jack too it wouldn't be teared. How about another cigarette?" The reporter gave him another one from the crumpled pack. Jiggs now stood against the wall. "I'll wait here," he said.

"Come on in," the reporter said. "They are bound to be here. It will be after midnight before they even find out that Grandlieu Street has been closed. . . . . . . That's a snappy pair of boots you got on there."

"Yair," Jiggs said. He looked down at his right foot again. "At least he wasn't a football player or maybe driving a truck.—I'll wait here. You can give me a call if Roger wants me." The reporter went on; Jiggs stood again on his left leg and scrubbed at his right instep with his cap. "What a town," he thought. "Where you got to wear a street closed sign on your back to walk around in it."

"Because at least I am a reporter until one minute past ten tomorrow," the reporter thought, mounting the shallow steps toward the lobby; "he said so himself. I reckon I will have to keep on being one until then. Because even if I am fired now, at this minute while I walk here, there wont be

anybody for him to tell to take my name off the payroll until
noon tomorrow. So I can tell him it was my conscience. I
can call him from the hotel here and tell him my conscience
would not let me go home and go to sleep." He recoiled,
avoiding here also the paperplumage, the parrotmask, a
mixed party, whiskey-and-ginreeking, and then gone, leaving
behind them the draggled cumulant hillocks of trampled
confetti minching across the tile floor before the minching
pans and brooms of paid monkeymen who for three nights
now will do little else; they vanished, leaving the reporter for
the instant marooned beside the same easelplat with which
the town bloomed—the photographs of man and machine
each above its neat legend:

Matt Ord, New Valois. Holder, World's Land Plane
     Speed Record
Al Myers. Calexco
Jimmy Ott. Calexco
R.Q. Bullitt. Winner Graves Trophy, Miami, Fla
Lieut. Frank Burnham

And here also the cryptic shieldcaught (i n r i) loops of
bunting giving an appearance temporary and tentlike to the
interminable long corridor of machine plush and gilded synthetic plaster running between anonymous and rentable
spaces or alcoves from sunrise to sunset across America, between the nameless faience womanface behind the phallic
ranks of cigars and the stuffed chairs sentineled each by its
spittoon and potted palm;—the congruous stripe of
Turkeyred beneath the recentgleamed and homeless shoes
running, on into an interval of implacable circumspection: a

silent and discreet inference of lysol and a bath—billboard
stage and vehicle for what in the old lusty days called themselves drummers: among the brass spittoons of elegance and
the potted palms of decorum, legion homeless and symbolic:
the immemorial flying buttresses of ten million American
Saturday nights, with shrewd heads filled with tomorrow's
cosmic alterations in the form of pricelists and the telephone
numbers of discontented wives and highschool girls. "Until
time to take the elevator up and telephone the bellhop for
gals," the reporter thought. "Yair," he thought, "tiered Q
pickles of one thousand worn oftcarried phoenixbastions of
rented cunts." But the lobby tonight was crowded with more
than these; already he saw them fallen definitely into two distinct categories: the one in Madison Avenue jackets, who
perhaps once held transport ratings and perhaps still hold
them, like the manufacturer who once wrote himself mechanic or clerk retains in the new chromiumGeddes sanctuary the ancient primary die or mimeograph machine with
which he started out, and perhaps have now only the modest
Q.B. wings which clip to the odorous lapel the temperate
silk ribbon stencilled Judge or Official without the transport
rating and perhaps the ribbon and the tweed but not even
the wings; and the other with faces both sober and silent because they cannot drink tonight and fly tomorrow and have
never learned to talk at any time, in blue serge cut apparently not only from the same bolt but folded at the same
crease on the same shelf, who hold the severe transport rating and are here tonight by virtue of painfullydrummed
chartertrips from a hundred little nameless bases known only
to the Federal Department of Commerce, about the land
and whose equipment consists of themselves and a me-

chanic and one aeroplane which is not new. The reporter
thrust on among them, with that semblance of filtering
rather than passing. "Yair," he thought, "you dont need to
look. It's the smell, you can tell the bastards because they
smell like pressingclubs instead of Harris tweed." Then he
saw her, standing beside a Spanish jar filled with sand
pocked by chewinggum and cigarettes and burnt matches,
in a brown worn hat and a stained trenchcoat from whose
pocket protruded a folded newspaper. "Yah," he thought,
"because a trenchcoat will fit anybody and so they can have
two of them and then somebody can always stay at home
with the kid." When he approached her she looked full at
him for a moment, with pale blank complete unrecognition,
so that while he crossed the crowded lobby toward her and
during the subsequent three hours while at first he and she
and Shumann and Jiggs, and later the little boy and the parachute jumper too, sat crowded in the taxicab while he
watched the implacable meterfigures compound, he seemed
to walk solitary and chill and without progress down a steel
corridor like a fly in a gunbarrel, thinking "Yah, Hagood told
me to go home and I never did know whether I intended to
go or not. But Jiggs told me she would be at the hotel but I
didn't believe that at all"; thinking (while the irrevocable figures clicked and clicked beneath the dim insistent bulb and
the child slept on his bony lap and the other four smoked the
cigarettes which he had bought for them and the cab spun
along the dark swampsmelling shell road out to the airport
and then back to town again)—thinking how he had not expected to see her again because tomorrow and tomorrow do
not count because that will be at the field, with air and earth

full of snarling and they not even alive out there because
they are not human. But not like this, in clad decorous atti-
tudes that the police will not even look once at, in the
human nightworld of halfpast ten oclock and then eleven
and then twelve: and then behind a million separate secret
closed doors we will slack ourselves profoundly defenseless
on our backs, opened for the profound unsleeping, the inescapable and compelling flesh. Standing there beside the
Pyrenæan chamberpot at twenty-two minutes past ten because one of her husbands flew this afternoon in a crate that
three years ago was all right, that three years ago was so all
right that ever since all the others have had to conjoin as one
in order to keep it so that the word 'race' would still apply, so
that now they cannot quit because if they once slow down
they will be overreached and destroyed by their own spawn-
ing, like the Bornean whatsitsname that has to spawn running to keep from being devoured by its own litter. "Yah," he
thought, "standing there waiting so he can circulate in his
blue serge suit and the other trenchcoat among the whiskey
and the tweed when he ought to be at what they call home
in bed except they aint human and dont have to sleep"; thinking how it seems that he can bear either of them, either one
of them alone. "Yair," he thought, "teared Q pickles of one
thousand cuntless nights. They will have to hurry before anybody can go to bed with her," walking straight into the pale
cold blank gaze which waked only when he reached his hand
and drew the folded paper from the trenchcoat's pocket.

"Dempsey asleep, huh?" he said, opening the paper, the
page which he could have recited offhand before he even
looked at it:

BURNHAM BURNS
VALOISIAN CLAIMS LOVENEST FRAMEUP
Myers Easy Winner in Opener at Feinman Airport
Laughing Boy in Fifth at Washington Park

"No news is good newspaper news," he said, folding the paper again. "Dempsey in bed, huh?"

"Yes," she said. "Keep it. I've seen it." Perhaps it was his face. "Oh, I remember. You work on a paper yourself. Is it this one? or did you tell me?"

"Yair," he said. "I told you. No, it aint this one." Then he turned too, though she had already spoken.

"This is the one that bought Jack the icecream today," she said. Shumann wore the blue serge, but there was no trenchcoat. He wore a new gray homburg hat, not raked like in the department store cuts but set square on the back of his head so that (not tall, with blue eyes in a square thin profoundly sober face) he looked out not from beneath it but from within it with open and fatal humorlessness, like an early Briton who has been assured that the Roman governor will not receive him without he wear the borrowed centurion's helmet; he looked at the reporter for a single unwinking moment even blanker than the woman's had been.

"Nice race you flew in there today," the reporter said.

"Yair?" Shumann said. Then he looked at the woman. The reporter looked at her too. She had not moved, yet she now stood in a more complete and somehow terrific immobility, in the stained trenchcoat, a cigarette burning in the grained and blackrimmed fingers of one hand, looking at Shumann with naked and urgent concentration. "Come on," Shumann said. "Let's go." But she did not move.

"You didn't get it," she said. "You couldn't—"

"No. They dont pay off until Saturday night," Shumann said. ("Yah," the reporter thought, clashing the tight hermetic door behind him as the automatic domelight came on; "ranked coffincubicles of dead tail; the Great American in one billion printings slavepostchained and scribblescrawled: annotations of eternal electrodeitch and bottomhope.")

"Deposit five cents for three minutes please," the bland machinevoice chanted. The metal stalk sweatclutched, the guttapercha bloom cupping his breathing back at him, he listened, fumbled, counting as the discreet click and cling died into wirehum.

"That's five," he bawled. "Hear them? Five nickels. Now dont cut me off in three hundred and eighty-one seconds and tell me to——Hello," he bawled, crouching, clutching the metal stalk as if he hung by it from the edge of a swimmingpool; "listen. Get this——Yair. At the Terrebonne—— Yair, after midnight; I know. Listen. Chance for the goddamn paper to do something at last beside run our ass ragged between what Grandlieu Street kikes tell us to print in their half of the paper and tell you what you cant print in our half and still find something to fill the blank spaces under Connotator of the World's Doings and Moulder of the Peoples' Thought ha ha ha ha——"

"What?" the editor cried. "Terrebonne Hotel? I told you when you left here three hours ago to——"

"Yair," the reporter said. "Almost three hours, that's all. Just a taxi ride to get to the other side of Grandlieu Street first, and then out to the airport and back because they dont have but a hundred beds for visiting pilots out there and

General Behindman needs all of them for his reception and
so we come on back to the hotel because this is where they
all are to tell him to come back Saturday night provided the
bastard dont kill him tomorrow or Saturday. And you can
thank whatever tutelary assscratcher you consider presides
over the fate destiny and blunders of that office that me or
somebody happened to come in here despite the fact that
this is the logical place to find what we laughingly call news
at ten oclock at night, what with half the airmeet proprietors
getting drunk here and all of Mardi Gras done already got
drunk here. And him that ought to been in bed three hours
ago because he's got to race again tomorrow only he cant
race tomorrow because he cant go to bed yet because he
hasn't got any bed to go to bed in because they haven't got
any money to hire a place with a floor in it with because he
only won thirty percent. of three hundred and twenty-five
dollars this afternoon and to the guys that own an airmeet
that aint no more than a borrowed umbrella and the parachute guy cant do them any good now because Jiggs collected his twenty bucks and——"

"What? What? Are you drunk?"

"No. Listen. Just stop talking a minute and listen. When
I saw her out at the airport today they were all fixed up for the
night like I tried to tell you but you said it was not news; yair,
like you said, whether a man sleeps or not or why he cant
sleep aint news but only what he does while he aint asleep,
provided of course that what he does is what the guys that are
ordained to pick and choose it consider news; yair, I tried to
tell you but I'm just a poor bastard of an ambulancechaser: I
aint supposed to know news when I see it at thirty-five bucks
a week or I'd be getting more——Where was I? O yair.——

had a room for tonight because they have been here since Wednesday and so they must have had somewhere that they could lock the door and take off some of their clothes or at least put the trenchcoat down and lay down themselves, because they had shaved somewhere: Jiggs has got a slash on his jaw that even at a barber college you dont get one like it; so they were all fixed up, only I never asked them what hotel because I knew it would not have a name, just a sign on the gallery post that the old man made on Saturday when his sciatica felt good enough for him to go down town only she wouldn't let him leave until he made the sign and nailed it up: and so what was the use in me having to say 'What street did you say? Where is that?' because I aint a racing pilot, I am a reporter ha ha ha and so I would not know where these places are, Yair, all fixed up, and so he come in on the money this afternoon and I was standing there holding the kid and she says, 'There.' just like that: 'There.' and then I know that she has not moved during the whole six and a half minutes or maybe six and forty-nine-fifty-two ten thousandths or whatever the time was; she just says 'There.' like that and so it was o.k. even when he come in from the field with the ship and we couldn't find Jiggs to help roll the ship into the hangar and he just says 'Chasing a skirt, I guess' and we put the ship away and he went to the office to get his one-O-seven-fifty and we stayed there waiting for the parachute guy to come down and he did and wiped the flour out of his eyes and says, 'Where's Jiggs?' 'Why?' she says. 'Why?' he says. 'He went to collect my money.' and she says, 'My God'——"

"Listen! Listen to me!" the editor cried. "Listen!"

"Yair, the mechanic. In a pair of britches that must have

zippers so he can take them off at night like you would peel two bananas, and the tops of a pair of boots this afternoon, because tonight I dont get it, even when I see them;—rivetted under the insteps of a pair of tennis shoes. He collected the parachute guy's twenty-five bucks for him while the parachute guy was still on the way back from work because the parachute guy gets twenty-five berries for the few seconds it takes except for the five bucks he has to pay the transport pilot to take him to the office you might say, and the eight cents a pound for the flour only today the flour was already paid for and so the whole twenty bucks was velvet. And Jiggs collected it and beat it because they owed him some jack and he thought that since Shumann had won the race that he would win the actual money too like the program said and not only be able to pay last night's bill at the whore house where they——"

"Will you listen to me? Will you? Will you?"

"Yair; sure. I'm listening. So I come on to Grandlieu Street thinking about how you had told me to go home and wr—go home, and wondering how in hell you expected me to get across Grandlieu between then and midnight and all of a sudden I hear this excitement and cursing and it is Jiggs where some guy has stepped on his foot and put a scratch on one of them new boots, only I dont get it then. He just tells me he saw her and Shumann going into the Terrebonne because that was all he knew himself; I dont reckon he stayed to hear much when he beat it back to town with the parachute guy's jack and bought the boots and then walked in with them on where they had just got in from the field where Shumann had tried to collect his one-O-seven-fifty and they wouldn't pay him. So I couldn't cross Grandlieu and so we

walked on to the Terrebonne even though this is the last
place in town a reporter's got any business being at halfpast
ten at night, what with all the airmeet getting drunk here,
and half of Mardi Gras already——but never mind; I already
told you that. So we come on over and Jiggs wont come in
and still I dont get it, even though I had noticed the boots. So
I come in and there she is, standing by this greaser chamberpot and the lobby full of drunk guys with ribbon badges and
these kind of coats that look like they need a shave bad, and
the guys all congratulating one another about how the airport cost a million dollars and how maybe in the three days
more they could find out how to spend another million and
make it balance; and he come up, Shumann come up, and
her stiller than the pot even and looking at him and he says
they dont pay off until Saturday and she says 'Did you try?
Did you try?' Yair, trying to collect an installment on the
hundred and seven bucks so they can go to bed, with the kid
already asleep on the sofa in the madam's room and the parachute guy waiting with him if he happened to wake up, and
so they walked up to the hotel from Amboise Street because
it aint far, they are both inside the city limits, to collect something on the money he was under the delusion he had won
and I said 'Amboise Street?' because in the afternoon she just
said they had a room down in French Town and she said
'Amboise Street' looking at me without batting an eye and if
you dont know what kind of beddinghouses they have on
Amboise Street your son or somebody ought to tell you: yair,
you rent the bed and the two towels and furnish your own
cover. So they went to Amboise Street and got a room; they
always do that because in the Amboise Streets you can sleep
tonight and pay tomorrow because a whore will leave a kid

sleep on credit. Only they hadn't paid for last night yet and so tonight they dont want to take up the bed again for nothing, what with the airmeet in town, let alone the natural course of Mardi Gras. So they left the kid asleep on the madam's sofa and they come on to the hotel and Shumann said they dont pay off until Saturday and I said 'Never mind; I got Jiggs outside' and they never even looked at me. Because I hadn't got it then that Jiggs had spent the money, you see: and so we went out to the taxi and Jiggs was still standing there against the wall and Shumann looked at him and says 'You can come on too. If I could eat them I would have done it at dinnertime' and Jiggs comes and gets in too, kind of sidling over and then ducking into the cab like it was a henhouse and hunkering down on the little seat with his feet under him and I still dont get it even yet, not even when Shumann says to him 'You better find a manhole to stand in until Jack gets into the cab.' So we got in and Shumann says 'We can walk' and I says 'Where? Out to Lanier Avenue to get across Grandlieu?' and so that was the first dollar-eighty and we eased up as soon as the door got unclogged a little; yair, they were having a rush; and we went in and there the kid was, awake now and eating a sandwich the madam had sent out for him, and the madam and a little young whore and the whore's fat guy in his shirtsleeves and his galluses down, playing with the kid and the fat guy wanting to buy the kid a beer and the kid setting there and telling them how his old man flew the best pylon in America and Jiggs hanging back in the hall and jerking at my elbow until I could hear what he was whispering: 'Say, listen. Find my bag and open it and you will find a pair of tennis shoes and a paper package that feels like it's got a—a—well, a bootjack in it and hand them out to me, will you?' and I says 'What? A what in it?' and then the parachute guy in the room says 'Who's that out there? Jiggs?' and nobody answered and the parachute guy says 'Come in here' and Jiggs kind of edged into the door where the parachute guy could just see his face and the guy says 'Come on' and Jiggs edges a little further in and the guy says 'Come on' and Jiggs edges into the light then, with his chin between his shirt pockets and his head turned to one side and the guy looking him slow from feet to his head and then back again and says 'The son of a bitch' and the madam says 'I think so myself. The idea of them dirty bastard kikes holding him up on a purchase of that size for just forty cents' and the parachute guy says 'Forty cents?' Yair, it was like this. The boots was twenty-two-fifty. Jiggs paid down two dollars and a dime on them and he had to pay the parachute guy's pilot five bucks and so he never had but twenty bucks left even when he beat the bus, and so he borrowed the forty cents from the madam; yair, he left the airport at five-thirty and did all that before the store closed at six; he got there just in time to stick one of the tennis shoes into the door before it shut. So we paid the madam and that was the next five-forty because the room for last night she just charged them three bucks for it because they set in her room so she could use the other one for business until midnight when the rush slacked up and so she just charged them three bucks just to use the room to sleep in and the other two bucks was busfare. And we had the kid and the parachute guy too now but the driver said it would be o.k. because it would be a long haul out to the airport, because the program said there was accommo- dations for a hundred visiting pilots out there and if there was more than two or three missing from the lobby of the

Terrebonne it was because they was just lost and hadn't come in yet, and besides you had told me you would fire me if I wasn't out there at daylight tomorrow morning—no; today now—and it was eleven then, almost tomorrow then, and besides it would save the paper the cabfare for me back to town. Yair, that's how I figured too because it seems like I aint used to airmeets either and so we took all the baggage, both of them and Jiggs' mealsack too, and went out there and that was the next two dollars and thirty-five cents, only the kid was asleep again by that time and so maybe one of the dollars was Pullman extra fare. And there was a big crowd still there, standing around and looking at the air where this guy Burnham had flew in it and at the scorched hole in the field where he had flew in that too, and we couldn't stay out there because they aint only got beds for a hundred visiting pilots and Colonel Feinman is using all of them for his reception. Yair, reception. You build the airport and you get some receptive women and some booze and you lock the entrances and the information and ticket windows and if they dont put any money into the tops of their stockings, it's a reception. So they cant sleep out there and so we come on back to town and that's the next two dollars and sixty-five cents because we left the first cab go and we had to telephone for another one and the telephone was a dime and the extra twenty cents was because we didn't stop at Amboise Street, we come on to the hotel because they are still here and he can still ask them for his jack, still believing that air racing is a kind of sport or something run by men that have got time to stop at almost one oclock in the morning and count up what thirty percent. of three hundred and twenty-five dollars is and give it to him for no other reason than that

they told him they would if he would do something first. And
so now is the chance for this connotator of the world's doings
and molder of the people's thought to——"

"Deposit five cents for three minutes please," the bland
machinevoice said. In the airless cuddy the reporter coin-
fumbled, sweatclutching the telephone; again the discreet
click and cling died into dead wirehum.

"Hello! Hello!" he bawled. "You cut me off; gimme
my——" But now the buzzing on the editor's desk had
sounded again; now the interval out of outraged and
apoplectic waiting: the wirehum clicked fullvoiced before
the avalanched, the undammed:

"Fired! Fired! Fired! Fired!" the editor screamed. He
leaned halfway across the desk beneath the greenshaded
light, telephone and receiver clutched to him like a tackled
halfback lying half across the goalline, as he had caught the
instrument up; as, sitting bolt upright in the chair, his knuckles white on the arms and his teeth glinting under his lip
while he glared at the telephone in fixed and waiting fury, he
had sat during the five minutes since putting the receiver
carefully back and waiting for the buzzer to sound again.
"Do you hear me?" he screamed.

"Yair," the reporter said. "Listen. I wouldn't even bother
with that son of a bitch Feinman at all; you can have the
right guy paged right here in the lobby. Or listen. You dont
even need to do that. All they need is just a few dollars to eat
and sleep on until tomorrow; just call the desk and tell them
to let me draw on the paper; I will just add the eleven-eighty
I had to spend to——"

"WILL you listen to me?" the editor said. "Please! Will
you?"

"—to ride out there and—....... Huh? Sure. Sure, chief. Shoot."

The editor gathered himself again; he seemed to extend and lie a little further and flatter across the desk even as the back with the goal safe, tries for an extra inch while already downed; now he even ceased to tremble. "No," he said; he said it slowly and distinctly. "No. Do you understand? NO." Now he too heard only dead wirehum, as if the other end of it extended beyond atmosphere, into cold space; as though he listened now to the profound sound of infinity, of void itself filled with the cold unceasing murmur of aeonweary and unflagging stars. Into the round target of light a hand slid the first tomorrow's galley: the stilldamp neat row of boxes which in the paper's natural order had no scarehead, containing, since there was nothing new in them since time began, likewise no alarm:—that crosssection out of timespace as though of a lightray caught by a speed lens for a second's fraction between infinity and furious and trivial dust:

**FARMERS REFUSE   BANKERS DENY
STRIKERS DEMAND   PRESIDENT'S YACHT
ACREAGE REDUCTION   QUINTUPLETS GAIN
EX-SENATOR RENAUD CELEBRATES TENTH
ANNIVERSARY AS RESTAURATEUR**

Now the wirehum came to life.

"You mean you wont——" the reporter said. "You aint going to——"

"No. No. I wont even attempt to explain to you why I will not or cannot. Now listen. Listen carefully. You are fired. Do you understand? You dont work for this paper. You dont work for anyone this paper knows. If I should learn tomorrow that you do, so help me God I will tear their advertisement out with my own hands. Have you a telephone at home?"

"No. But there's one at the corner; I co——"

"Then go home. And if you call this office or this building again tonight I will have you arrested for vagrancy. Go home."

"All right, chief. If that's how you feel about it, O.K. We'll go home; we got a race to fly tomorrow, see?—Chief! Chief!"

"Yes?"

"What about my eleven-eighty? I was still working for you when I sp——"

Night in the Vieux Carré

Now they could cross Grandlieu Street; there was traffic in it now; to clash and clang of light and bell trolley and automobile crashed and glared across the intersection, rushing in a light curbchanneled spindrift of tortured and draggled serpentine and trodden confetti pending the dawn's whitewings—spent tinseldung of Momus' Nilebarge clatterfalque; ordered and marked by light and bell and carrying the two imitationleather bags and the drill mealsack they could now cross, the four others watching the reporter who, the little boy still asleep on his shoulder, stood at the extreme of the curbedge's channelbrim, in poised and swooping immobility like a scarecrow weathered gradually out of the earth which had supported it erect and intact and now poised for the first light vagrant air to blow it into utter dissolution. He translated himself into a kind of flapping gallop, gaining fifteen or twenty feet on the others before they could move, passing athwart the confronting glares of automobiles apparently without contact with earth like one of those apocryphal nighttime batcreatures whose nest or home no man ever saw, which are seen only in midswoop caught for a second in a lightbeam between nothing and nowhere. "Somebody take Jack from him," the woman said. "I am afr——"

"Of him?" the parachute jumper said, carrying one of the bags, his other hand under her elbow. "A guy would no more hit him than he would a glass barberpole. Or a paper sack of empty beerbottles in the street."

"He might fall down though and cut the kid all to pieces," Jiggs said. Then he said (it was still good, it pleased him no less even though this was the third time): "When he gets to the other side he might find out that they have opened the cemetery too and that would not be so good for Jack." He handed the sack to Shumann and passed the woman and the jumper, stepping quick on his short bouncing legs, the boots twinkling in the aligned tense immobility of the headlights, and overtook the reporter and reached up for the boy. "Gimme," he said. The reporter glared down at him without stopping, with a curious glazed expression like that of one who has not slept much lately.

"I got him," he said. "He aint heavy."

"Yair; sure," Jiggs said, dragging the still sleeping boy down from the other's shoulder like a bolt of wingfabric from a shelf as they stepped together onto the other curb. "But you want to have your mind free to find the way home."

"Yair," the reporter cried. They paused, turning, waiting for the others; the reporter glared down with that curious dazed look at Jiggs who carried the boy now with no more apparent effort than he had carried the aeroplane's tail, half-turned also, balanced like a short pair of tailor's shears stuck lightly upright into the tabletop, leaning a little forward like a dropped bowieknife. The other three still walked in the street—the woman who somehow even contrived to wear the skirt beneath the sexless trenchcoat as any one of the three men would; the tall parachute jumper with his handsome face now wearing an expression of sullen speculation; and Shumann behind them, in the neat serge suit and the new hat which even yet had the appearance of resting exactly as the machine stamped and molded it, on the hatblock in the store—the three of them with that same air which in Jiggs was merely oblivious and lightlyworn insolvency but which in them was that irrevocable homelessness of three immigrants walking down the steerage gangplank of a ship. As the woman and the parachute jumper stepped onto the curb light and bell clanged again and merged into the rising gearwhine as the traffic moved; Shumann sprang forward and onto the curb with a stiff light movement of unbelievable and rigid celerity, without a hair's abatement of expression or hatangle; again, behind them now, the light harried spindrift of tortured confetti and serpentine rose from the gutter in sucking gusts. The reporter glared at them all now with his dazed, strained and urgent face. "The bastards!" he cried. "The son of a bitches!"

"Yair," Jiggs said. "Which way now?" For an instant longer the reporter glared at them. Then he turned, as though put into motion not by any spoken word but by the sheer solid weight of their patient and homeless passivity, into the dark mouth of the street now so narrow of curb that they followed in single file, walking beneath a shallow overhang of irongrilled balconies. The street was empty, unlighted save by the reflection from Grandlieu Street behind them, smell-

ing of mud and of something else richly anonymous somewhere between coffeegrounds and bananas. Looking back
Jiggs tried to spell out the name, the letters inletted into the
curbedge in tileblurred mosaic, unable to discern at once
that it was not only a word, a name which he had neither
seen nor heard in his life, but that he was looking at it upside
down. "Jesus," he thought, "it must have took a Frenchman
to be polite enough to call this a street, let alone name it" carrying the sleeping boy on his shoulder and followed in turn
by the three others and the four of them hurrying quietly
after the hurrying reporter as though Grandlieu Street and
its light and movement were Lethe itself just behind them
and they four shades this moment out of the living world and
being hurried, grave quiet and unalarmed, on toward complete oblivion by one not only apparently long enough in res-
idence to have become a citizen of the shadows, but who
from all outward appearances had been born there too. The
reporter was still talking, but they did not appear to hear him,
as though they had arrived too recently to have yet unclogged their ears of human speech in order to even hear the
tongue in which the guide spoke. Now he stopped again,
turning upon them again his wild urgent face. It was another
intersection: two narrow roofless tunnels like exposed minegalleries marked by two pale oneway arrows which seemed
to have drawn to themselves and to hold in faint suspension
what light there was. Then Jiggs saw that to the left the street
ran into something of light and life — a line of cars along the
curb beneath an electric sign, a name, against which the
shallow dark grillwork of the eternal balconies hung in
weightless and lacelike silhouette. This time Jiggs stepped

from the curb and spelled out the street's name. "Toulouse," he spelled. "Too loose," he thought. "Yair. Swell. Our house last night must have got lost on the way home." So at first he was not listening to the reporter, who now held them immobile in a tableau reminiscent (save for his hat) of the cartoon pictures of city anarchists; Jiggs looked up only to see him rushing away toward the lighted sign; they all looked, watching the thin long batlike shape as it fled on.

"I dont want anything to drink," Shumann said. "I want to go to bed." The parachute jumper put his hand into the pocket of the woman's trenchcoat and drew out a pack of cigarettes, the third of those which the reporter had bought before they left the hotel the first time. He lit one and jetted smoke viciously from his nostrils.

"I heard you tell him that," he said.

"Booze?" Jiggs said. "Jesus, is that what he was trying to tell us?" They watched the reporter, the gangling figure in the flapping suit running loosely toward the parked cars; they saw the newsboy emerge from somewhere, the paper already extended and then surrendered, the reporter scarcely pausing to take it and pay.

"That's the second one he has bought tonight since we met him," Shumann said. "I thought he worked on one." The parachute jumper inhaled and jetted the vicious smoke again.

"Maybe he cant read his own writing," he said. The woman moved abruptly; she came to Jiggs and reached for the little boy.

"I'll take him a while," she said. "You and whatever his name is have carried him all evening." But before Jiggs could even release the boy the parachute jumper came and took hold of the boy too. The woman looked at him. "Get away, Jack," she said.

"Get away yourself," the jumper said. He lifted the boy from both of them, not gentle and not rough. "I'll take him. I can do this much for my board and keep." He and the woman looked at one another across the sleeping boy.

"Laverne," Shumann said, "give me one of the cigarettes." The woman and the jumper looked at one another.

"What do you want?" she said. "Do you want to walk the streets tonight? Do you want Roger to sit in the railroad station tonight and then expect to win a race tomorrow? Do you want Jack to——"

"Did I say anything?" the jumper said. "I dont like his face. But all right about that. That's my business. But did I say anything? Did I?"

"Laverne," Shumann said, "give me that cigarette." But it was Jiggs who moved; he went to the jumper and took the child from him.

"Jesus, gimme," he said. "You never have learned how to carry him." From somewhere among the dark dead narrow streets there came a sudden burst of sound, of revelry: shrill, turgid, wallmuted, as though emerging from beyond a low doorway or from a cave—some place airless and filled with smoke. Then they saw the reporter. He appeared from beneath the electric sign, emerging too from out a tilefloored and -walled cavern containing nothing like an incomplete gymnasium showerroom, and lined with two rows of discreet and curtained booths from one of which a faunfaced waiter with a few stumps of rotting teeth had emerged and recognised him.

"Listen," the reporter had said. "I want a gallon of absinth. You know what kind. I want it for some friends but I am going to drink it too and besides they aint Mardi Gras tourists. You tell Pete that. You know what I mean?"

"Sure mike," the waiter said. He turned and went on to the rear and so into a kitchen, where at a zinccovered table a man in a silk shirt, with a shock of black curls, eating from a single huge dish, looked up at the waiter with a pair of eyes like two topazes while the waiter repeated the reporter's name. "He says he wants it good," the waiter said in Italian. "He has friends with him. I guess I will have to give him gin."

"Absinth?" the other said, also in Italian. "Fix him up. Why not?"

"He said he wanted the good."

"Sure. Fix him up. Call mamma." He went back to eating. The waiter went out a second door; a moment later he returned with a gallon jug of something without color and followed by a decent withered old lady in an immaculate apron. The waiter set the jug on the sink and the old lady took from the apron's pocket a small phial. "Look and see if it's the paregoric she has," the man at the table said without looking up or ceasing to chew. The waiter leaned and looked at the phial from which the old lady was pouring into the jug. She poured about an ounce; the waiter shook the jug and held it to the light.

"A trifle more, madonna," he said. "The color is not quite right." He carried the jug out; the reporter emerged from beneath the sign, carrying it; the four at the corner watched him approach at his loose gallop, as though on the verge not of falling down but of completely disintegrating at the next stride.

"Absinth!" he cried. "New Valois absinth! I told you I

knew them. Absinth! We will go home and I will make you some real New Valois drinks and then to hell with them!" He faced them, glaring, with the actual jug now gesticulant. "The bastards!" he cried. "The son of a bitches!"

"Watch out!" Jiggs cried. "Jesus, you nearly hit that post with it!" He shoved the little boy at Shumann. "Here; take him," he said. He sprang forward, reaching for the jug. "Let me carry it," he said.

"Yair; home!" the reporter cried. He and Jiggs both clung to the jug while he glared at them all with his wild bright face. "Hagood didn't know he would have to fire me to make me go there. And get this, listen! I dont work for him now and so he never will know whether I went there or not!"

As the cage door clashed behind him, the editor himself reached down and lifted the facedown watch from the stack of papers, from that cryptic staccato crosssection of an instant crystallised and now dead two hours, though only the moment, the instant: the substance itself not only not dead, not complete, but in its very insoluble enigma of human folly and blundering possessing a futile and tragic immortality:

**FARMERS   BANKERS   STRIKERS   ACREAGE
WEATHER   POPULATION**

Now it was the elevator man who asked the time. "Half past two," the editor said. He put the watch back, placing it without apparent pause or calculation in the finicking exact center of the line of caps, so that now, in the shape of a cheap metal disc, the cryptic stripe was parted neatly in the exact center by the blank backside of the greatest and most inescapable enigma of all. The cage stopped, the door slid back. "Good night," the editor said.

"Good night, Mr Hagood," the other said. The door clashed behind him again; now in the glass street doors into which the reporter had watched himself walk five hours ago, the editor watched his reflection—a shortish sedentary man in worn cheap neartweed knickers and rubbersoled golfshoes, a silk muffler, a shetland jacket which unmistakably represented money and from one pocket of which protruded the collar and tie which he had removed probably on a second or third tee sometime during the afternoon, topped by a bare bald head and the horn glasses—the face of an intelligent betrayed asceticism, the face of a Yale or perhaps a Cornell senior outrageously surprised and overwhelmed by a sudden and vicious double decade—which marched steadily upon him as he crossed the lobby until just at the point where either he or it must give way, when it too flicked and glared away and he descended the two shallow steps and so into the chill and laggard predawn of winter. His roadster stood at the curb, the hostler from the allnight garage beside it, the neatgleamed and vaguely obstetrical shapes of golfclubheads projecting, raked slightly, above the lowered top and repeating the glint and gleam of other chromium about the car's dullsilver body. The hostler opened the door but Hagood gestured him in first.

"I've got to go down to French Town," he said. "You drive on to your corner." The hostler slid, lean and fast, past the golfbag and the gears and under the wheel. Hagood entered stiffly, like an old man, letting himself down into the low seat, whereupon without sound or warning the golfbag struck him across the head and shoulder with an apparently calculated and lurking viciousness, emitting a series of dry clicks as though produced by the jaws of a beast domesticated though not tamed, half in fun and half in deadly seriousness, like a pet shark. Hagood flung the bag back and then caught it just before it clashed at him again. "Why in hell didn't you put it into the rumble?" he said.

"I'll do it now," the hostler said, opening the door.

"Never mind now," Hagood said. "Let's get on. I have to go clear across town before I can go home."

"Yair, I guess we will all be glad when Moddy Graw is over," the hostler said. The car moved; it accelerated smoothly and on its fading gearwhine it drifted down the alley, poising without actually pausing; then it swung into the Avenue, gaining speed—a machine expensive, complex, delicate and intrinsically useless, created for some obscure psychic need of the species if not the race, from the virgin resources of a continent, to be the individual muscles bones and flesh of a new and legless kind—into the empty avenue between the purple-and-yellow paper bunting caught from post to post by cryptic shields symbolic of laughter and mirth now vanished and departed. It rushed along the dark lonely street, its displacement and the sum of money it represented concentrated and reduced to a single suavely illuminated dial on which numerals without significance increased steadily toward some yet unrevealed crescendo of ultimate triumph whose only witnesses were waifs. It slowed and stopped as smoothly and skilfully as it had started; the hostler slid out before it came to a halt. "O.K., Mr Hagood," he said. "Good night."

"Good night," Hagood said. As he slid across to the wheel the golfbag feinted silently at him. This time he slammed it over and down into the other corner. The car moved again, though now it was a different machine. It got into motion with a savage overpowered lurch as if something of it besides the other and younger man had quitted it when it stopped; it rolled on and into Grandlieu Street unchallenged now by light or bell. Instead, only the middle eye on each post stared dimly and steadily yellow, the four corners of the intersection marked now by four milkcolored jets from the fireplugs and standing one beside each plug, motionless and identical, four men in white like burlesqued internes in comedies, while upon each gutterplaited stream now drifted the flotsam and jetsam of the dead evening's serpentine and confetti. The car drifted on across the intersection and into that quarter of narrow canyons, the exposed minegalleries hung with iron lace, going faster now, floored now with cobbles and roofed by the low overcast sky and walled by a thick and tremendous uproar as though all reverberation hung like invisible fog in the narrow streets, to be waked into outrageous and monstrous sound even by streamlining and airwheels. He slowed into the curb at the mouth of an alley in which even as he got out of the car he could see the shape of a lighted second storey window printing upon the flag paving the balcony's shadow, and then in the window's rectangle the shadow of an arm which even from here he could see holding the shadow of a drinkingglass as, closing the car door, he turned upon the curb's chipped mosaic inlet *The Drowned* and walked up the alley in outrage but not surprise. When he came opposite the window he could see the living arm itself, though long before that he had begun to hear the reporter's voice. Now he could hear nothing else, scarcely his own voice as he stood beneath the balcony, shouting, beginning to scream, until without warning a short trimlegged man bounced suddenly to the balustrade and leaned outward a blunt face and a tonsure like a priest's as Hagood glared up at him and thought with raging impotence, "He told me they had a horse too. Damn damn damn!"

"Looking for somebody up here, doc?" the man on the balcony said.

"Yes!" Hagood screamed, shouting the reporter's name again.

"Who?" the man on the balcony said, cupping his ear downward. Again Hagood screamed the name. "Nobody up here by that name that I know of," the man on the balcony said; then he said, "Wait a minute." Perhaps it was Hagood's amazed outraged face; the other turned his head and he too bawled the name into the room behind him. "Anybody here named that?" he said. The reporter's voice ceased for a second, no more, then it shouted in the same tone which Hagood had been able to hear even from the end of the alley:

"Who wants to know?" But before the man on the balcony could answer, it shouted again: "Tell him he aint here. Tell him he's moved away. He's married. He's dead." then the voice, for its type timbre and volume, roared: "Tell him he's gone to work!" The man on the balcony looked down again.

"Well, mister," he said, "I guess you heard him about as plain as I did."

"No matter," Hagood said. "You come down."

"Me?"

"Yes!" Hagood shouted. "You!" So he stood in the alley and watched the other go back into the room which he himself had never seen. He had never before been closer to what

the reporter who had worked directly under him for twenty
months now called home than the file form which the reporter had filled out on the day he joined the paper. That
room, that apartment which the reporter called bohemian,
he had hunted down in this section of New Valois's vieux
carré and then hunted down piece by piece the furniture
which cluttered it, with the eager and deluded absorption of
a child hunting colored easter eggs. It was a gaunt cavern
roofed like a barn, with scuffed and worn and even rotted
floorboards and scrofulous walls and cut into two uneven
halves, bedroom and studio, by an old theatre curtain and
cluttered with slovenlymended and useless tables draped
with imitation batik bearing precarious lamps made of
liquorbottles, and other objects of oxidised metal made for
what original purpose no man knew, and hung with more
batik and machinemade Indian blankets and indecipherable
basrelief plaques vaguely religio-Italian primitive. It was
filled with objects whose desiccated and fragile inutility bore
a kinship to their owner's own physical being as though he
and they were all conceived in one womb and spawned in
one litter—objects which possessed that quality of veteran
prostitutes: of being overlaid by the ghosts of so many anonymous proprietors that even the present titleholder held
merely rights but no actual possession—a room apparently
exhumed from a theatrical morgue and rented intact from
one month to the next.

One day, it was about two months after the reporter had
joined the paper without credentials or any past, documen-
tary or hearsay, at all, with his appearance of some creature
evolved by forced draft in a laboratory and both beyond and
incapable of any need for artificial sustenance, like a tum-

bleweed, with his eager doglike air and his child's aptitude
for being not so much where news happened exactly but for
being wherever were the most people at any given time rushing about the vieux carré for his apartment and his furniture
and the decorations—the blankets and batik and the objects
which he would buy and fetch into the office and then listen
with incorrigible shocked amazement while Hagood would
prove to him patiently how he had paid two or three prices
for them;—one day Hagood looked up and watched a
woman whom he had never seen before enter the city room.
"She looked like a locomotive," he told the paper's owner
later with bitter outrage. "You know: when the board has
been devilled and harried by the newsreels of Diesel trains
and by the reporters that ask them about the future of rail-
roading until at last the board takes the old engine, the one
that set the record back in nineteen-two or nineteen-ten or
somewhere and sends it to the shops and one day they unveil
it (with the newsreels and the reporters all there, too) with
horseshoe rose wreaths and congressmen and thirty-six highschool girls out of the beauty show in bathing suits, and it is
a new engine on the outside only, because everyone is glad
and proud that inside it is still the old fast one of nineteen-
two or -ten. The same number is on the tender and the old
fine, sound, timeproved workingparts, only the cab and the
boiler are painted robin'segg blue and the rods and the bell
look more like gold than gold does and even the supercharger dont look so very noticeable except in a hard light,
and the number is in neon now: the first number in the
world to be in neon?" He looked up from his desk and saw
her enter on a blast of scent as arresting as mustard gas and
followed by the reporter looking more than ever like a

shadow whose projector had eluded it weeks and weeks ago—the fine big bosom like one of the walled impervious towns of the middleages whose origin antedates writing, which have been taken and retaken in uncountable fierce assaults which overran them in the brief fury of a moment and vanished, leaving no trace, the broad tomatocolored mouth, the eyes pleasant shrewd and beyond mere disillusion, the hair of that diamondhard and imperviously recent luster of a gilt service in a shopwindow, the goldstudded teeth square and white and big like those of a horse—all seen beneath a plump rich billowing of pink plumes so that Hagood thought of himself as looking at a canvas out of the vernal equinox of pigment when they could not always write to sign their names to them—a canvas conceived in and executed out of that fine innocence of sleep and open bowels capable of crowning the rich foul unchaste earth with rosy cloud where lurk and sport oblivious and incongruous cherubim. "I just dropped into town to see who he really works for," she said. "May I—Thanks." She took the cigarette from the pack on the desk before he could move, though she did wait for him to strike and hold the match. "And to ask you to sort of look out for him. Because he is a fool, you see. I dont know whether he is a newspaperman or not. Maybe you dont know yet, yourself. But he is the baby." Then she was gone—the scent, the plumes; the room which had been full of pink vapor and golden teeth darkened again, became niggard—and Hagood thought, "Baby of what?" because the reporter had told him before and now assured him again that he had neither brothers nor sisters, that he had no ties at all save the woman who had passed through the city room and apparently through New Valois too without stopping, with something of that aura of dwarfed distances and selfsufficient bulk of a light cruiser passing through a canallock, and the incredible name. "Only the name is right," the reporter told him. "Folks dont always believe it at first, but it's correct as far as I know."—"But I thought she said her name was—" and Hagood repeated the name the woman had given. "Yair," the reporter said. "It is now."—"You mean she has—" Hagood said. "Yair," the reporter said. "She's changed it twice since I can remember. They were both good guys, too." So then Hagood believed that he saw the picture—the woman not voracious, not rapacious; just omnivorous like the locomotive's maw of his late symbology; he told himself with savage disillusion, Yes. Come here to see just who he really worked for. What she meant was she came here to see that he really had a job and whether or not he was going to keep it. He believed now that he knew why the reporter cashed his paycheck before leaving the building each Saturday night; he could almost see the reporter, running now to reach the postoffice station before it closed—or perhaps the telegraph office; in the one case the flimsy blue strip of money order, in the other the yellow duplicate receipt—so that on that first midweek night when the reporter opened the subject diffidently, Hagood set a precedent out of his own pocket which he did not break for almost a year, cursing the big woman whom he had seen but once, who had passed across the horizon of his life without stopping yet forever after disarranging it, like the airblast of the oblivious locomotive crossing a remote and trashfilled suburban street. But he said nothing until the reporter came and requested a loan twice the size of an entire week's pay, and even then he did not open the matter; it was his face which caused the reporter to explain; it was for a weddingpresent. "A wedding-present?" Hagood said. "Yair," the reporter said. "She's been good to me. I reckon I better send her something, even if she wont need it." — "Wont need it?" Hagood cried. "No. She wont need what I could send her. She's always been lucky that way." — "Wait," Hagood said. "Let me get this straight. You want to buy a weddingpresent. I thought you told me you didn't have any sisters or br——" — "No," the reporter said. "It's for mamma." — "Oh," Hagood said after a time, though perhaps it did not seem very long to the reporter; perhaps it did not seem long before Hagood spoke again: "I see. Yes. Am I to congratulate you?" — "Thanks," the reporter said. "I dont know the guy. But the two I did know were o.k." — "I see," Hagood said. "Yes. Well. Married. The two you did know. Was one of them your——But no matter. Dont tell me. Dont tell me!" he cried. "At least it is something. Anyway, she did what she could for you!" Now it was the re-porter looking at Hagood with courteous interrogation. "It will change your life some now," Hagood said. "Well, I hope not," the reporter said. "I dont reckon she has done any worse this time than she used to. You saw yourself she's still a finelooking old gal and a good goer still, even if she aint any longer one of the ones you will find in the dance marathons at six a.m. So I guess it's o.k. still. She always has been lucky that way." — "You hope......." Hagood said. "You....... Wait," he said. He took a cigarette from the pack on the desk, though at last the reporter himself leaned and struck the match for him and held it. "Let me get this straight. You mean you haven't been......that that money you bor-rowed from me, that you send......." — "Send what where?" the reporter said after a moment. "Oh, I see. No. I aint sent her money. She sends me money. And I dont reckon that just getting married again will——" Hagood did not even sit back in the chair. "Get out of here!" he screamed. "Get out! Out!" For a moment longer the reporter looked down at him with that startled interrogation, then he turned and retreated. But before he had cleared the railing around the desk Hagood was calling him back in a voice hoarse and restrained; he returned to the desk and watched the editor snatch from a drawer a pad of note forms and scrawl on the top one and thrust pad and pen toward him. "What's this, chief?" the reporter said. "It's a hundred and eighty dollars," Hagood said in that tense careful voice, as though speaking to a child. "With interest at six percent. per annum and payable at sight. Not even on demand: on sight. Sign it."—"Jesus," the reporter said. "Is it that much already?"—"Sign it," Hagood said. "Sure, chief," the reporter said. "I never did mean to try to beat you out of it."

"So that's his name," Jiggs said. "That what?"

"That nothing!" Hagood said. They stood side by side on the old uneven flags which the New Valoisians claim rang more than once to the feet of the pirate Lafitte, looking up toward the window and the loud drunken voice beyond it. "It's his last name. Or the only name he has except the one initial as far as I or anyone else in this town knows. But it must be his; I never heard of anyone else named that and so no one intelligent enough to have anything to hide from would deliberately assume it. You see? Anyone, even a child, would know it is false."

"Yair," Jiggs said. "Even a kid wouldn't be fooled by it." They looked up at the window.

"I know his mother," Hagood said. "Oh, I know what you

are thinking. I thought the same thing myself when I first saw him: what anyone would think if he were to begin to explain where and when and why he came into the world, like what you think about a bug or a worm: 'All right! All right! For God's sake, all right!' And now he has doubtless been trying ever since, I think it was about half past twelve, to get drunk and I daresay successfully."

"Yair," Jiggs said. "You're safe there. He's telling Jack how to fly, about how Matt Ord gave him an hour's dual once. About how when you takeoff and land on them concrete Fs out at the airport he says it's like flying in and out of a, organization maybe; he said organization or organasm but maybe he never knew himself what he was trying to say; something about a couple of gnats hanging around a couple of married elephants in bed together like they say it takes them days and days and even weeks to get finished. Yair, him and Jack both, because Laverne and Roger have gone to bed in the bed with the kid and so maybe him and Jack are trying to get boiled enough to sleep on the floor, because Jesus, he spent enough on that taxi to have taken us all to the hotel. But nothing would do but we must come home with him; yair, he called it a house too; and on the way he rushes into this dive and rushes out with a gallon of something that he is hollering is absinth only I never drank any absinth but I could have made him all he wanted of it with a bathtub and enough grain alcohol and a bottle of paregoric or maybe it's laudanum. But you can come up and try it yourself. Besides, I better get on back; I am kind of keeping an eye on him and Jack, see?"

"Watching them?" Hagood said.

"Yair. It wont be no fight though; like I told Jack, it

would be like pushing over your grandmother. It happened that Jack kept on seeing him and Laverne this afternoon standing around on the apron or coming out of the —" Hagood turned upon Jiggs.

"Do I," Hagood cried with thin outrage, "do I have to spend half my life listening to him telling me about you people and the other half listening to you telling me about him?" Jiggs' mouth was still open; he closed it slowly; he looked at Hagood steadily with his hot bright regard, his hands on his hips, lightpoised on his bronco legs, leaning a little forward.

"You dont have to listen to anything I can tell you if you dont want to, mister," he said. "You called me down here. I never called you. What is it you want with me or him?"

"Nothing!" Hagood said. "I only came here in the faint hope that he would be in bed, or at least sober enough to come to work tomorrow."

"He says he dont work for you. He says you fired him."

"He lied!" Hagood cried. "I told him to be there at ten oclock tomorrow morning. That's what I told him."

"Is that what you want me to tell him, then?"

"Yes! Not tonight. Dont try to tell him tonight. Wait until tomorrow, when he. . . . . . . You can do that much for your night's lodging, cant you?" Again Jiggs looked at him with that hot steady speculation.

"Yair. I'll tell him. But it wont be just because I am trying to pay him back for what he done for us tonight. See what I mean?"

"I apologise," Hagood said. "But tell him. Do it anyway you want to, but just tell him, see that he is told before he leaves here tomorrow. Will you?"

"O.K.," Jiggs said. He watched the other turn and go back down the alley, then he turned too and entered the house, the corridor, and mounted the cramped dark treacherous stairs and into the drunken voice again. The parachute jumper sat on an iron cot disguised thinly by another Indian blanket and piled with bright faded pillows about which dust seemed to lurk in a thin nimbuscloud even at the end of the couch which the jumper had not disturbed. The reporter stood beside a slopped table on which the gallon jug sat and a dishpan containing now mostly dirty icewater, though a few fragments of the actual ice still floated in it. He was in his shirtsleeves, his collar open and the knot of his tie slipped downward and the ends of the tie darkly wet, as if he had leaned them downward into the dishpan; against the bright vivid even though machinedyed blanket on the wall behind him he resembled some slain curious trophy of a western vacation half finished by a taxidermist and then forgotten and then salvaged again.

"Who was it?" he said. "Did he look like if you would want to see him right after supper on Friday night you would have to go around to the church annex where the boy scouts are tripping one another up from behind?"

"What?" Jiggs said. "I guess so." Then he said, "Yair. That's him." The reporter looked at him, holding in his hand a glass such as chainstore jam comes in.

"Did you tell him I was married? Did you tell him I got two husbands now?"

"Yair," Jiggs said. "How about going to bed?"

"Bed?" the reporter cried. "Bed? When I got a widowed guest in the house that the least thing I can do for him is to get drunk with him because I cant do anything else because

I am in the same fix he is only I am in this fix all the time and not just tonight?"

"Sure," Jiggs said. "Let's go to bed." The reporter leaned against the table and with his bright reckless face he watched Jiggs go to the bags in the corner and take from the stained canvas sack a paperwrapped parcel and open it and take out a brandnew bootjack; he watched Jiggs sit on one of the chairs and try to remove the right boot; then at the sound he turned and looked with that bright speculation at the parachute jumper completely relaxed on the cot, his long legs crossed and extended, laughing at Jiggs with vicious and humorless steadiness. Jiggs sat on the floor and extended his leg toward the reporter. "Give it a yank," he said.

"Sure," the jumper said. "We'll give it a yank for you." The reporter had already taken hold of the boot; the jumper struck him aside with a backhanded blow. The reporter staggered back into the wall and watched the jumper, his handsome face tense and savage in the lamplight, his teeth showing beneath the slender moustache, take hold of the boot and then lift his foot suddenly toward Jiggs' groin before Jiggs could move. The reporter half fell into the jumper, jolting him away so that the jumper's foot only struck Jiggs' turned flank.

"Here!" he cried. "You aint playing!"

"Playing?" the jumper said. "Sure I'm playing. That's all I do—like this." The reporter did not see Jiggs rise from the floor at all; he just saw Jiggs in midbounce, as though he had risen with no recourse to his legs at all, and Jiggs' and the jumper's hands flick and lock as with the other hand Jiggs now hurled the reporter back into the wall.

"Quit it, now," Jiggs said. "Look at him. What's the fun

in that, huh?" He looked back over his shoulder at the reporter. "Go to bed," he said. "Go on, now. You got to be at
work at ten oclock. Go on." The reporter did not move. He
leaned back against the wall, his face fixed in a thin grimace
of smiling as though glazed. Jiggs sat on the floor again, his
right leg extended again, holding it extended between his
hands. "Come on," he said. "Give them a yank." The reporter took hold of the boot and pulled; abruptly he too was
sitting on the floor facing Jiggs, listening to himself laughing.
"Hush," Jiggs said. "Do you want to wake up Roger and Laverne and the kid? Hush now. Hush."

"Yair," the reporter whispered. "I'm trying to quit. But I
cant. See? Just listen at me."

"Sure you can quit," Jiggs said. "Look. You done already
quit. Aint you? See now?"

"Yair," the reporter said. "But maybe it's just freewheel-
ing." He began to laugh again, and then Jiggs was leaning
forward, slapping his thigh with the flat of the bootjack until
he stopped.

"Now," Jiggs said. "Pull." The boot loosened, since it had
already been worked at; Jiggs slipped it off. But when the left
one came it gave way so suddenly that the reporter went over
on his back, though this time he did not laugh; he lay there
saying,

"It's o.k. I aint going to laugh," then he was looking up at
Jiggs standing over him in a pair of cotton socks which, like
the homemade putties of the morning, consisted of legs and
insteps only.

"Get up," Jiggs said, lifting the reporter.

"All right," the reporter said. "Just make the room stop."
He began to struggle to stay down, but Jiggs hauled him up

and he leaned outward against the arms which held him on his feet, toward the couch, the cot. "Wait till it comes around again," he cried; then he lunged violently, sprawling onto the cot and then he could feel someone tumbling him onto the cot and he struggled again to be free, saying thickly through a sudden hot violent liquid mass in his mouth, "Look out! Look out! I'm on now. Let go!" Then he was free, though he could not move yet. Then he saw Jiggs lying on the floor next the wall, his back to the room and his head pillowed on the canvas sack and the parachute jumper at the slopped table, pouring from the jug. The reporter got up, unsteadily, though he spoke quite distinctly: "Yair. That's the old idea. Little drink, hey?" He moved toward the table, walking carefully, his face wearing again the expression of bright and desperate recklessness, speaking apparently in soliloquy to an empty room: "But nobody to drink with now. Jiggs gone to bed and Roger gone to bed and Laverne cant drink tonight because Roger wont let her drink. See?" Now he looked at the jumper across the table, above the jug, the jam glasses, the dishpan, with that bright dissolute desperation though he still seemed to speak into an empty room: "Yair. It was Roger, see. Roger was the one that wouldn't let her have anything to drink tonight, that took the glass out of her hand after a friend gave it to her. And so she and Roger have gone to bed. See?" They looked at one another.

"Maybe you wanted to go to bed with her yourself?" the jumper said. For a moment longer they looked at one another. The reporter's face had changed. The bright recklessness was still there, but now it was overlaid with that abject desperation which, lacking anything better, is courage.

"Yes!" he cried. "Yes!" flinging himself backward and

crossing his arms before his face at the same time; at first he did not even realise that it was only the floor which had struck him until he lay prone again, his arms above his face and head and looking between them at the feet of the parachute jumper who had not moved. He watched the jumper's hand go out and strike the lamp from the table and then when the crash died he could see nothing and hear nothing, lying on the floor perfectly and completely passive and waiting. "Jesus," he said quietly, "for a minute I thought you were trying to knock the jug off." But there was no reply, and again his insides had set up that fierce maelstrom to which there was no focalpoint, not even himself. He lay motionless and waiting and felt the quick faint airblast and then the foot, the shoe, striking him hard in the side, once, and then he heard the jumper's voice from above him speaking apparently from somewhere within the thick instability of the room, the darkness, whirling and whirling away, in a tone of quiet detachment saying the same words and in the same tone in which he had spoken them to Jiggs in the brothel six hours ago. They seemed to continue, to keep on speaking, clapping quietly down at him even after he knew by sound that the jumper had gone to the cot and stretched out on it; he could hear the quiet savage movements as the other arranged the dusty pillows and drew the blanket up. "That must be at least twelve times," the reporter thought. "He must have called me a son of a bitch at least eight times after he went to sleep.—Yair," he thought, "I told you. I'll go, all right. But you will have to give me time, until I can get up and move.—Yair," he thought, while the long vertiginous darkness completed a swirl more profound than any yet; now he felt the thick cold oil start and spring from his pores and which, when his dead hand found his dead face, did not sop up nor wipe away beneath the hand but merely doubled as though each drop were the atom which instantaneously divides not only into two equal parts but into two parts each of which is equal to the recent whole; "yesterday I talked myself out of a job, but tonight I seem to have talked myself out of my own house." But at last he began to see: it was the dim shape of the window abruptly against some outer lightcolored space or air; vision caught, snagged and clung desperately and blindly like the pinafore of a child falling from a fence or a tree. On his hands and knees and still holding to the window by vision he found the table and got to his feet. He remembered exactly where he had put the key, carefully beneath the edge of the lamp, but now with the lamp gone his still nerveless hand did not feel the key at all when he knocked it from the table: it was hearing alone: the forlorn faint clink. He got down and found it at last and rose again, carefully, and wiped the key on the end of his necktie and laid it in the center of the table, putting it down with infinite care as though it were a dynamite cap, and found one of the sticky glasses and poured from the jug by sound and feel and raised the glass, gulping, while the icy almost pure alcohol channeled fiercely down his chin and seemed to blaze through his cold wet shirt and onto and into his flesh. It tried to come back at once; he groped to the stairs and down them, swallowing and swallowing the vomit which tried to fill his throat; and there was something else that he had intended to do which he remembered only when the door clicked irrevocably behind him and the cold thick predawn breathed against his damp shirt which had no coat to cover it and warm it. And now he could not recall at once what he had intended to do, where he had intended to go, as though destination and purpose were some theoretical point like latitude or time which he had passed in the hall, or something like a stamped and forgotten letter in the coat which he had failed to bring. Then he remembered; he stood on the cold flags, shaking with slow and helpless violence inside his wet shirt, remembering that he had started for the newspaper to spend the rest of the night on the floor of the now empty city room (he had done it before), having for the time forgotten that he was now fired. If he had been sober he would have tried the door, as people will, out of that vague hope for even though not belief in, miracles. But, drunk, he did not. He just began to move carefully away, steadying himself along the wall until he should get into motion good, waiting to begin again to try to keep the vomit swallowed, thinking quietly out of peaceful and profound and detached desolation and amazement: "Four hours ago they were out and I was in, and now it's turned around exactly backward. It's like there was a kind of cosmic rule for poverty like there is for water-level, like there has to be a certain weight of bums on park benches or in railroad waitingrooms waiting for morning to come or the world will tilt up and spill all of us wild and shrieking and grabbing like so many shooting stars, off into nothing." But it would have to be a station, walls, even though he had long since surrendered to the shaking and felt no cold at all anymore. There were two stations, but he had never walked to either of them and he could not decide nor remember which was the nearer, when he stopped abruptly, remembering the Market, thinking of coffee. "Coffee," he said. "Coffee. When I have had some coffee, it will be tomorrow. Yair. When you have had coffee, then it is already tomorrow and so you dont have to wait for it."

He walked pretty well now, breathing with his mouth wide open as if he hoped (or were actually doing it) to soothe and quiet his stomach with the damp and dark and the cold. Now he could see the Market—a broad low brilliant wallless cavern filled with ranked vegetables as bright and impervious in appearance as artificial flowers, among which men in sweaters and women in men's sweaters and hats too sometimes, with Latin faces still swollen with sleep and vapored faintly about the mouth and nostrils by breathing still warm from slumber, paused and looked at the man in shirtsleeves and loosened collar, with a face looking more than ever like that of a corpse roused and outraged out of what should have been the irrevocable and final sleep. He went on toward the coffee stall; he felt fine now. "Yair, I'm all right now," he thought, because almost at once he had quit trembling and shaking, and when at last the cup of hot pale liquid was set before him he told himself again that he felt fine; indeed, the very fact of his insistence to himself should have been intimation enough that things were not all right. And then he sat perfectly motionless, looking down at the cup in that rapt concern with which one listens to his own insides. "Jesus," he thought. "Maybe I tried it too quick. Maybe I should have walked around a while longer." But he was here, the coffee waited before him; already the counterman was watching him coldly. "And Jesus, I'm right; after a man has had his coffee it's tomorrow: it has to be!" he cried, with no sound, with that cunning selfdeluding logic of a child. "And tomorrow it's just a hangover; you aint still drunk tomorrow; tomorrow you cant feel this bad." So he raised the cup as he had the final glass before he left home; he felt the hot liquid channeling down his chin too and striking through his shirt against his flesh; with his throat surging and trying to gag and his gaze holding desperately to the low cornice above the coffeeurn he thought of the cup exploding from his mouth, shooting upward and without trajectory like a champagne-cork; he put the cup down, already moving though not quite running, out of the stall and between the bright tables, passing from one to another by his hands like a monkey runs until he brought up against a table of strawberry boxes, holding to it without knowing why he had stopped nor when, while a woman in a black shawl behind the table repeated,

"How many, mister?" After a while he heard his mouth saying something, trying to.

"Qu'est-ce qu'il voulait?" a man's voice said from the end of the table.

"D' journal d' matin," the woman said.

"Donne-t-il," the man said. The woman stooped and reappeared with a paper, folded back upon an inner sheet, and handed it to the reporter.

"Yair," he said. "That's it." But when he tried to take it he missed it; it floated down between his and the woman's hands, opening onto the first page. She folded it right now and he took it, swaying, holding to the table with the other hand, reading from the page in a loud declamatory voice: "Bankers strike! Farmers yacht! Quintuplets acreage! Reduction gains!——No; wait." He swayed, staring at the shawled woman with gaunt concentration. He fumbled in his pocket; the coins rang on the floor with the same sound which the key made, but now as he began to stoop the cold floor struck

him a shocking blow on the face and then hands were holding him again while he struggled to rise. Now he was plunging toward the entrance; he caromed from the last table
without even feeling it, the hot corrupted coffee gathering
inside him like a big heavy bird beginning to fly as he
plunged out the door and struck a lamppost and clung to it
and surrendered as life, sense, all, seemed to burst out of his
mouth as though his entire body were trying in one fierce or-
gasm to turn itself wrongsideout.

Now it was dawn. It had come unremarked; he merely
realised suddenly that he could now discern faintly the words
on the paper and that he now stood in a gray palpable substance without weight or light, leaning against the wall
which he had not yet tried to leave. "Because I dont know
whether I can make it yet or not," he thought, with peaceful
and curious interest as if he were engaged in a polite parlor
game for no stakes; when he did move at last he seemed to
blow leaflight along the graying wall to which he did not
cling exactly but rather moved in some form of light slow at-
trition, like the leaf without quite enough wind to keep it in
motion. The light grew steadily, without seeming to come
from any one source or direction; now he could read the
words, the print, quite well though they still had a tendency
to shift and flow in smooth elusion of sense, meaning while
he read them aloud: "Quintuplets bank. . . . No; there aint
any pylon—Wait. Wait. . . . Yair, it was a pylon only it was
pointed down and buried at the time and they were not quintuplets yet when they banked around it.——Farmers bank.
Yair. Farmer's boy, two farmers' boys, at least one from Ohio
anyway she told me. And the ground they plow from Iowa;
yair, two farmers' boys downbanked; yair, two buried pylons

in the one Iowadrowsing womandrowsing pylondrowsing
. . . . No; wait." He had reached the alley now and he
would have to cross it since his doorway was in the opposite
wall: so that now the paper was in the hand on the side
which now clung creeping to the wall and he held the page
up into the gray dawn as though for one last effort, concen-
trating sight, the vision without mind or thought, on the sym-
metrical line of boxheads: FARMERS REFUSE   BANKERS
DENY   STRIKERS DEMAND   PRESIDENT'S YACHT
ACREAGE REDUCTION   QUINTUPLETS GAIN   EX-
SENATOR RENAUD CELEBRATES TENTH ANNIVERSARY
AS RESTAURATEUR—the fragile web of ink and paper, as-
sertive, proclamative; profound and irrevocable if only in the
sense of being profoundly and irrevocably unimportant—the
dead instant's fruit of forty tons of machinery and an entire
nation's antic delusion. The eye, the organ without thought
speculation or amaze, ran off the last word and then, ceasing
again, vision went on ahead and gained the door beneath the
balcony and clung and completely ceased. "Yair," the reporter thought. "I'm almost there but still I dont know if I am
going to make it or not."

Tomorrow

It was a foot in his back prodding him that waked Jiggs. He rolled over to face the room and the daylight and saw Shumann standing over him, dressed save for his shirt, and the parachute jumper awake too, lying on his side on the couch with the Indian blanket drawn to his chin and across his feet the rug which last night had been on the floor beside the cot. "It's half past eight," Shumann said. "Where's what's his name?"

"Where's who?" Jiggs said. Then he sat up, bounced up into sitting, his feet in the socklegs projecting before him as he looked about the room in surprised recollection. "Jesus, where is he?" he said. "I left him and Jack—Jesus, his boss came down here about three oclock and said for him to be somewhere at work at ten oclock." He looked at the parachute jumper, who might have been asleep save for his open eyes. "What became of him?" he said.

"How should I know?" the jumper said. "I left him lying

[97]

there on the floor, about where you are standing," he said to Shumann. Shumann looked at the jumper too.

"Were you picking on him again?" he said.

"Yair he was," Jiggs said. "So that's what you were staying awake until I went to sleep for." The jumper did not answer. They watched him throw the blanket and the rug back and rise, dressed as he had been the night before—coat vest and tie—save for his shoes; they watched him put the shoes on and stand erect again and contemplate his now wrinkled trousers in bleak and savage immobility for a moment, then turn toward the faded theatre curtain.

"Going to wash," he said. Shumann watched Jiggs, seated now, delve into the canvas sack and take out the tennis shoes and the bootlegs which he had worn yesterday and put his feet into the shoes. The new boots sat neatly, just the least bit wrinkled about the ankles, against the wall where Jiggs' head had been. Shumann looked at the boots and then at the worn tennis shoes which Jiggs was lacing, but he said nothing: he just said,

"What happened last night? Did Jack——"

"Nah," Jiggs said. "They were all right. Just drinking. Now and then Jack would try to ride him a little, but I told him to let him alone. And Jesus, his boss said for him to be at work at ten oclock. Have you looked down stairs? Did you look under the bed in there? Maybe he——"

"Yair," Shumann said. "He aint here." He watched Jiggs now forcing the tennis shoes slowly and terrifically through the bootlegs, grunting and cursing. "How do you expect them to go on over the shoes?"

"How in hell would I get the strap on the outside of the shoes if I didn't?" Jiggs said. "You ought to know what become of him; you wasn't drunk last night, were you? I told his boss I would——"

"Yair," Shumann said. "Go back and wash." With his legs drawn under him to rise Jiggs paused and glanced at his hands for an instant.

"I washed good at the hotel last night," he said. He began to rise, then he stopped and took from the floor a halfsmoked cigarette and bounced up, already reaching into his shirt pocket as he came up facing the table. With the stub in his mouth and the match in his hand, he paused. On the table, amid the stained litter of glasses and matches burnt and not burnt and ashes which surrounded the jug and the dishpan, lay a pack of cigarettes, another of those which the reporter had bought last night. Jiggs put the stub into his shirt pocket and reached for the pack. "Jesus," he said, "during the last couple months I have got to where a whole cigarette aint got any kick to it." Then his hand paused again, but for less than a watchtick, and Shumann watched it go on to the jug's neck while the other hand broke free from the table's sticky top the glass, the same from which the reporter had drunk in the darkness.

"Leave that stuff alone," Shumann said. He looked at the blunt watch on his naked wrist. "It's twenty to nine. Let's get out of here."

"Yair," Jiggs said, pouring into the glass. "Get your clothes on; let's go check them valves. Jesus, I told the guy's boss I would——Say, I found out last night what his name is. Jesus, you wouldn't never guess in. . . . . . ." He stopped; he and Shumann looked at one another.

"Off again, huh?" Shumann said.

"I'm going to take one drink, that I saved out from last

night to take this morning. Didn't you just say let's get out to the field? How in hell am I going to get anything to drink out there, even if I wanted it, when for Christ's sake the only money I have had in three months I was accused of stealing it? When the only guy that's offered me a drink in three months we took both his beds away from him and left him the floor to sleep on and now we never even kept up with him enough to deliver a message from his boss where he is to go to work——"

"One drink, huh?" Shumann said. "There's a slop jar back there; why not get it and empty the jug into it and take a good bath?" He turned away. Jiggs watched him lift the curtain aside and pass beyond it. Then Jiggs began to raise the glass, making already the preliminary grimace and shudder, when he paused again. This time it was the key where the reporter had carefully placed it and beside which Shumann had set the broken lamp which he had raised from the floor. Touching the key, Jiggs found it too vulcanised lightly to the table's top by spilt liquor.

"He must be here, then," he said. "But for Christ's sake where?" He looked about the room again; suddenly he went to the couch and lifted the tumbled blanket and looked under the cot. "He must be somewheres though," he thought. "Maybe behind the baseboard. Jesus, he wouldn't make no more bulge behind it than a snake would." He went back to the table and raised the glass again; this time it was the woman and the little boy. She was dressed, the trench-coat belted; she gave the room a single pale comprehensive glance, then she looked at him, brief, instantaneous, blank. "Drinking a little breakfast," he said.

"You mean supper," she said. "You'll be asleep in two hours."

"Did Roger tell you we have mislaid the guy?" he said.

"Go on and drink it," she said. "It's almost nine oclock. We have got to pull all those valves today." But again he did not get the glass to his mouth. Shumann was also dressed now; across the arrested glass Jiggs watched the jumper go to the bags and jerk them and then the boots out into the floor and then turn upon Jiggs, snarling,

"Go on. Drink it."

"Dont either of them know where he went?" the woman said.

"I dont know," Shumann said. "They say they dont."

"I told you No," the jumper said. "I didn't do anything to him. He flopped down there on the floor and I put the light out and went to bed and Roger woke me up and he was gone and it's damned high time we were doing the same thing if we are going to get those valves miked and back in the engine before three oclock."

"Yair," Shumann said, "he can find us if he wants us. We are easier for him to find than he is for us to find." He took one of the bags; the jumper already had the other. "Go on," he said, without looking at Jiggs. "Drink it and come on."

"Yair," Jiggs said. "Let's get started." He drank now and set the glass down while the others moved toward the stairs and began to descend. Then he looked at his hands; he looked at them as if he had just discovered he had them and had not yet puzzled out what they were for. "Jesus, I had better wash," he said. "You all go ahead; I'll catch you before you get to the bus stop."

"Sure; tomorrow," the jumper said. "Take the jug too. No; leave it. If he's going to lay around drunk all day long too, better here than out there in the way." He was last; he kicked the boots savagely out of his path. "What are you going to do with these? carry them in your hands?"

"Yair," Jiggs said. "Until I get them paid for."

"Paid for? I thought you did that yesterday, with my——"

"Yair," Jiggs said. "So did I."

"Come on, come on," Shumann said from the stairs. "Go on, Laverne." The jumper went on to the stairs. Shumann now herded them all before him. Then he paused and looked back at Jiggs, dressed, neat, profoundly serious beneath the new hat which Jiggs might still have been looking at through plate glass. "Listen," he said. "Are you starting out on a bat today? I aint trying to stop you because I know I cant, I have tried that before. I just want you to tell me so I can get somebody else to help Jack and me pull those valves."

"Dont you worry about me," Jiggs said. "Jesus, dont I know we are in a jam as well as you do? You all go on; I'll wash up and catch you before you get to Main Street." They went on; Shumann's hat sank from sight. Then Jiggs moved with rubbersoled and light celerity. He caught up the boots and passed on beyond the curtain and into a cramped alcove hung with still more blankets and pieces of frayed and faded dyed or painted cloth enigmatic of significance and inscrutable of purpose, and containing a chair, a table, a washstand, a chest of drawers bearing a celluloid comb and two ties such as might be salvaged from a trashbin but for the fact that anyone who would have salvaged them would not wear ties, and a bed neatly madeup, so neatly restored that it shouted the fact that it had been recently occupied by a woman who did not live there. Jiggs went to the washstand but it was not his hands and face that he bathed. It was the boots, examining with grim concern a long scratch across the instep of the right one where he believed that he could even discern the reversed trademark of the assaulting heeltap, scrubbing at the mark with the damp towel. "Maybe it wont show through a shine," he thought. "Anyway I can be glad the bastard wasn't a football player." It did not improve any now, however, so he wiped both the boots, upper and sole, and hung the now filthy towel carefully and neatly back and returned to the other room. He may have looked at the jug in passing but first he put the boots carefully into the canvas sack before going to the table. He could have heard sounds, even voices, from the alley beneath the window if he had been listening. But he was not. All he heard now was that thunderous silence and solitude in which man's spirit crosses the eternal repetitive rubicon of his vice in the in-stant after the terror and before the triumph becomes dis-may—the moral and spiritual waif shrieking his feeble I-am-I into the desert of chance and disaster. He raised the jug; his hot bright eyes watched the sticky glass run almost half full; he gulped it, raw, scooping blindly the stale and trashladen water from the dishpan and gulping that too; for one fierce and immolated instant he thought about hunting and finding a bottle which he could fill and carry with him in the bag along with the boots, the soiled shirt, the sweater, the cigarbox containing a cake of laundry soap and a cheap straight razor and a pair of pliers and a spool of safetywire, but he did not. "Be damned if I will," he cried silently, even while his now ruthless inside was telling him that within the hour he would regret it; "be damned if I will steal any man's whiskey behind his back," he cried, catching up the sack and hurrying down the stairs, fleeing at least from temptation's protagonist, even if it was rather that virtue which is desire's temporary assuagement than permanent annealment, since he did not want the drink right now and so when he did begin to want it, he would be at least fifteen miles away from that particular jug. It was not the present need for another drink that he was running from. "I aint running from that," he told himself, hurrying down the corridor toward the street door. "It's because even if I am a bum there is some crap I will not eat," he cried out of the still white glare of honor and even pride, jerking the door open and then leaping up and outward as the reporter, the last night's missing host, tumbled slowly into the corridor at Jiggs' feet as he had at the feet of the others when the parachute jumper opened the door five minutes before and Shumann dragged the reporter up and the door of its own weight swung to behind them and the reporter half lay again in the frame of it, his nondescript hair broken down about his brow and his eyes closed and peaceful and his shirt and awry tie stiff and sour with vomit until Jiggs in turn jerked open the door and once more the reporter tumbled slowly sideways into the corridor as Shumann caught him and Jiggs hurdled them both as the door swung to with its own weight and locked itself. Whereupon something curious and unpresaged happened to Jiggs. It was not that his purpose had flagged or intention and resolution had reversed, switched back on him. It was as though the entire stable world across which he hurried from temptation, victorious and in good faith and unwarned, had reversed ends while he was in midair above the two men in the doorway; that his own body had become corrupt too and without consulting him at all had made that catlike turn in midair and presented to him the blank and now irrevocable panel upon which like on the screen he saw the jug sitting on the table in the empty room above plain enough to have touched it. "Catch that door!" he cried; he seemed to bounce back to it before even touching the flags, scrabbling at its blank surface with his hands. "Why didn't somebody catch it?" he cried. "Why in hell didn't you holler?" But they were not even looking at him; now the parachute jumper stooped with Shumann over the reporter. "What?" Jiggs said. "Breakfast, huh?" They did not even look at him.

"Go on," the jumper said. "See what he's got or get away and let me do it."

"Wait," Jiggs said. "Let's find some way to get him back into the house first." He leaned across them and tried the door again. He could even see the key now, still on the table beside the jug—an object trivial in size, that a man could almost swallow without it hurting him much probably and which now, even more than the jug, symbolised taunting and fierce regret since it postulated frustration not in miles but in inches; the gambit itself had refused, confounding him and leaving him hung up on a son of a bitch who couldn't even get into his own house.

"Come on," the jumper said to Shumann. "See what he's got—unless somebody has already beat us to him."

"Yair," Jiggs said, putting his hand on the reporter's flank. "But if we could just find some way to get him back into the house——" The jumper caught him by the shoulder and jerked him backward; again Jiggs caught balance, bouncing back, and saw the woman catch the jumper's arm as the jumper reached toward the reporter's pocket.

"Get away yourself," she said. The jumper rose; he and the woman glared at one another—the one cold, hard, calm; the other tense, furious, restrained. Shumann had risen too; Jiggs looked quietly and intently from him to the others and back again.

"So you're going to do it yourself," the jumper said.

"Yes. I'm going to do it myself." They stared at one another for an instant longer, then they began to curse each other in short hard staccato syllables that sounded like slaps while Jiggs, his hands on his hips and leaning a little forward on his lightpoised rubber soles, looked from them to Shumann and back again.

"All right," Shumann said. "That'll do now." He stepped between them, shoving the jumper a little. Then the woman stooped and while Jiggs turned the reporter's inert body from thigh to thigh she took from his pockets a few crumpled bills and a handfull of silver.

"There's a five and four ones," Jiggs said. "Let me count that change."

"Three will pay the bus," Shumann said. "Just take three more."

"Yair," Jiggs said. "Seven or eight will be a plenty. Look. Leave him the five and one of the ones for change." He took the five and one of the ones from the woman's hand and folded them and thrust them into the reporter's fob pocket and was about to rise when he saw the reporter looking at him, lying sprawled in the door with his eyes open and quiet and profoundly empty—that vision without contact yet with mind or thought, like two dead electric bulbs set into his skull. "Look," Jiggs said, "he's——" He sprang up, then he saw the jumper's face for the second before the jumper caught the woman's wrist and wrenched the money from her hand and flung it like a handfull of gravel against the reporter's peaceful and openeyed and sightless face and said in a tone of thin and despairing fury,

"I will eat and sleep on Roger and I will eat and sleep on you. But I wont eat and sleep on your ass, see?" He took up his bag and turned; he walked fast; Jiggs and the little boy watched him turn the alley mouth and vanish. Then Jiggs looked back at the woman who had not moved and at Shumann kneeling and gathering up the scattered coins and bills from about the reporter's motionless legs.

"Now we got to find some way to get him into the house," Jiggs said. They did not answer. But then he did not seem to expect or desire any answer. He knelt too and began to pick up the scattered coins. "Jesus," he said. "Jack sure threw them away. We'll be lucky to find half of them." But still they seemed to pay him no heed.

"How much was it?" Shumann said to the woman, extending his palm toward Jiggs.

"Six dollars and seventy cents," the woman said. Jiggs put the coins into Shumann's hand; as motionless as Shumann, Jiggs' hot eyes watched Shumann count the coins by sight.

"All right," Shumann said. "That other half."

"I'll just pick up some cigarettes with it," Jiggs said. Now Shumann didn't say anything at all; he just knelt with his hand out. After a moment Jiggs put the last coin into it. "O.K.," Jiggs said. His hot bright eyes were now completely unreadable; he did not even watch Shumann put the money into his pocket, he just took up his canvas bag. "Too bad we aint got any way to get him off the street," he said.

"Yair," Shumann said, taking up the other bag. "We aint,

though. So let's go." He went on; he didn't even look back. "It's a valvestem has stretched," he said. "I'll bet a quarter. That must be why she ran hot yesterday. We'll have to pull them all."

"Yair," Jiggs said. He walked behind the others, carrying the canvas bag. He didn't look back either yet; he stared at the back of Shumann's head with intent secret speculation blank and even tranquil; he spoke to himself out of a sardonic reserve almost of humor: "Yair. I knew I would be sorry. Jesus, you would think I would have learned by now to save being honest for Sunday. Because I was all right until.......and now to be hung up on a bastard that......." He looked back. The reporter still lay propped in the doorway; the quiet thoughtful empty eyes seemed still to watch them gravely, without either surprise or reproach. "Jesus," Jiggs said aloud, "I told that guy last night it wasn't paregoric: it was laudanum or something......." because for a little while now he had forgot the jug, he was thinking about the reporter and not about the jug, until now. "And it wont be long now," he thought, with a sort of desperate outrage, his face perfectly calm, the boots striking through the canvas sack, against his legs at each step as he walked behind the other three, his eyes hot blank and dead as if they had been reversed in his skull and only the blank backsides showed while sight contemplated the hot wild secret coiling of drink netted and snared by the fragile web of flesh and nerves in which he lived, resided. "I will call the paper and tell them he is sick," he said out of that specious delusion of need and desire which even in this inviolable privacy brushed ruthlessly aside all admission of or awareness of lying or truth: "Maybe some of them will know some way to get in. I will tell him and Laverne that they asked me to wait and show them

where. . . . . . ." They reached the alley's mouth. Without
pausing Shumann craned and peered up the street where
the jumper had vanished. "Get on," Jiggs said. "We'll find
him at the bus stop. He aint going to walk out there no matter how much his feelings are hurt." But the jumper was not
at the bus stop. The bus was about to depart but the jumper
was not in it. Another had gone ten minutes before and Shumann and the woman described the jumper to the starter
and he had not been in that one either. "He must have decided to walk out, after all," Jiggs said, moving toward the
step. "Let's grab a seat."

"We might as well eat now," Shumann said. "Maybe he
will come along before the next bus leaves."

"Sure," Jiggs said. "We could ask the bus driver to start
taking off the overhead."

"Yes," the woman said, suddenly. "We can eat out there."

"We might miss him," Shumann said. "And he hasn't——"

"All right," she said; she spoke in a cold harsh tone, without looking at Jiggs. "Do you think that Jack will need more
watching this morning than he will?" Now Jiggs could feel
Shumann looking at him too, thoughtfully from within the
machinesymmetry of the new hat. But he did not move; he
stood immobile, like one of the dummy figures which are
wheeled out of slumdistrict stores and pawnshops at eight
a.m., quiet waiting and tranquil; and bemused too, the in-
turned vision watching something which was not even
thought supplying him out of an inextricable whirl of half-
caught pictures, like a roulette wheel bearing printed sentences in place of numbers, with furious tagends of plans
and alternatives—telling them he had heard the jumper say
he was going back to the place on Amboise street and that

he, Jiggs, would go there and fetch him—of escaping even for five minutes and striking the first person he met and then the next and the next and the next until he got a half dollar; and lastly and this steadily, with a desperate conviction of truth and regret, that if Shumann would just hand him the coin and say go get a shot, he would not even take it, or lacking that, would take the one drink and then no more out of sheer gratitude for having been permitted to escape from impotence and need and thinking and calculation by means of which he must even now keep his tone casual and innocent.

"Who, me?" he said. "Hell, I drank enough last night to do me a long time. Let's get on; he must have deadheaded out somehow."

"Yair," Shumann said, still watching him with that open and deadly seriousness. "We got to pull those valves and mike them. Listen. If things break right today, tonight I'll get you a bottle. O.K.?"

"Jesus," Jiggs said. "Have I got to get drunk again? Is that it? Come on; let's get a seat." They got in. The bus moved. It was better then, because even if he had the half dollar he could not buy a drink with it until the bus either stopped or reached the airport, and also he was moving toward it at last; he thought again out of the thunder of solitude, the instant of exultation between the terror and the dismay: "They cant stop me. There aint enough of them to stop me. All I got to do is wait."—"Yair," he said, leaning forward between Shumann's and the woman's heads above the seatback in front of the one on which he and the boy sat, "he's probably already on the ship. I'll go right over and get on those valves and I can send him back to the restaurant." But they did not find the jumper at once at the airport either, though Shumann stood for a while and looked about the forenoon's deserted plaza as though he had expected to see the parachute jumper still in the succeeding elapsed second from that in which he had walked out of sight beyond the alley's mouth. "I'll go on and get started," Jiggs said. "If he's in the hangar I'll send him on to the restaurant."

"We'll eat first," Shumann said. "You wait."

"I aint hungry," Jiggs said. "I'll eat later. I want to get started——"

"No," the woman said; "Roger, dont——"

"Come on and eat some breakfast," Shumann said. It seemed to Jiggs that he stood a long time in the bright hazy sunlight with his jaws and the shape of his mouth aching a little, but it was not long probably, and anyway his voice seemed to sound all right too.

"O.K.," he said. "Let's go. They aint my valves. I aint going to have to ride behind them at three oclock this afternoon." The rotundra was empty, the restaurant empty too save for themselves. "I just want some coffee," he said.

"Eat some breakfast," Shumann said. "Come on, now."

"I aint any hungrier now than I was out there by that lamppost two minutes ago," Jiggs said. But his voice was still all right. "I just said I would come in, see," he said. "I never said I would eat, see." Shumann watched him bleakly.

"Listen," he said. "You have had—was it two or three drinks this morning? Eat something. And tonight I will see that you have a couple or three drinks if you want. You can even get tight if you want. But now let's get those valves out." Jiggs sat perfectly still, looking at his hands on the table and then at the waitress' arm propped beside him with waiting, wristnestled by four woolworth bracelets, the fingernails five spots of crimson glitter as if they had been bought and clipped onto the fingerends too.

"All right," he said. "Listen too. What do you want? A guy with two or three drinks in him helping you pull valves, or a guy with a gut full of food on top of the drinks, asleep in a corner somewhere? Just tell me what you want, see? I'll see you get it. Because listen. I just want coffee. I aint even telling you; I'm just asking you. Jesus, would please do any good?"

"All right," Shumann said. "Just three breakfasts then," he said to the waitress. "And two extra coffees.——Damn Jack," he said. "He ought to eat too."

"We'll find him at the hangar," Jiggs said. They found him there, though not at once; when Shumann and Jiggs emerged from the toolroom in their dungarees and waited outside the chickenwire door for the woman to change and join them, they saw first five or six other dungaree figures gathered about a sandwich board which had not been there yesterday, set in the exact center of the hangar entrance — a big board lettered heavily by hand and possessing a quality cryptic and peremptory and for the time incomprehensible as though the amplifyer had spoken the words:

NOTICE

All contestants, all pilots and parachute jumpers and all others eligible to win cash prizes during this meet, are requested to meet in Superintendent's office at 12 noon today. All absentees will be considered to acquiesce and submit to the action and discretion of the race committee.

The others watched quietly while Shumann and the woman read it.

"Submit to what?" one of the others said. "What is it? Do you know?"

"I dont know," Shumann said. "Is Jack Holmes on the field yet? Has anybody seen him this morning?"

"There he is," Jiggs said. "Over at the ship, like I told you." Shumann looked across the hangar. "He's already got the cowling off. See?"

"Yair," Shumann said. He moved at once. Jiggs spoke to the man beside whom he stood, almost without moving his lips:

"Lend me half a buck," he said. "I'll hand it back tonight. Quick." He took the coin; he snatched it; when Shumann reached the aeroplane Jiggs was right behind him. The jumper, crouched beneath the engine, looked up at them, briefly and without stopping, as he might have glanced up at the shadow of a passing cloud.

"You had some breakfast?" Shumann said.

"Yes," the jumper said, not looking up again.

"On what?" Shumann said. The other did not seem to have heard. Shumann took the money from his pocket—the remaining dollar bill, three quarters and some nickels, and laid two of the quarters on the engine mount at the jumper's elbow. "Go and get some coffee," he said. The other did not seem to hear, busy beneath the engine. Shumann stood watching the back of his head. Then the jumper's elbow struck the engine mount. The coins rang on the concrete floor and Jiggs stooped, ducking, and rose again, extending the coins before Shumann could speak or move.

"There they are," Jiggs said, not loud; he could not have been heard ten feet away: the fierceness, the triumph. "There you are. Count them. Count both sides so you will be sure." After that they did not talk anymore. They worked quiet and fast, like a circus team, with the trained team's economy of motion, while the woman passed them the tools as needed; they did not even have to speak to her, to name the tool. It was easy now, like in the bus; all he had to do was to wait as the valves came out one by one and grew in a long neat line on the workbench and then, sure enough, it came.

"It must be nearly twelve," the woman said. Shumann finished what he was doing. Then he looked at his watch and stood up, flexing his back and legs. He looked at the jumper.

"You ready?" he said.

"You are not going to wash up and change?" the woman said.

"I guess not," Shumann said. "It will be that much more time wasted." He took the money again from his pocket and gave the woman the three quarters. "You and Jiggs can get a bite when Jiggs gets the rest of the valves out. And, say—" he looked at Jiggs "—dont bother about trying to put the micrometer on them yourself. I'll do that when I get back. You can clean out the supercharger; that ought to hold you until we get back." He looked at Jiggs. "You ought to be hungry now."

"Yair," Jiggs said. He had not stopped; he did not watch them go out. He just squatted beneath the engine with the spraddled tenseness of an umbrellarib, feeling the woman looking at the back of his head. He spoke now without fury, without triumph, to himself: without sound: "Yair, beat it. You cant stop me. You couldn't stop me but for a minute even if you tried to hold me between your legs." He was not thinking of the woman as Laverne, as anyone: she was just the last and now swiftlyfading residuum of the *it*, the *they*, watching the back of his head as he removed the super-charger without even knowing that she was already defeated.

"Do you want to eat now?" she said. He didn't answer. "Do you want me to bring you a sandwich?" He didn't answer. "Jiggs," she said. He looked up and back, his eyebrows rising and vanishing beyond the cap's peak, the hot bright eyes blank, interrogatory, arrested.

"What? How was that?" he said. "Did you call me?"

"Yes. Do you want to go and eat now or do you want me to bring you something?"

"No. I aint hungry yet. I want to get done with this supercharger before I wash my hands. You go on." But she didn't move yet; she stood looking at him.

"I'll leave you some money and you can go when you are ready, then."

"Money?" he said. "What do I need with money up to my elbows in this engine?" She turned away then. He watched her pause and call the little boy, who came out of a group across the hangar and joined her; they went on toward the apron and disappeared. Then Jiggs rose; he laid the tool down carefully, touching the coin in his pocket through the cloth, though he did not need to since he had never ceased to feel it; he was not thinking about her, not talking to her; he spoke without triumph or exultation, quietly: "Goodbye, you snooping bitch," he said.

But they had not been able to tell if the reporter had seen them or not, though he probably could neither see nor hear; certainly the thin youngish lightcolored negress who came up the alley about half past nine, in a modish though not new hat and coat and carrying a wicker marketbasket covered neatly with a clean napkin, decided almost immediately that he could not. She looked down at him for perhaps ten seconds with complete and impersonal speculation, then she waggled one hand before his face and called him by name: and when she reached into his pockets she did not move or shift his body at all; her hand reached in and drew out the two folded bills where Jiggs had put them with a single motion limber and boneless and softly rapacious as that of an octopus, then the hand made a second limber swift motion, inside her coat now, and emerged empty. It was her racial and sex's nature to have taken but one of the bills, no matter how many there might have been—either the five or the one, depending upon her own need or desire of the moment or upon the situation itself—but now she took them both and stood again, looking down at the man in the doorway with a kind of grim though still impersonal sanctimoniousness. "If he found any of hit left hit wouldn't learn him no lesson," she said, aloud. "Laying out here in the street, drunk. Aint no telling where he been at, but hit couldn't a been much for them to let him git back out and that much money in his pocket." She took a key from somewhere beneath the coat and unlocked the door and caught him back in her turn as he began to tumble slowly and deliberately into the corridor, and entered herself. She was not gone long and now she carried the dishpan of dirty water, which she flung suddenly into his face and caught him again as he gasped and started. "I hopes you had sense enough to left your pocketbook in the house fo you decided to take a nap out here," she cried, shaking him. "If you didn't, I bound all you got left now is the pocketbook." She carried him up the cramped stairs almost bodily, like that much firehose, and left him apparently unconscious again on the cot and went beyond the curtain and looked once with a perfectly in-scrutable face at the neat bed which but one glance told her was not her handiwork. From the basket she took an apron and a bright handkerchief; when she returned to the reporter she wore the apron and the handkerchief about her head in place of the hat and coat, and she carried the dishpan filled now with fresh water, and soap and towels; she had done this before too, apparently, stripping the fouled shirt from the man who was her employer for this half hour of the six week-days, and both washing him off and slapping him awake dur-ing the process until he could see and hear again. "It's past ten oclock," she said. "I done lit the gas so you can shave."

"Shave?" he said. "Didn't you know? I dont have to ever shave again. I'm fired."

"The more reason for you to git up from here and try to look like something." His hair, soaked, was plastered to his skull, yet it fitted no closer to the bones and ridges and joints than the flesh of his face did, and now his eyes did indeed look like holes burned with a poker in a parchment diploma, some postgraduate certificate of excess; naked from the waist up, it seemed as if you not only saw his ribs front and side and rear but that you saw the entire ribcage complete from any angle like you can see both warp and woof of screen wire from either side. He swayed laxly beneath her limber soft and ungentle hands, articulate and even collected though moving for a while yet in the twilight between the delusion of drunkenness and the delusion of sobriety.

"Are they gone?" he said. The negress' face and manner did not change at all.

"Is who gone?" she said.

"Yair," he said, drowsily. "She was here last night. She

slept yonder in the bed last night. There was just one of them slept with her and there could have been both of them. But she was here. And it was him himself that wouldn't let her drink, that took the glass out of her hand. Yair. I could hear all the long soft waiting sound of all womanmeat in bed beyond the curtain." At first, for the moment, the negress did not even realise what it was touching her thigh until she looked down and saw the sticklike arm, the brittle light and apparently senseless hand like a bundle of dried twigs too, blundering and fumbling stiffly at her while in the gaunt eyesockets the eyes looked like two spots of dying daylight caught by water at the bottom of abandoned wells. The negress did not become coy nor outraged; she avoided the apparently blind or possibly just still insensible hand with a single supple shift of her hips, speaking to him, calling him by name, pronouncing the m.i.s.t.e.r. in full, in the flat lingering way of negroes, like it had two sets of two or three syllables each.

"Now then," she said, "if you feel like doing something yourself, take a holt of this towel. Or see how much of whatever money you think you had folks is left you, besides leaving you asleep on the street."

"Money?" he said. He waked completely now, his mind did, though even yet his hands fumbled for a while before finding the pocket while the negress watched him, standing now with her hands on her hips. She said nothing else, she just watched his quiet bemused and intent face as he plumbed his empty pockets one by one. She did not mention company again; it was he who cried, "I was out there, asleep in the alley. You know that, you found me. I left here, I was out there asleep because I forgot the key and I couldn't get in again; I was out there a long time even before daylight. You know I was." Still she said nothing, watching him. "I remember just when I quit remembering!"

"How much did you have when you quit remembering?"

"Nothing!" he said. "Nothing. I spent it all. See?" When he got up she offered to help him back to the bedroom, but he refused. He walked unsteadily still, but well enough, and when after a time she followed him she could hear him through the beaverboard wall of the alcove somewhat larger than a clothescloset and which she entered too and set water to heat on the gas plate beside which he was shaving, and prepared to make coffee. She gave the undisturbed bedroom another cold inscrutable look and returned to the front room and restored the tumbled cot, spreading the blanket and the pillows and picked up the soiled shirt and the towel from the floor and paused, laying the shirt on the couch but still carrying the towel, and went to the table and looked at the jug now with that bemused inscrutable expression. She wiped one of the sticky glasses with finicking care and poured into it from the jug almost what a thimble would have held and drank it, the smallest finger of that hand crooked delicately, in a series of birdlike and apparently extremely distasteful sips. Then she gathered up what she could conveniently carry of the night's misplaced litter and returned beyond the curtain, though when she went to where she had set the basket on the floor against the wall with the hat and coat lying upon it, you could not hear her cross the floor at all nor stoop and take from the basket an empty pint bottle sparklingly clean as a sterilised milkbottle. By ordinary she would not have filled the flask at any single establishment of her morning round, on the contrary filling the bottle little by little with a sort of niggard and foresighted husbandry and arriving at home in midafternoon with a pint of liquid weird, potent, anonymous and strange, but once more she seemed to find the situation its own warrant, returning and putting the filled flask back into the basket still without any sound. The reporter heard only the broom for a time, and other muted sounds as though the room were putting itself to rights by means of some ghostly and invisible power of its own, until she came at last to the alcove's doorway, where he stood tying his tie, with the hat and coat on again and the basket beneath its neat napkin again on her arm.

"I'm through," she said. "The coffee's ready, but you better not waste no time over drinking hit."

"All right," he said. "I'll have to make another loan from you."

"You wont need but a dime to get to the paper. Aint you got even that much left?"

"I aint going to the paper. I'm fired, I tell you. I want two dollars."

"I has to work for my money. Last time I lent you hit took you three weeks to start paying me back."

"I know. But I have to have it. Come on, Leonora. I'll pay you back Saturday." She reached inside her coat; one of the bills was his own.

"The key's on the table," she said. "I washed hit off too." It lay there, on the table clean and empty save for the key; he took it up and mused upon it with that face which the few hours of violent excess had altered from that of one brightly and peacefully dead to that of one coming back from, or looking out of, hell itself.

"But it's all right," he said. "It dont matter. It aint anything." He stood in the clean empty room where there was not even a cigarettestub or a burned match to show any trace. "Yair. She didn't even leave a hair pin," he thought. "Or maybe she dont use them. Or maybe I was drunk and they were not even here"; looking down at the key with a grimace faint and tragic which might have been called smiling while he talked to himself, giving himself the advice which he knew he was not going to take when he insisted on borrowing the two dollars. "Because I had thirty before I spent the eleven-eighty and then the five for the absinth. That left about thirteen." Then he cried, not loud, not moving: "Besides, maybe she will tell me. Maybe she intended to all the time but they couldn't wait for me to come to," without even bothering to tell himself that he knew he was lying, just saying quietly and stubbornly, "All right. But I'm going anyway. Even if I dont do anything but walk up where she can see me and stand there for a minute." He held the key in his hand now while the door clicked behind him, standing for a moment longer with his eyes shut against the impact of light, of the thin sun, and then opening them, steadying himself against the doorframe where he had slept, remembering the coffee which the negress had made and he had forgot about until now, while the alley swam away into mirageshapes, tilting like the sea or say the lakesurface, against which the ordeal of destination, of hope and dread, shaped among the outraged nerves of vision the bright vague pavilionglitter beneath the whipping purple-and-gold pennons. "It's all right," he said. "It aint nothing but money. It dont matter." It was not two when he reached the airport, but already the parkinglots along the boulevard were filling, with the young men paid doubtless out of some wearily initialled national

fund, in the purple-and-gold caps lent or perhaps compul-
sory, clinging to runningboards, moving head-and-shoulders
above the continuous topline of alreadyparked cars as
though they consisted of torsos alone and ran on wires for no
purpose and toward no discernible destination. A steady
stream of people flowed along the concrete gutters, converging toward the entrances, but the reporter did not follow. To
the left was the hangar where they would be now, but he did
not go there either; he just stood in the bright hazy damp-
filled sunlight, with the pennons whipping stiffly overhead
and the wind which blew them seeming to blow through
him too, not cold, not unpleasant: just whipping his clothing
about him as if it blew unimpeded save by the garment,
through his ribcage and among his bones. "I ought to eat,"
he thought. "I ought to," not moving yet as though he hung
static in a promise made to someone which he did not believe even yet that he was going to break. The restaurant was
not far; already it seemed to him that he could hear the clash
and clatter and the voices and smell the food, thinking of the
three of them yesterday while the little boy burrowed with
flagging determination into the second plate of icecream.
Then he could hear the sounds, the noise, and smell the
food itself as he stood looking at the table where they had sat
yesterday, where a family group from a grandmother to an infant in arms now sat. He went to the counter. "Breakfast," he
said.

"What do you want to eat?" the waitress said.

"What do people eat for breakfast?" he said, looking at
her—a porcelainfaced woman whose hair complexion and
uniform appeared to have been made of various shades of
that material which oldtime bookkeepers used to protect

their sleeves with—and smiling: or he would have called it smiling. "That's right. It aint breakfast now, is it?"

"What do you want to eat?"

"Roast beef," his mind said at last. "Potatoes," he said. "It dont matter."

"Sandwich or lunch?"

"Yes," he said.

"Yes what? You wanna order dont you wanna?"

"Sandwich," he said.

"Mash one!" the waitress cried.

"And that's that," he thought, as though he had discharged the promise; as though by ordering, acquiescing to the idea, he had eaten the food too. "And then I will. . . . . . ." Only the hangar was not the mirage but the restaurant, the counter, the clash and clatter, the sound of food and of eating; it seemed to him that he could see the group: the aeroplane, the four dungaree figures, the little boy in dungarees too, himself approaching: *I hope you found everything you wanted before you left? Yes, thank you. It was thirteen dollars. Just till Saturday—No matter; it dont matter; dont even think of it* Now suddenly he heard the amplifyer too in the rotundra; it had been speaking for some time but he had just noticed it:

"——second day of the Feinman Airport dedication invitation meet held under the official rules of the American Aeronautical Association and through the courtesy of the city of New Valois and of Colonel H.I. Feinman, Chairman of the Sewage Board of New Valois. Events for the afternoon as follows——" He quit listening to it then, drawing from his pocket the pamphlet program of yesterday and opening it at the second fading imprint of the mimeograph:

Friday

2:30 P.M.	Spot Parachute Jump. Purse $25.00
3:00 P.M.	Scull Speed Dash. 375 cu. in. Qualifying speed 180 m.p.h. Purse $325.00 (1, 2, 3, 4)
3:30 P.M.	Aerial Acrobatics. Jules Despleins, France. Lieut. Frank Burnham, United States.
4:30 P.M.	Scull Speed Dash. 575 cu. in. Qualifying speed, 200 m.p.h. Purse $650.00 (1, 2, 3, 4)
5:00 P.M.	Delayed Parachute Drop.
8:00 P.M.	Special Mardi Gras Evening Event. Rocket Plane. Lieut. Frank Burnham

He continued to look at the page long after the initial impact of optical surprise had faded. "That's all," he said. "That's all she would have to do. Just tell me they. . . . . . . It aint the money. She knows it aint that. It aint the money with me anymore than it is with them," he said; the man had to speak to him twice before the reporter knew he was there. "Hello," he said.

"So you got out here after all," the other said. Behind the man stood another, a short man with a morose face, carrying a newspaper camera.

"Yes," the reporter said. "Hi, Jug," he said to the second man. The first looked at him, curiously.

"You look like you have been dragged through hell by the heels," he said. "You going to cover this today too?"

"Not that I know of," the reporter said. "I understand I am fired. Why?"

"I was about to ask you. Hagood phoned me at four this morning, out of bed. He told me to come out today and if you were not here, to cover it. But mostly to watch out for you if you came and to tell you to call him at this number." He took a folded strip of paper from his vest and gave it to the reporter. "It's the country club. He said to call him as soon as I found you."

"Thanks," the reporter said. But he did not move. The other looked at him.

"Well, what do you want to do? You want to cover it or you want me to?"

"No. I mean, yes. You take it. It dont matter. Jug knows better what Hagood wants than you or I either."

"O.K.," the other said. "Better call Hagood right away, though."

"I will," the reporter said. Now the food came: the heaped indestructible plate and the hand scrubbed, with vicious coral nails, the hand too looking like it had been conceived formed and baked in the kitchen, or perhaps back in town and sent out by light and speedy truck along with the scrolled squares of pastry beneath the plate glass counter; he looked at both the food and the hand from the crest of a wave of pure almost physical flight. "Jesus, sister," he said, "I was joking with the wrong man, wasn't I?" But he drank the coffee and ate some of the food; he seemed to watch himself creeping slowly and terrifically across the plate like a mole, blind to all else and deaf now even to the amplifyer; he ate a good deal of it, sweating, seeming to chew forever and ever before getting each mouthful in position to be swallowed. "I guess that'll be enough," he said at last. "Jesus, it will have to be," he said. He was in the rotundra now and moving toward the gates into the stands before he remembered and turned and breasted the stream toward the entrance and so outside and into the bright soft hazy sunlight with its quality of having been recently taken out of water and not yet thoroughly dried and full of the people, the faces, the cars coming up and discharging and moving on. Across the plaza the hangar-wing seemed to sway and quiver like a grounded balloon. "But I feel better," he thought. "I must. They would not have let me eat all that and not feel better because I cant possibly feel as bad as I still think I do." He could hear the voice again now from the amplifyer above the entrance:

"——wish to announce that due to the tragic death of Lieutenant Frank Burnham last night, the airport race committee has discontinued the evening events. . . . The time is now one-forty-two. The first event on today's program will. . . . . . ." The reporter stopped.

"One-forty-two," he thought. Now he could feel something which must have been the food he had just eaten beating slow and steady against his skull which up to this time had been empty, had hardly troubled him at all except for the sensation of being about to float off like one of the small balloons escaped from the hand of a child at a circus, trying to remember what hour the program had allotted to the three hundred and seventy-five cubic inch race, thinking that perhaps when he got into the shade he could bear to look at the program again. "Since it seems I am bound to offer her the chance to tell me that they stole. . . . . . .not the money. It's not the money. It's not that." Now the shade of

the hangar fell upon him and he could see the program
again, the faint mimeographed letters beating and pulsing
against his cringing eyeballs and steadying at last so that he
could read his watch. It would be an hour still before he
could expect to find her alone. He turned and followed the
hangarwall and passed beyond it. Across the way the parking-
lot was almost full and there was another stream here, moving toward the bleachers, though he stood on the edge of it
while his eyeballs still throbbed and watched the other fringe
of them slowing and clotting before one of the temporary
wooden refreshment booths which had sprung up about the
borders of the airport property as the photographs of the
pilots and machines had bloomed in the shopwindows
downtown for some time before he began to realise that
something besides the spectacle (still comparatively new) of
outdoors drinking must be drawing them. Then he thought
he recognised the voice and then he did recognise the raked
filthy swagger of the cap and moved, pressing, filtering, on
and into the crowd and so came between Jiggs' drunken bel-
ligerent face and the Italian face of the booth's proprietor
who was leaning across the counter and shouting,

"Bastard, huh? You theenk bastard, hey?"

"What is it?" the reporter said. Jiggs turned and looked at
him for a moment of hot blurred concentration without
recognition; it was the Italian who answered.

"For me, nothing!" he shouted. "He come here, he have
one drink, two drink; he no need either one of them but o.k.;
he pay; that o.k. for me. Then he say he wait for friend, that
he have one more drink to surprise friend. That not so good
but my wife she give it to him and that maka three drink he
dont need and I say, You pay and go, eh? Beat it. And he say,

O.K., goodbye and I say Why you no pay, eh? and he say That drink to surprise friend; looka like it surprise you too, eh? and I grab to hold and call policaman because I dont want for trouble with drunk and he say bastard to me before my wife——" Still Jiggs did not move. Even while holding himself upright by the counter he gave that illusion of tautly sprung steel set delicately on a hair trigger.

"Yair," he said. "Three drinks, and just look what they done to me!" on a rising note which stopped before it became idiotic laughter; whereupon he stared again at the reporter with that blurred gravity, watching while the reporter took the second of the two dollar bills which the negress had loaned him and gave it to the Italian. "There you are, Columbus," Jiggs said. "Yair. I told him. Jesus, I even tried to tell him your name, only I couldn't remember it." He looked at the reporter with hot intensity, like an astonished child. "Say, that guy last night told me your name. Is that it, sure enough? you swear to Christ, no kidding?"

"Yair," the reporter said. He put his hand on Jiggs' arm. "Come on. Let's go." The spectators had moved on now. Behind the counter the Italian and his wife seemed to pay them no more attention. "Come on," the reporter said. "It must be after two. Let's go help get the ship ready and then I'll buy another drink." But Jiggs did not move, and then the reporter found Jiggs watching him with something curious, calculating and intent, behind the hot eyes; they were not blurred now at all, and suddenly Jiggs stood erect before the reporter could steady him.

"I was looking for you," Jiggs said.

"I came along at the right time, didn't I, for once in my

life. Come on. Let's go to the hangar. I imagine they are waiting for you there. Then I will buy a——"

"I dont mean that," Jiggs said. "I was kidding the guy. I had the quarter, all right. I've had all I want. Come on." He led the way, walking a little carefully yet still with the light springlike steps, bumping and butting through the gateward stream of people, the reporter following, until they were beyond it and clear; anyone who approached them now would have to do so deliberately and should have been visible a hundred yards away, though neither of them saw the parachute jumper who was doing just that.

"You mean the ship's all ready?" the reporter said.

"Sure," Jiggs said. "Roger and Jack aint even there. They have gone to the meeting."

"Meeting?"

"Sure. Contestants' meeting. To strike, see? But listen——"

"To strike?"

"Sure. For more jack. It aint the money: it's the principle of the thing. Jesus, what do we need with money?" Jiggs began to laugh again on that harsh note which stopped just as it became laughing and started before it was mirth. "But that aint it. I was looking for you." Again the reporter looked at the hot unreadable eyes. "Laverne sent me. She said to give me five dollars for her." The reporter's face did not change at all. Neither did Jiggs': the hot impenetrable eyes, the membrane and fiber netting and webbing the unrecking and the undismayed. "Roger was in the money yesterday; you'll get it back Saturday. Only if it was me, I wouldn't even wait for that. Just let her underwrite you, see?"

"Underwrite me?"

"Sure. Then you wouldn't even have to bother to put anything back into your pocket. All you would have to do would be to button up your pants." Still the reporter's face did not change, his voice did not change, not loud, without amazement, anything.

"Do you reckon I could?"

"I dont know," Jiggs said. "Didn't you ever try it? It's done every night somewhere, so I hear. Probably done right here in New Valois, even. And if you cant, she can show you how." The reporter's face did not change; he was just looking at Jiggs and then suddenly Jiggs moved, sudden and complete; the reporter saw the hot secret eyes come violently alive and, turning, the reporter also saw the parachute jumper's face. That was a little after two oclock; Shumann and the jumper had been in the Superintendent's office from twelve until fifteen to one. They passed through the same discreet door which Jiggs had used the afternoon before and went on through the anteroom and into a place like a board room in a bank—a long table with a row of comfortable chairs behind it, in which perhaps a dozen men who might have been found about any such table back in town sat, and another group of chairs made out of steel and painted to resemble wood, in which with a curious gravity something like that of the older and better behaved boys in a reform school on Christmas eve, sat the other men who by ordinary at this hour would have been working over the aeroplanes in the hangar—the pilots and parachute jumpers, in greasy dungarees or leather jackets almost as foul, the quiet sober faces looking back as Shumann and the jumper entered. Just as the blue serge of last night was absent, so were the tweed coats and the ribbon badges with one exception.

This was the microphone's personified voice. He sat with neither group, his chair that which should have been at the end of the table but which he had drawn several feet away as though preparing to tip it back against the wall. But he was as grave as either group; the scene was exactly that of the conventional conference between the millowners and the delegation from the shops, the announcer representing the labor lawyer—that man who was once a laborer himself but from whose hands now the callouses have softened and whitened away so that, save for something nameless and ineradicable—a quality incorrigibly dissentive and perhaps even bizarre—about his clothing which distinguishes him forever from the men behind the table as well as from the men before it as the badge of the labor organization in his lapel establishes him forever as one of them, he might actually sit behind the table too. But he did not. But the very slightness of the distance between him and the table postulated a gap more unbridgable even than that between the table and the second group, as if he had been stopped in the midst of a violent movement, if not of protest at least of dissent, by the entrance into the room of the men in whose absent names he dissented. He nodded to Shumann and the jumper as they found chairs, then he turned to the thickfaced man at the center of the table.

"They're all here now," he said. The men behind the table murmured to one another.

"We must wait for him," the thickfaced man said. He raised his voice. "We are waiting for Colonel Feinman, men," he said. He took a watch from his vest; three or four others looked at their watches. "He instructed us to have everyone present at twelve oclock. He has been delayed. You can smoke, if you like." Some of the second group began to smoke, passing lighted matches, speaking quietly like a school class which has been told that it can talk for a moment:

"What is it?"

"I dont know. Maybe something about Burnham."

"Oh, yair. Probably that's it."

"Hell, they dont need all of us to——"

"Say, what do you suppose happened?"

"Blinded, probably."

"Yair. Blinded."

"Yair. Probably couldn't read his altimeter at all. Or maybe forgot to watch it. Flew it right into the ground."

"Yair. Jesus, I remember one time I was......." They smoked. Sometimes they held the cigarettes like dynamite caps so as not to spill the ash, looking quietly about the clean new floor; sometimes they spilled the ashes discreetly down their legs. But finally the stubs were too short to hold. One of them rose; the whole room watched him cross to the table and take up an ashtray made to resemble a radial engine and bring it back and start it passing along the three rows of chairs like a church collection plate. Shumann looked at his watch and it was twenty-five minutes past twelve. He spoke quietly, to the announcer, as though they were alone in the room:

"Listen, Hank. I've got all my valves out. I have got to put the micrometer on them before I——"

"Yair," the announcer said. He turned to the table. "Listen," he said. "They are all here now. And they have got to get the ships ready for the race at three; Mr Shumann there has got all his valves out. So cant you tell them without waiting for F——Colonel Feinman? They will agree, all right. I told you that. There aint anything else they can—I mean they will agree."

"Agree to what?" the man beside Shumann said. But the chairman, the thickfaced man, was already speaking.

"Colonel Feinman said——"

"Yair." The announcer spoke patiently. "But these boys have got to get their ships ready. We've got to be ready to give these people that are buying the tickets out there something to look at." The men behind the table murmured again, the others watching them quietly.

"Of course we can take a straw vote now," the chairman said. Now he looked at them and cleared his throat. "Gentlemen, the committee representing the business men of New Valois who have sponsored this meet and offered you the opportunity to win these cash prizes——" The announcer turned to him.

"Wait," he said. "Let me tell them." He turned now to the grave almost identical faces of the men in the hard chairs; he spoke quietly too. "It's about the programs. The printed ones—you know. With the setup for each day. They were all printed last week and so they have still got Frank's name on them——" The chairman interrupted him now:

"And the committee wants to express here and now to you other pilots who were con——" Now he was interrupted by one of the men beside him:

"—and on behalf of Colonel Feinman."

"Yes.—and on behalf of Colonel Feinman.—contemporaries and friends of Lieutenant Burnham, its sincere regret at last night's unfortunate accident."

"Yair," the announcer said; he had not even looked toward the speaker, he just waited until he had got through. "So they—the committee—feel that they are advertising something they cant produce. They feel that Frank's name should come off the program. I agree with them there and I know you will too."

"Why not take it off, then?" one of the second group said.

"Yes," the announcer said. "They are going to. But the only way they can do that is to have new programs printed, you see." But they did not see yet. They just looked at him, waiting. The chairman cleared his throat, though at the moment there was nothing for him to interrupt.

"We had these programs printed for your benefit and convenience as contestants, as well as that of the spectators, without whom I dont have to remind you there would be no cash prizes for you to win. So you see, in a sense you contestants are the real benefactors of these printed programs. Not us; the schedule of these events can be neither information nor surprise to us, since we were privy to the arranging of them even if we are not to the winning—since we have been given to understand (and I may add, have seen for ourselves) that air racing has not yet reached the, ah, scientific heights of horse racing——" He cleared his throat again; a thin polite murmur of laughter rose from about the table and died away. "We had these programs printed at considerable expense, none of which devolved on you, yet they were planned and executed for your—I wont say profit, but convenience and benefit. We had them printed in good faith that what we guaranteed in them would be performed; we knew no more than you did that that unfortunate ac——"

"Yes," the announcer said. "It's like this. Somebody has got to pay to have new programs printed. These g—this. . . . . . . they say w—the contestants and announcers and everybody drawing jack from the meet, should do it." They did not make a sound, the still faces did not change expression; it was the announcer himself, speaking now in a tone urgent, almost pleading, where no dissent had been offered or intimated: "It's just two and a half percent. We're all in it; I'm in it too. Just two and a half percent.; when it comes out of prizemoney, like they say you wont notice it because you haven't got it anyway until after the cut is taken out. Just two and a half percent., and——" The man in the second group spoke for the second time:

"Or else?" he said. The announcer did not answer. After a moment Shumann said,

"Is that all?"

"Yes," the announcer said. Shumann rose.

"I better get back on my valves," he said. Now when he and the jumper crossed the rotunda the crowd was trickling steadily through the gates. They worked into line and shuffled up to the gates too before they learned that they would have to have grandstand tickets to pass. So they turned and worked back out of the crowd and went out and around toward the hangar, walking now in a thin deep drone from somewhere up in the sun, though presently they could see them—a flight of army pursuit singleseaters circling the field in formation to land and then coming in, fast, bluntnosed, fiercelyraked, viciously powerful. "They're over souped," Shumann said. "They will kill you if you dont watch them. I wouldn't want to do that for two-fifty-six a month."

"You wouldn't be cut two and a half percent. while you

were out to lunch though," the jumper said savagely. "What's two and a half percent. of twenty-five bucks?"

"It aint the whole twenty-five," Shumann said. "I hope Jiggs has got that supercharger ready to go back." So they had almost reached the aeroplane before they discovered that it was the woman and not Jiggs at work on it and that she had put the supercharger back on with the engine head still off and the valves still out. She rose and brushed her hair back with the flat of her wrist, though they had asked no question.

"Yes," she said. "I thought he was all right. I went out to eat and left him here."

"Have you seen him since?" Shumann said. "Do you know where he is now?"

"What the hell does that matter?" the jumper said in a tense furious voice. "Let's get the damned supercharger off and put the valves in." He looked at the woman, furious, re-strained. "What has this guy done to you? give you a dose of faith in mankind like he would syphilis or consumption or whatever it is, that will even make you trust Jiggs?"

"Come on," Shumann said. "Let's get the supercharger off. I guess he didn't check the valve stems either, did he?"

"I dont know," she said.

"Well, no matter. They lasted out yesterday. And we haven't time now. But maybe we can get on the line by three if we dont stop to check them." They were ready before that; they had the aeroplane on the apron and the engine running before three, and then the jumper who had worked in grim fury turned away, walking fast even though Shumann called after him. He went straight to where Jiggs and the reporter stood. He could not have known where to find them yet he went straight to them as though led by some blind instinct

out of fury; he walked into Jiggs' vision and struck him on the
jaw so that the surprise the alarm and the shock were almost
simultaneous, hitting him again before he finished falling
and then whirled as the reporter caught his arm.

"Here! here!" the reporter cried. "He's drunk! You cant
hit a——" But the jumper didn't say a word; the reporter saw
the continuation of the turning become the blow of the fist.
He didn't feel the blow at all. "I'm too light to be knocked
down or even hit hard," he thought; he was still telling himself that while he was being raised up again and while the
hands held him upright on his now boneless legs and while
he looked at Jiggs sitting up now in a small stockade of legs
and a policeman shaking him. "Hello, Leblanc," the reporter said. The policeman looked at him now.

"So it's you, hey?" the policeman said. "You got some
news this time, aint you? Something to put in the paper that
people will like to read. Reporter knocked down by irate victim, hey? That's news." He began to prod Jiggs with the side
of his shoe. "Who's this? Your substitute? Get up. On your
feet now."

"Wait," the reporter said. "It's all right. He wasn't in it.
He's one of the mechanics here. An aviator."

"I see," the policeman said, hauling at Jiggs' arm. "Aviator, hey? He dont look very high to me. Or maybe it was a
cloud hit him in the jaw, hey?"

"Yes. He's just drunk. I'll be responsible; I tell you he
wasn't even in it; the guy hit him by mistake. Leave him be,
Leblanc."

"What do I want with him?" the policeman said. "So
you're responsible, are you? Get him up out of the street,
then." He turned and began to shove at the ring of people.

"Go; beat it; get on, now," he said. "The race is about to start. Go on, now." So presently they were alone again, the reporter standing carefully, balancing, on his weightless legs ("Jesus," he thought, "I'm glad now I am light enough to float"), feeling gingerly his jaw, thinking with peaceful astonishment, "I never felt it at all. Jesus, I didn't think I was solid enough to be hit that hard but I must have been wrong." He stooped, still gingerly, and began to pull at Jiggs' arm until after a time Jiggs looked up at him blankly.

"Come on," the reporter said. "Let's get up."

"Yair," Jiggs said. "Yair. Get up."

"Yes," the reporter said. "Come on, now." Jiggs rose slowly, the reporter steadying him; he stood blinking at the reporter.

"Jesus," he said. "What happened?"

"Yes," the reporter said. "But it's all right now. It's all over now. Come on. Where do you want to go?" Jiggs moved, the reporter beside him, supporting him; suddenly Jiggs recoiled; looking up the reporter also saw the hangar door a short distance away.

"Not there," Jiggs said.

"Yes," the reporter said. "We dont want to go there." They turned; the reporter led the way now, working them clear again of the people passing toward the stands. He could feel his jaw beginning now, and looking back and upward he watched the aeroplanes come into position one by one as beneath them each dropping body bloomed into parachute. "And I never even heard the bomb," he thought. "Or maybe that was what I thought hit me." He looked at Jiggs walking stiffly beside him, as though the spring steel of his legs had been reft by enchantment of temper and were now mere dead iron. "Listen," he said. He stopped and stopped Jiggs too, looking at him and speaking to him tediously and carefully as though Jiggs were a child. "I've got to go to town. To the paper. The boss sent for me to come in, see? Now you tell me where you want to go. You want to go somewhere and lie down a while? Maybe I can find a car where you can——"

"No," Jiggs said. "I'm all right. Go on."

"Yes. Sure. But you ought. . . . . . ." Now all the parachutes were open; the sunny afternoon was filled with downcupped blooms like inverted water hyacinths; the reporter shook Jiggs a little. "Come on, now. What's next now? after the chute jumps?"

"What?" Jiggs said. "Next? What next?"

"Yes. What? Cant you remember?"

"Yair," Jiggs said. "Next." For a full moment the reporter looked down at Jiggs with a faint lift of one side of his mouth as though favoring his jaw, not of concern nor regret nor even hopelessness so much as of faint and quizzical foreknowledge.

"Yes," he said. He took the key from his pocket. "Can you remember this, then?" Jiggs looked at the key, blinking. Then he stopped blinking.

"Yair," he said. "It was on the table right by the jug. And then we got hung up on the bastard laying there in the door and I let the door shut behind. . . . . . ." He looked at the reporter, peering at him, blinking again. "For Christ's sake," he said. "Did you bring it too?"

"No," the reporter said.

"Hell. Gimme the key; I will go and——"

"No," the reporter said. He put the key back into his pocket and took out the change which the Italian had given him, the three quarters. "You said five dollars. But I haven't got that much. This is all I have. But that will be all right because if it was a hundred it would be the same; it would not be enough because all I have never is, you see? Here." He put the three quarters into Jiggs' hand. For a moment Jiggs looked at his hand without moving. Then the hand closed; he looked at the reporter while his face seemed to collect, to become sentient.

"Yair," he said. "Thanks. It's o.k. You'll get it back Saturday. We're in the money now; Roger and Jack and the others struck this afternoon, see. Not for the money: for the principle of the thing, see?"

"Yes," the reporter said. He turned and went on. Now he could feel his jaw quite distinctly through the faint grimace of smiling, the grimace thin bitter and wrung. "Yes. It aint the money. That aint it. That dont matter." He heard the bomb this time and saw the five aeroplanes dart upward, diminishing, as he reached the apron, beginning to pass the spaced amplifyers and the rich voice:

"——second event. Three-seventy-five cubic inch class. Some of the same boys that gave you a good race yesterday, except Myers, who is out of this race to save up for the five-fifty later this afternoon. But Ott and Bullitt are out there, and Roger Shumann who surprised us all yesterday by taking second in a field that——" He found her almost at once; she had not changed from the dungarees this time. He extended the key, feeling his jaw plainer and plainer through his face's grimace.

"Make yourselves at home," he said. "As long as you want to. I'm going to be out of town for a few days. So I may not even see you again. But you can just drop the key in an envelope and address it to the paper. And make yourselves at home; there is a woman comes every morning but Sunday to clean up. . . . . . ." The five aeroplanes came in on the first lap: the snarl, the roar banking into a series of downwind scuttering pops as each one turned the pylon and went on.

"You mean you're not going to need the place yourself at all?" she said.

"No. I wont be there. I am going out of town on an assignment."

"I see. Well, thanks. I wanted to thank you for last night, but——"

"Yair," he said. "So I'll beat it. You can say goodbye to the others for me."

"Yes. But are you sure it wont——"

"Sure. It's all right. You make yourselves at home." He turned; he began to walk fast, thinking fast, "Now if I only can just——" He heard her call him twice; he thought of trying to run on his boneless legs and knew that he would fall, hearing her feet just behind him now, thinking, "No. No. Dont. That's all I ask. No. No." Then she was beside him; he stopped and turned, looking down at her.

"Listen," she said. "We took some money out of your——"

"Yes. I knew. It's o.k. You can hand it back. Put it in the envelope with the——"

"I intended to tell you as soon as I saw you today. It was——"

"Yair; sure." He spoke loudly now, turning again, fleeing before yet beginning to move. "Anytime. Goodbye now."

"——it was six-seventy. We left. . . . . . ." Her voice died away; she stared at him, at the thin rigid grimace which could hardly have been called smiling but which could have been called nothing else. "How much did you find in your pocket this morning?"

"It was all there," he said. "Just the six-seventy was missing. It was all right." He began to walk. The aeroplanes came in and turned the field pylon again as he was passing through the gate and into the rotunda. When he entered the bar the first face he saw was that of the photographer whom he had called Jug.

"I aint going to offer you a drink," the photographer said, "because I never buy them for nobody. I wouldn't even buy Hagood one."

"I dont want a drink," the reporter said. "I just want a dime."

"A dime? Hell, that's damn near the same as a drink."

"It's to call Hagood with. That will look better on your expense account than a drink would." There was a booth in the corner; he called the number from the slip which the substitute had given him. After a while Hagood answered. "Yair, I'm out here," the reporter said. "Yair, I feel o.k. . . . . Yair, I want to come in. Take something else, another assignment. . . . . Yair, out of town if you got anything, for a day or so if you——Yair. Thanks, chief. I'll come right on in." He had to walk through the voice again to pass through the rotunda, and again it met him outside though for the moment he did not listen to it for listening to himself: "It's all the same! I did the same thing myself! I dont intend to pay Hagood either! I lied to him about money too!" and the answer, loud too: "You lie, you bastard. You're lying, you son of a bitch." So he was hearing the amplifyer before he knew that he was listening, just as he had stopped and half-turned before he knew that he had stopped, in the bright thin sunlight

filled with mirageshapes which pulsed against his painful
eyelids: so that when two uniformed policemen appeared
suddenly from beyond the hangar with Jiggs struggling between them, his cap in one hand and one eye completely
closed now and a long smear of blood on his jaw, the reporter
did not even recognise him; he was now staring at the amplifyer above the door as though he were actually seeing in it
what he merely heard:

"——Shumann's in trouble; he's out of the race; he's
turning out to. . . . . . . He's cut his switch and he's going to
land; I dont know what it is but he's swinging wide; he's trying to keep clear of the other ships and he's pretty wide and
that lake's pretty wet to be out there without any motor——
Come on, Roger; get back into the airport, guy!——He's in
now; he's trying to get back onto the runway to land and it
looks like he'll make it all right but the sun is right in his eyes
and he swung mighty wide to keep clear of——I dont know
about this——I dont. . . . . . . Hold her head up, Roger! Hold
her head up! Hold——" The reporter began to run; it was not
the crash that he heard: it was a single long exhalation of
human breath as though the microphone had reached out
and caught that too out of all the air which people had ever
breathed. He ran back through the rotundra and through the
suddenly clamorous mob at the gate, already tugging out his
policecard; it was as though all the faces, all the past twenty-
four hours' victories and defeats and hopes and renunciations
and despairs, had been blasted completely out of his life as if
they had actually been the random sheets of that organ to
which he dedicated his days, caught momentarily upon one
senseless member of the scarecrow which he resembled, and
then blown away. A moment later, above the heads streaming

up the apron and beyond the ambulance and the firetruck and the motorcycle squad rushing across the field, he saw the aeroplane lying on its back, the undercarriage projecting into the air rigid and delicate and motionless as the legs of a dead bird. Two hours later, at the bus stop on the Grandlieu Street corner, from where she and Shumann stood a few feet away, the woman could see the reporter standing quietly as he had emerged from the bus and surrendered the four tickets for which he had paid. She could not tell who or what he was looking at: his face was just peaceful, waiting, apparently inattentive even when the parachute jumper limped over to him, dragging savagely the leg which even through the cloth of the trousers appeared thick stiff and ungainly with the emergency dressing from the airport's surgery, result of having been drifted by an unforeseen windgust over the stands and then slammed into one of the jerrybuilt refreshment booths when landing his parachute.

"Look here," he said. "This afternoon. I was mad at Jiggs. I never meant to sock you. I was worried and mad. I even thought it was still Jiggs' face until too late."

"It's all right," the reporter said. It was not smiling: it was just peaceful and serene. "I guess I just got in the way."

"I didn't plan to. If you want any satisfaction——"

"It's all right," the reporter said. They didn't shake hands; the jumper just turned after a moment and dragged his leg back to where he had been standing, leaving the reporter as before, in that attitude of peaceful waiting. The woman looked at Shumann again.

"Then if the ship's all right, why wont Ord fly it himself, race it himself?" she said.

"Maybe he dont have to," Shumann said. "If I had his

Ninety-Two I wouldn't need this ship either. I guess Ord would do the same. Besides, I—we haven't got it yet. So there aint anything to worry about. Because if it is a bum, Ord wont let us have it. Yair, you see? if we can get it, that's proof that it's o.k. because Ord wouldn't——" She was looking down now, motionless save for her hands, with the heel of one of which she was striking lightly the other's palm. Her voice was flat, hard, and low, not carrying three feet:

"We. We. He has boarded and fed us for a day and night now, and now he is even going to get us another ship to fly. And all I want is just a house, a room; a cabin will do, a coal-shed where I can know that next Monday and the Monday after that and the Monday after that——. . . . . . . Do you suppose he would have something like that he could give to me?" She turned; she said, "We better get on and get that stuff for Jack's leg." The reporter had not heard her, he had not been listening; now he found that he had not even been watching; his first intimation was when he saw her walking toward him. "We're going on to your house," she said. "I guess we'll see you and Roger when we see you. You have changed your plan about leaving town, I imagine?"

"Yes," the reporter said. "I mean no. I'm going home with a guy on the paper to sleep. Dont you bother about me." He looked at her, his face gaunt, serene, peaceful. "Dont you worry. I'll be o.k."

"Yes," she said. "About that money. That was the truth. You can ask Roger and Jack."

"It's all right," he said. "I would believe you even if I knew you had lied."

And Tomorrow

So you see how it is," the reporter said. He looked down at Ord too, as he seemed doomed to look down at everyone with whom he seemed perennially and perpetually compelled either to plead or just to endure: perhaps enduring and passing the time until that day when time and age would have thinned still more what blood he had and so permit him to see himself actually as the friendly and lonely ghost peering timidly down from the hayloft at the other children playing below. "The valves went bad and then he and Holmes had to go to that meeting so they could tell them that thirty percent. exceeded the code or something: and then Jiggs went and then they didn't have time to check the valvestems and take out the bad ones and then the whole engine went and the rudderpost and a couple of longerons and tomorrow's the last day. That's tough luck, aint it?"

"Yes," Ord said. They all three still stood. Ord had probably invited them to sit out of habit, courtesy, when they first came in though probably he did not remember now doing so any more than the reporter and Shumann could remember declining if they had declined. But probably neither invitation nor refusal had passed at all, that the reporter had brought into the house, the room, with him that atmosphere of a fifteenth century Florentine stage scene—an evening call with formal courteous words in the mouth and naked rapiers under the cloaks. In the impregnably new glow of two roseshaded lamps which looked like the ones that burn for three hours each night in a livingroom suite in the storewindows dressed by a junior manclerk, they all stood now as they had come from the airport, the reporter in that single suit which apparently composed his wardrobe, and Shumann and Ord in greasestained suede jackets which a third person could not have told apart, standing in the livingroom of Ord's new neat little flowercluttered house built with the compact economy of an aeroplane itself, with the new matched divan and chairs and tables and lamps arranged about it with the myriad compactness of the dials and knobs of an instrument panel. From somewhere toward the rear they could hear a dinnertable being set, and a woman's voice singing obviously to a small child. "All right," Ord said. He did not move; his eyes seemed to watch them both without looking at either, as though they actually were armed invaders. "What do you want me to do?"

"Listen," the reporter said. "It's not the money, the prize; I dont have to tell you that. You were one too, not so long ago, before you met Atkinson and got a break. Hell, look at you now, even when you got Atkinson and all you have to do is just build them without even seeing a pylon closer to it than the grandstand, without ever taking your other foot off the ground except to get into bed. But do you? Yair; maybe it

was somebody else pulling that Ninety-Two around those pylons at Chicago last summer that day; maybe that wasn't
Matt Ord at all. So you know it aint the money, the damn
cash: Jesus Christ, he aint got the jack he won yesterday yet.
Because if it was just the money, if he just had to have it and
he come to you and told you, you would lend it to him. Yair,
I know. I dont have to tell you. Jesus, I dont have to tell anybody that after today, after up there in that office at noon.
Yair; listen. Suppose instead of them up there on those damn
hard chairs today it had been a gang of men hired to go down
into a mine say, not to do anything special down there but
just to see if the mine would cave in on top of them, and five
minutes before they went down the bigbellied guys that own
the mine would tell them that everybody's pay had been cut
two and a half percent. to print a notice how the elevator or
something had fell on one of them the night before: would
they go down? Naw. But did these guys refuse to fly that race?
Maybe it was not a valve that Shumann's ship swallowed but
a peanut somebody in the grandstand threw down on the
apron. Yair; they could have kept back the ninety-seven and
a half and give them the two and a half and it would——"

"No," Ord said. He spoke with complete and utter final-
ity. "I wouldn't even let Shumann make a field hop in it. I
wouldn't let any man, let alone fly it around a closed course.
Even if it was qualified." Now it was as though with a word
Ord had cut through the circumlocution like through a
light net and that the reporter, without breaking stride, had
followed him onto new ground as bleak and forthright as a
prizering.

"But you have flown it. I dont mean that Shumann can

fly as good as you can; I dont believe anybody can do that even though I know mine aint even an opinion: it's just that hour's dual you give me talking. But Shumann can fly anything that will fly. I believe that. And we will get it qualified; the license is still o.k."

"Yes. The license is o.k. But the reason it hasn't been revoked yet is the Department knows I aint going to let it off the ground again. Only to revoke it would not be enough: it ought to be broken up and then burned, like you would kill a maddog. Hell, no. I wont do it. I feel sorry for Shumann but not as sorry as I would feel tomorrow night if that ship was over at Feinman Airport tomorrow afternoon."

"But listen, Matt," the reporter said. Then he stopped. He did not speak loud, and with no especial urgency, yet he emanated the illusion still of having longsince collapsed yet being still intact of his own weightlessness like a dandelion burr moving where there is no wind; in the soft pink glow his face appeared gaunter than ever, as though following the excess of the past night, his vital spark now fed on the inner side of the actual skin itself, paring it steadily thinner and more and more transparent, as parchment is made. Now his face was completely inscrutable. "So even if we could get it qualified, you wouldn't let Shumann fly it."

"Right," Ord said. "It's tough on him. I know that. But he dont want to commit suicide."

"Yair," the reporter said. "He aint quite got to where wont nothing else content him. Well, I guess we better get on back to town."

"Stay and eat some dinner," Ord said. "I told Mrs Ord you fellows——"

"I reckon we better get on back," the reporter said. "It looks like we will have all day tomorrow with nothing to do but eat."

"We could eat and then drive over to the hangar and I will show you the ship and try to explain——"

"Yair," the reporter said pleasantly. "But what we want is one that Shumann can look at from inside the cockpit three oclock tomorrow afternoon. Well, sorry we troubled you." The station was not far; they followed a quiet graveled village street in the darkness, the Franciana February darkness already heavy with spring—the Franciana spring which emerges out of the Indian summer of fall almost, like a mistimed stage resurrection which takes the curtain even before rigor mortis has made its bow, where the decade's phenomenon of ice occurs simultaneous with bloomed stalk and budded leaf. They walked quietly; even the reporter was not talking now—the two of them who could have had nothing in common save the silence which for the moment the reporter permitted them—the one volatile, irrational, with his ghostlike quality of being beyond all mere restrictions of flesh and time, of possessing no intrinsic weight or bulk himself and hence being everywhere to supply that final straw's modicum of surprise and even disaster to the otherwise calculable doings of calculable people; the other singlepurposed, fatally and grimly without any trace of introversion or any ability to objectivate or ratiocinate as though like the engine, the machine for which he apparently existed, he functioned, moved, only in the vapor of gasoline and the filmslick of oil—the two of them taken in conjunction and because of this dissimilarity capable of almost anything; walking, they seemed to communicate by some means or agency of the purpose, the disaster, toward which without yet being conscious of it apparently, they moved. "Well," the reporter said. "That's about what we expected."

"Yair," Shumann said. They walked on in silence again; it was as though the silence were the dialogue and the actual speech the soliloquy, the marshalling of thought:

"Are you afraid of it?" the reporter said. "Let's get that settled; we can do that right now."

"Tell me about it again," Shumann said.

"Yes. The guy brought it down here from Saint Louis for Matt to rebuild it; it wouldn't go fast enough for him. He had it all doped out, about how they would pull the engine and change the body a little and put in a big engine and Matt told him he didn't think that was so good, that the ship had all the engine then it had any business with and the guy asked Matt whose ship it was and Matt said it was the guy's and the guy asked Matt whose money it was and so Matt said o.k. Only Matt thought they ought to change the body more than the guy thought they ought to and at last Matt refused to have anything to do with it unless the guy compromised with him and even then Matt didn't think so much of it, he didn't want to butcher it up because it was a good ship, even I can tell that by looking at it. And so they compromised because Matt told him he would not test it otherwise, besides getting the license back on it and the guy saying how he seemed to have been misinformed in what he had heard about Matt and so Matt told him o.k., if he wanted to take the ship to somebody else he would put it back together and not even charge the guy storage space on it. So finally the guy agreed to let Matt make the changes he absolutely insisted on and then he wanted Matt to guarantee the ship and

Matt told the guy his guarantee would be when Matt got into the cockpit and took it off and the guy said he meant to turn a pylon with it and Matt told the guy maybe he had been misinformed about him and maybe he had better take the ship to somebody else and so the guy cooled down and Matt made the changes and put in the big engine and he brought Sales, the inspector, out there and they stressed it and Sales o.k.'d the job and then Matt told the guy he was ready to test it. The guy had been kind of quiet for some time now, he said o.k., he would go into town and get the money while Matt was testing it, flying it in, and so Matt took it off." They didn't stop walking, the reporter talking quietly: "Because I dont know much; I just had an hour's dual with Matt because he gave it to me one day: I dont know why he did it and I reckon he dont either. So I dont know: only what I could understand about what Matt said, that it flew o.k. because Sales passed it; it flew o.k. and it stalled o.k. and did everything it was supposed to do up in the air, because Matt wasn't even expecting it when it happened: he was coming in to land, he said how he was getting the stick back and the ship coming in fine and then all of a sudden his belt caught him and he saw the ground up in front of his nose instead of down under it where it ought to been, and how he never took time to think, he just jammed the stick forward like he was trying to dive it into the ground and sure enough the nose came up just in time; he said the slipstream on the tailgroup made a—a——"

"Burble," Shumann said.

"Yair. Burble. He dont know if it was going slow to land or being close to the ground that changed the slipstream, he just levelled it off with the stick jammed against the firewall until it lost speed and the burble went away and he got the stick back and blasted the nose up with the gun and he managed to stay inside the field by groundlooping it. And so they waited a while for the guy to get back from town with the money and after a while Matt put the ship back in the hangar and it's still there. So you say now if you think you better not."

"Yair," Shumann said. "Maybe it's weight distribution."

"Yair. That may be it. Maybe we will find out right away it's just that, maybe as soon as you see the ship you will know." They came to the quiet little station lighted by a single bulb, almost hidden in a mass of oleander and vines and palmettos. In either direction the steady green eye of a switchlamp gleamed faintly on the rails where they ran, sparsely strung with the lighted windows of houses, through a dark canyon of mosshung liveoaks. To the south, on the low night overcast, lay the glare of the city itself. They had about ten minutes to wait.

"Where you going to sleep tonight?" Shumann said.

"I got to go to the office for a while. I'll go home with one of the guys there."

"You better come on home. You got enough rugs and things for us all to sleep. It wouldn't be the first time Jiggs and Jack and me have slept on the floor."

"Yes," the reporter said. He looked down at the other; they were little better than blurs to one another; the reporter said in a tone of hushed quiet amazement: "You see, it dont matter where I would be. I could be ten miles away or just on the other side of that curtain, and it would be the same. Jesus, it's funny: Holmes is the one that aint married to her and if I said anything like that to him I would have to dodge—if I had time. And you are married to her, and I can....... Yair. You can go on and hit me too. Because maybe if I was to even sleep with her, it would be the same. Sometimes I think about how it's you and him and how maybe sometimes she dont even know the difference, one from another, and I would think how maybe if it was me too she wouldn't even know I was there at all."

"Here, for Christ's sake," Shumann said. "You'll have me thinking you are ribbing me up in this crate of Ord's so you can marry her maybe."

"Yair," the reporter said; "all right. I'd be the one. Yair. Because listen. I dont want anything. Maybe it's because I just want what I am going to get, only I dont think it's just that. Yair, I'd just be the name, my name, you see: the house and the beds and what we would need to eat. Because, Jesus, I'd just be walking: it would still be the same: you and him, and I'd just be walking, on the ground; I would maybe keep up with Jiggs and that's all. Because it's thinking about the day after tomorrow and the day after that and after that and me smelling the same burnt coffee and dead shrimp and oysters and waiting for the same light to change like me and the red light worked on the same clock so I could cross and get home and go to bed so I could get up and start smelling the coffee and fish and waiting for the light to change again; yair, smelling the paper and the ink too where it says how among those who beat or got beat at Omaha or Miami or Cleveland or Los Angeles was Roger Shumann and family. Yes. I would be the name; I could anyway buy her the pants and the nightgowns and it would be my sheets on the bed and even my towels.—Well, come on. Aint you going to sock me?" Now the far end of the canyon of liveoaks sprang into more profound impenetrability yet as the headlight of the train fell upon it and then swept down the canyon itself. Now Shumann could see the other's face.

"Does this guy you are going to stay with tonight expect you?" he said.

"Yes. I'll be all right. And listen. We better catch the eight-twenty back here."

"All right," Shumann said. "Listen. About that money——"

"It's all right," the reporter said. "It was all there."

"We put a five and a one back into your pocket. But if it was gone, I'll make it good Saturday, along with the other. It was our fault for leaving it there. But we couldn't get in; the door had locked when it shut."

"It dont matter," the reporter said. "It's just money. It dont matter if you dont ever pay it back." The train came up, slowing, the lighted windows jarred to a halt. The car was full, since it was not yet eight oclock, but they found two seats at last, in tandem, so they could not talk anymore until they got out in the station. The reporter still had a dollar of the borrowed five; they took a cab. "We'll go by the paper first," he said. "Jiggs ought to be almost sober now." The cab, even at the station, ran at once into confetti, emerging beneath dingy gouts of the purple-and-gold bunting three days old now dropped across the smokegrimed façade of the station like flotsam left by a spent and falling tide and murmuring even yet of the chalkwhite, the forlorn, the glare and pulse of Grandlieu Street miles away. Now the cab began to run between loops of it from post to post of lamps; the cab ran now between the lofty and urbane palms and turned slowing and then drew up at the twin glass doors. "I wont be but a minute," the reporter said. "You can stay here in the cab."

"We can walk from here," Shumann said. "The police station aint far."

"We'll need the cab to get around Grandlieu," the reporter said. "I wont be long." He walked into no reflection now, since darkness was behind him; the doors swung to. The elevator door was slightly ajar and he could see the stack of papers beneath the facedown watch and he could smell the stinking pipe but he did not pause, taking the steps two at a time, and on into the cityroom; beneath his green eyeshade Hagood looked up and saw the reporter. But this time the reporter neither sat down nor removed his hat: he stood, loomed, into the green diffusion above the desklamp, looking down at Hagood with gaunt and quiet immobility as though he had been blown for a second against the desk by a wind and would in another second be blown onward once more.

"Go home and go to bed," Hagood said. "The story you phoned in is already set up."

"Yes," the reporter said. "I must have fifty dollars, chief." After a while Hagood said,

"Must, do you?" He did not move at all. "Must, eh?" he said. The reporter did not move either.

"I cant help it. I know that I. . . . . . .yesterday, whenever it was. When I thought I was fired. I got the message, all right. I ran into Cooper about noon and I didn't call you until after three. And I didn't report in here, like I said. But I did phone in the story; I will come back in about an hour and clean it. . . . . . . But I got to have fifty dollars."

"It's because you know I wont fire you," Hagood said. "Is that it?" The reporter said nothing. "All right. Come on. What is it this time? I know, all right. But I want to hear it

from you — or are you still married or moved away or dead?"
The reporter did not move; he spoke quietly, apparently into
the green lampshade like it was a microphone:

"The cops got him. It happened just about the time Shumann nosed over, and so I. . . . . . . So he's in the can. And
they will need some jack too until Shumann gets his money
tomorrow night."

"So," Hagood said. He looked up at the still face above
him which for the time had that calm sightless contempla-
tion of a statue. "Why dont you let these people alone?" he
said. Now the blank eyes waked; the reporter looked at Hagood for a full minute. His voice was as quiet as Hagood's.

"I cant," he said.

"You cant?" Hagood said. "Did you ever try to?"

"Yes," the reporter said in his dead flat voice, looking at
the lamp again; that is, Hagood knew that the reporter was
not looking at him. "I tried." After a moment Hagood turned,
heavily. His coat hung on the back of his chair. He took his
wallet from it and counted fifty dollars onto the desk and
pushed it over to the reporter and saw the bony, clawlike
hand come into the lamp's glare and take up the money.
"Do you want me to sign anything now?" the reporter said.

"No," Hagood said without looking up. "Go home and
go to bed. That's all I want."

"I'll come in later and clean up the story."

"It's already in galley," Hagood said. "You go home." The
reporter moved away from the desk quietly enough, but as he
entered the corridor it was as though the wind which had
blown him against Hagood's desk and left him there had now
begun to blow him again; he was passing the elevator shaft
toward the stairs with only a glance at it when the door

clashed back and someone got out, whereupon he turned and entered, reaching with one hand into his pocket as with the other he lifted the top paper beneath the sliding face-down watch. But he did not even glance at it now; he thrust it, folded, into his pocket as the cage stopped and the door clashed open.

"Well, I see where another of them tried to make a head-line out of himself this afternoon," the elevator man said.

"Is that so?" the reporter said. "Better close that door; I think you got a draft in there." He ran into the swinging re-flection in the glass doors this time, on his long loose legs, with the long loose body which had had no food since noon and little enough before that but which, weightless anyway, had the less to carry now. Shumann opened the cab door for him. "Bayou Street police station," the reporter told the driver. "Make it snappy."

"We could walk," Shumann said.

"Hell, I got fifty bucks now," the reporter said. They trav-eled crosstown now; the cab could rush fast down each block of the continuous alley, pausing only at the intersections where, to the right, canyonniched, the rumor of Grandlieu Street swelled and then faded in repetitive and indistin-guishable turmoil, flicking on and past as though the cab ran along the rimless periphery of a ghostly wheel spoked with light and sound. "Yair," the reporter said, "I reckon they took Jiggs to the only quiet place in New Valois for a man to sober up in. He'll be sober now." He was sober; a turnkey fetched him in to where the reporter and Shumann waited at the desk. His eye was closed now and his lip swollen though the blood had been cleaned away except where it had dried on his shirt.

"Got enough for a while?" Shumann said.

"Yair," Jiggs said. "Give me a cigarette, for God's sake." The reporter gave him the cigarette and held the match while Jiggs tried to bring the cigarette into the flame, jerking and twitching until at last the reporter grasped Jiggs' hand and steadied it to make the contact.

"We'll get a piece of steak and put it on your eye," the reporter said.

"You better put it inside of him," the desk man said.

"How about that?" the reporter said. "You want to eat?" Jiggs held the cigarette in both shaking hands.

"All right," Jiggs said.

"What?" the reporter said. "Would you feel better if you ate something?"

"All right," Jiggs said. "Do we go now or do I go back in there?"

"No, we're going right now," the reporter said. He said to Shumann, "You take him on to the cab; I'll be right out." He turned to the desk. "What's it, Mac? Drunk or vag?"

"You springing him, or the paper?"

"I am."

"Call it vag," the desk man said. The reporter took out Hagood's money and laid ten dollars on the desk.

"O.K.," he said. "Will you give the other five to Leblanc? I borrowed it off of him out at the airport this afternoon." He went out too. Shumann and Jiggs waited beside the cab. The reporter saw now the once raked and swaggering cap crumpled and thrust into Jiggs' hip pocket and that the absence of the raked and filthy object from Jiggs' silhouette was like the dropped flag from the shot buck's—the body still ran, still retained a similitude of power and even speed, would even run on for yards and even perhaps miles, and then for years in a gnawing burrowing of worms, but that which tasted air and drank the sun was dead. "The poor bastard," the reporter thought; he still carried the mass of bills as he had thrust them into and withdrawn them from his pocket. "You're o.k. now," he said, loudly, heartily. "Roger can stop somewhere and get you something to eat and then you will be all right. Here." He nudged his hand at Shumann.

"I wont need it," Shumann said. "Jack collected his eighteen-fifty for the jump this afternoon."

"Yair; I forgot," the reporter said. Then he said, "But what about tomorrow? We'll be gone all day, see? Here, take it; you can leave it with her in case. . . . . . . You can just keep it and pay it all back, then."

"Yair," Shumann said. "Thanks then." He took the crumpled wad without looking at it and put it into his pocket and pushed Jiggs into the cab.

"Besides, you can pay the cab, too," the reporter said. "We forgot about that. — I told him where to go. See you in the morning." He leaned to the window; beyond Shumann Jiggs sat in the other corner, smoking the cigarette out of both shaking hands. The reporter spoke in a tone repressed, conspiratorial: "Train leaves at eight-twenty-two. O.K.?"

"O.K.," Shumann said.

"I'll have everything fixed up and meet you at the station."

"O.K.," Shumann said. The cab moved on. Through the back window Shumann saw the reporter standing at the curb in the glare of the two unmistakable pariahgreen globes on either side of the entrance, still, gaunt, the garments which hung from the skeleton frame seeming to stir faintly and steadily even when and where there was no wind, as though having chosen that one spot out of the entire sprawled and myriad city he stood there without impatience or design: patron (even if no guardian) saint of all waifs, all the homeless the desperate and the starved. Now the cab turned its back on Grandlieu Street, though presently it turned parallel to it or to where it must be now, since now there was no rumor, no sound, save the lightglare on the sky which held to their right even after the cab turned and now ran toward where the street should be; Shumann did not know they had crossed it until they plunged suddenly into the region of narrow gashes between balconies, crossing intersections marked by the ghostly oneway arrows. "We must be almost there," he said. "You want to stop and eat?"

"All right," Jiggs said.

"Do you or dont you?"

"Yair," Jiggs said. "Whatever you want me to do." Then Shumann looked at him and saw him trying to hold the cigarette to his mouth with both hands, and that the cigarette was dead.

"What do you want?" Shumann said.

"I want a drink," Jiggs said quietly.

"Do you have to have one?"

"I guess I dont if I cant get one." Shumann watched him holding the dead cigarette to his mouth, drawing at it.

"If I give you a drink, will you eat something?"

"Yair. I'll do anything." Shumann leaned forward and tapped on the glass. The driver turned his head.

"Where can I get something to eat?" Shumann said. "A bowl of soup?"

"You'll have to go back up toward Grandlieu for that."

"Aint there any place close around here?"

"You can get a ham sandwich at these wop stores, if you can find one open."

"All right. Stop at the next one you see, will you?" It was not far; Shumann recognised the corner, though he asked to be sure as they got out. "Noy-dees Street aint far from here, is it?"

"Noyades?" the driver said. "That's it in the next block there. On the right."

"We'll get out here then," Shumann said. He drew out the crumpled money which the reporter had given him, glancing down at the plump neat figure five in the corner. "That makes eleven-seventy," he thought, then he discovered a second bill crumpled into the first one; he passed it to the driver, still looking at the compact "5" on the one in his hand. "Damn," he thought. "That's seventeen dollars", as the driver spoke to him:

"It's just two-fifteen. Aint you got anything smaller than this?"

"Smaller?" Shumann said. He looked at the bill in the driver's hand, held so that the light from the meter fell upon it. It was a ten. "No," he thought; he didn't even swear now. "It's twenty-two dollars." The store was a room the size shape and temperature of a bankvault. It was illuminated by one kerosene lamp which seemed to cast not light but shadows, out of whose brown Rembrandtgloom the hushed bellies of ranked cans gleamed behind a counter massed with an unbelievable quantity of indistinguishable objects which the proprietor must vend by feel alone to distinguish not only object from object but object from chiaroscuro. It smelled of cheese and garlic and of heated metal; sitting on either side

of a small fiercelyburning kerosene heater a man and a
woman, both wrapped in shawls and distinguishable by gen-
der only because the man wore a cap and whom Shumann
had not seen until now, looked up at him. The sandwich was
the end of a hard French loaf, with ham and cheese. He gave
it to Jiggs and followed him out, where Jiggs stopped again
and stood looking at the object in his hand with a sort of ox-
like despair.

"Could I have the drink first?" he said.

"You eat while we walk home," Shumann said. "I'll give
you the drink later."

"It would be better if I had the drink first," Jiggs said.

"Yes," Shumann said. "You thought that this morning
too."

"Yair," Jiggs said. "That's right." He became motionless
again, looking at the sandwich.

"Go on," Shumann said. "Eat it."

"All right," Jiggs said. He began to eat; Shumann
watched him bring the sandwich to his mouth with both
hands and turn his face sideways to bite into it; he could see
Jiggs shaking and jerking all over now as he worried the bite
off and began to chew; chewing, Jiggs looked full at Shumann, holding the bitten sandwich in both grimed hands before his breast as though it were a crucifix, chewing with his
mouth open, looking full at Shumann until Shumann realised that Jiggs was not looking at him at all, that the one
good eye was merely open and filled with a profound and
hopeless abnegation as if the despair which both eyes should
have divided between them had now to be concentrated and
contained in one alone, and that Jiggs' face was now slicked
over with something which in the faint light resembled oil in

the instant before Jiggs began to vomit. Shumann held him up, holding the sandwich clear with the other hand, while Jiggs' stomach continued to go through the motions of refusal long after there was nothing left to abdicate.

"Try to stop it now," Shumann said.

"Yair," Jiggs said. He dragged his sleeve across his mouth.

"Here," Shumann said. He extended his handkerchief. Jiggs took it, but at once he reached his hand again, groping. "What?" Shumann said.

"The sandwich."

"Could you hold it down if you had a drink?"

"I could do anything if I had a drink," Jiggs said.

"Come on," Shumann said. When they entered the alley they could see the outfall of light from the window beyond the balcony as Hagood had seen it last night, though there was now no armshadow, no voice. Shumann halted beneath the balcony. "Jack," he said. "Laverne." But still there was nothing to see: just the parachute jumper's voice from beyond the window:

"It's off the latch. Lock it when you come in." When they came up the stairs the jumper was sitting on the cot, in his underclothes, his clothing arranged neatly on a chair and his foot on the chair too while with a stained wad of cotton he swabbed liquid from a bottle into the long raw abrasion like a paintsmear from his ankle to his thigh. On the floor lay the bandage and tape which he had worn in from the airport. He had already arranged the cot for the night; the blanket was turned neatly back and the rug from the floor spread over the foot.

"You better sleep in the bed tonight," Shumann said. "That blanket will give that skinned place hell." The jumper did not answer, bent over his leg, swabbing the medicine in with a sort of savage concentration. Shumann turned; he seemed to notice for the first time the sandwich in his hand and then to remember Jiggs who now stood quietly beside his canvas bag, watching Shumann quietly and patiently with the one eye, with that patient inarticulate quality of a dog. "Oh yes," Shumann said, turning on toward the table. The jug still sat there, though the glasses and the dishpan were gone and the jug itself appeared to have been washed. "Get a glass and some water," he said. When the curtain fell behind Jiggs Shumann laid the sandwich on the table and looked at the jumper again. After a moment the jumper looked up at him.

"Well?" the jumper said. "What about it?"

"I guess I can get it," Shumann said.

"You mean you didn't see Ord?"

"Yair. We found him."

"Suppose you do get it. How are you going to get it qualified in time to race tomorrow?"

"I dont know," Shumann said. He lit a cigarette. "He said he could get that fixed up. I dont know, myself."

"How? Does the race committee think he is Jesus too, the same as the rest of you do?"

"I said I dont know," Shumann said. "If we cant get it qualified, that's all there is to it. But if we can. . . . . . ." He smoked. The jumper swabbed carefully and viciously at his leg. "There's two things I could do," Shumann said. "It will qualify under five hundred and seventy-five cubic inches. I could enter it in that and loaf back on half throttle and take third without having to make a vertical turn, and the purse tomorrow is eight-ninety. Or I could enter the other, the Trophy. It will be the only thing out there that will even stay in sight of Ord. And Ord is just in it so his home folks can see him fly; I dont believe he would beat that Ninety-Two to death just to win two thousand dollars. Not on a five mile course. Because it must be fast. We would be fixed then."

"Yes; fixed. She'd owe Ord about five thousand for the crate and the motor. What's wrong with it?"

"I dont know. I didn't ask Ord. All I know is what Ord told him—" he made a brief indescribable motion with his head as though to indicate the room but which indicated the reporter as plainly as if Shumann had spoken his name—"he said the controls cross when it lands. Whether it's slowing up or whether it's the air off the ground. Because he said that Ord stalled it out when he. . . . . . . Or maybe a different weight distribution, a couple of sandbags in the——"

"Yair. Or maybe when he gets it qualified tomorrow he will have them move the pylons up to around four thousand feet and hold the race up there instead of at General Behindman's country club." He ceased and bent over his leg again, then Shumann also saw Jiggs. He had apparently been in the room for some time, standing beside the table with two of the jam glasses, one of them containing water, in his hands. Shumann went to the table and poured into the empty glass and looked at Jiggs who now mused upon the drink.

"Aint that enough?" Shumann said.

"Yair," Jiggs said, rousing; "yair." When he poured water from the other glass into the drink the two rims clicked together with a faint chattering; Shumann watched him set the water glass down, where it chattered again on the table before he released it, and then with both hands attempt to raise the other one to his lips. As the glass approached Jiggs' whole head began to jerk so that he could not make contact with his mouth, the rim of the glass clicking against his teeth while he tried to still it. "Jesus," he said quietly, "Jesus. I tried for two hours to sit on the bed because when I would walk up and down the guy would come and holler at me through the bars."

"Here," Shumann said. He put his hand on the glass and stopped it and tilted it; he could watch Jiggs swallowing now and the liquid trickling down his bluestubbled chin from each corner of his mouth and splotching dark on his shirt until Jiggs pushed the glass away, panting.

"Wait," he said. "It's wasting. Maybe if you wont look at me I can drink it."

"And then get on the sandwich again," Shumann said. He took the jug from the table and looked back at the jumper again. "Go on and take the bed tonight," he said. "You'll have that leg infected under a blanket. Are you going to put the bandage back on?"

"I'll sleep in a cuckold's bed but not in a pimp's," the jumper said. "Go on. Get yourself a piece to take to hell with you tomorrow."

"I can take third in the five-seventy-five without even crossing the airport," Shumann said. "Anyway, by the time it is qualified I'll know whether I can land it or not.—How about putting that bandage back on?" But the jumper did not answer nor even look at him. The blanket was already turned back; with the injured leg swinging stiffly he turned on the ball of his buttocks and swung into the cot and drew the blanket up in one motion; for a while longer Shumann looked at him, the jug against his leg. Then he realised that for some time he had been hearing Jiggs chewing and he looked at him and saw Jiggs squatting on the floor beside the canvas bag, chewing, holding the sandwich in both hands. "You, too," Shumann said. "You going to sleep there?" Jiggs looked up at him with the one eye. His whole face was swollen and puffed now; he chewed slowly and gingerly, looking up at Shumann with that doglike quality abject, sad, and at peace. "Go on," Shumann said. "Get settled. I'm going to turn out the light." Without ceasing to chew Jiggs disengaged one hand and dragged the canvas sack over and lay down, his head upon it. Shumann could still hear him chewing as he groped in the darkness toward the curtain and lifted it and passed beyond it and groped on to the lamp beside the bed, moving quietly now, and snapped it on and found the woman, the boy asleep beside her, watching him. She lay in the middle of the bed with the boy between her and the wall. Her clothes were laid neatly too on a chair and then Shumann saw the nightgown, the only silk one she had, lying across the chair too; and stooping to set the jug beneath the bed he paused and then lifted from the floor the cotton shorts which she wore, or had worn, from where they had either been dropped or flung, and put them on the chair too and removed his jacket and began to unbutton his shirt while she watched him, the bedclothes huddled to her chin.

"So you got the ship," she said.

"I dont know. We're going to try." He removed the watch from his wrist and wound it carefully and put it on the table; when the faint clicking ceased he could hear again from beyond the curtain the sound of Jiggs chewing. He set his feet in turn on the corner of the chair and unlaced his shoes, feeling her watching him. "I can take at least third in the five-seventy-five without passing the pylons close enough for anybody on them to read the ship's number. And that's fifteen percent. of eight-ninety. Or there's two thousand in the Trophy and I dont believe Ord will——"

"Yes. I heard you through the curtain. But why?" He set the shoes neatly side by side and stepped out of his trousers and shook them into crease by the cuffs and folded them and put them on the chest of drawers beside the celluloid comb and brush and the cravat and stood also in shorts. "And the ship is all right except you wont know until you are in the air whether or not you can take it off and you wont know until you are back on the ground and standing up again whether or not you can land it."

"I guess I can land it, all right." He lit a cigarette and then stood with his hand on the light switch, looking at her. She had not moved, lying with the covers drawn smooth and nunlike up to her chin; again from beyond the curtain he could hear Jiggs chewing, mouthing at the hard sandwich with that painful patience.

"You're lying," she said. "We got along before."

"Because we had to. This time we dont have to."

"But it's seven months yet."

"Yair. Just seven months. And one more meet, and the only ship we have with a shot engine and two wrenched longerons." He looked at her a moment longer; at last she opened the covers; as he snapped off the light his retina carried into the darkness the imprint of one bare shoulder and breast down to the waist. "Want to move Jack to the middle?" he said. She did not answer, though it was not until he drew the covers up himself that he discovered that she was lying rigid, her flank tense and hard with rigid muscles where his own touched it as he settled himself. He withdrew the cigarette and held it suspended above his mouth, hearing Jiggs chewing beyond the curtain and then the jumper's voice: "Jesus God, stop eating that! You sound just like a dog!"

"Here, take it easy," Shumann said. "I haven't got it qualified yet, even."

"You bastard," she said in a tense rigid whisper. "You rotten pilot, you bastard rotten pilot. Hanging off there with a dead stick so you wouldn't interfere in their damn race and then mushing in over that seawall and you wouldn't even hold its head up! you wouldn't even hold——" Her hand shot out and snatched the cigarette from him; he felt his own fingers wrench and bend and then saw the red coal twinkle and arc across the dark and strike the invisible floor.

"Here," he whispered. "Let me pick it up off the——" But now the hard hand struck his cheek, clutching and scrabbling about his jaw and throat and shoulder until he caught it and held it, wrenching and jerking.

"You bastard rotten, you rotten——" she panted.

"All right," he said. "Steady, now." She ceased, breathing hard and fast. But he still held the wrist, wary and without gentleness too. "All right, now.—You want to take your pants off?"

"They're already off."

"Oh yair," he said. "I forgot." When she made her first parachute jump they had not been together very long. She was the one who suggested that he teach her to jump, and he already had a parachute, the exhibition kind; when he used it he either flew the aeroplane or made the jump, depending on whether the casual partner with whom he would join forces for a day or a week or a season were a pilot himself or not. She made the suggestion herself and he showed her, drilled her, in the simple mechanics of climbing out onto the wing with the parachute harness buckled on and then dropping off and letting her own weight pull the parachute from the case attached to the wing. The act was billed for a Saturday afternoon in a small Kansas town and he did not know that she was frightened until they were in the air and the money collected and the crowd waiting and she had begun to climb out along the wing. She wore skirts; they had decided that her exposed legs would not only be a drawing card but that in the skirt no one would doubt that she was a woman, and now she was clinging to the inner bay strut and looking back at him with an expression that he was later to realise was not at all fear of death but on the contrary a wild and now mindless repudiation of bereavement as if it were he who was the one about to die and not her. He sat in the back cockpit with the aeroplane in position, holding the wing up under her weight, gesturing her on out toward the wingtip, almost angrily, when he saw her leave the strut and with that blind and completely irrational expression of protest and wild denial on her face and the hem of the skirt whipping out of the parachute harness about her loins climb, not back into the front seat which she had left but on toward the one in which he sat holding the aeroplane level, scrambling and sprawling into the cockpit (he saw her knuckles perfectly white where she gripped the cockpit's edge) astride his legs and facing him. In the same instant of realising (as with one hand she ripped her skirthem free of the safetywire with which they had fastened it bloomer-fashion between her legs) that she was clawing blindly and furiously not at the belt across his thighs but at the fly of his trousers he realised that she had on no undergarment, pants. She told him later that the reason was that she was afraid that from fear she might soil one of the few undergarments which she now possessed. So he tried to fight her off for a while, but he had to fly the aeroplane, keep it in position over the field, and besides (they had been together only a few months then) soon he had two opponents; he was outnumbered, he now bore in his own lap, between himself and her wild and frenzied body, the perennially undefeated, the victorious; it was some blind instinct out of the long swoon while he waited for his backbone's fluid marrow to congeal again that he remembered to roll the aeroplane toward the wing to which the parachute case was attached because the next that he remembered was the belt catching him across the legs as, looking up he saw the parachute floating between him and the ground, and looking down he saw the bereaved, the upthrust, the stalk: the annealed rapacious heartshaped crimson bud. He had to land the aeroplane, the rest he learned later: how she had come down with the dress, pulled or blown free of the parachute harness, up about her armpits and had been dragged along the ground until overtaken by a yelling mob of men and youths, in the center of which she now lay dressed from the waist down in dirt and parachute straps and stockings. When he fought through the mob to where she was she had been arrested by three village officers one of whose faces Shumann remarked even then with a violent foreboding—a youngish man with a hard handsome face sadistic rather than vicious, who was using the butt of a pistol to keep the mob back and who struck at Shumann with it with the same blind fury. They carried her to jail, the younger one threatening her with the pistol now; already

Shumann realised that in the two other officers he had only
bigotry and greed to contend with, it was the younger one
that he had to fear—a man besotted and satiated by his tri-
umphs over abased human flesh which his corrupt and
picayune office supplied him, seeing now and without fore-
warning the ultimate shape of his jaded desires fall upon him
out of the sky, not merely naked but clothed in the very tra-
ditional symbology—the ruined dress with which she was
trying wildly to cover her loins, and the parachute harness—
of female bondage. They would neither arrest Shumann too
nor allow him access to her. After he was driven back along
with the mob by the younger officer's pistol from the jail
door—a square building of fierce new brick into which he
saw her, struggling still, vanish—a single glimpse of her indomitable and terrified face beyond the younger officer's
shoulder as the now alarmed older officers hurried her inside—for the time he became one of the mob though even
then, mad with rage and terror, he knew that it was merely
because his and the mob's immediate object happened to be
the same—to see, touch her, again. He knew too that the two
older craven officers were at least neutral, pulled to his side
by their own physical fear of the mob, and that actually the
younger one had for support only his dispensation for im-
punitive violence with which the dingy cadaver of the law in-
vested him. But it seemed to be enough. It was for the next
hour anyway, during which, followed by his ragamuffin train
of boys and youths and drunken men, he accomplished his
nightmare's orbit about the town, from mayor to lawyer to
lawyer to lawyer and back again. They were at supper, or
about to sit down to it or just finishing; he would have to tell
his story with the round eyes of children and the grim im-

placable faces of wives and aunts watching him while the
empowered men from whom he sought what he sincerely
believed to be justice and no more forced him step by step to
name what he feared, whereupon one of them threatened to
have him arrested for criminal insinuations against the
town's civil structure. It was a minister (and two hours after
dark) who finally telephoned to the mayor. Shumann
learned only from the overheard conversation that the au-
thorities were apparently seeking him now; five minutes later
a car called for him, with one of the two older officers in it
and two others whom he had not seen yet. "Am I under arrest too?" he said. "You can try to get out and run if you want
to," the officer said. That was all. The car stopped at the jail
and the officer and one of the others got out. "Hold him," the
officer said. "I'll hold him, all right," the second deputy said.
So Shumann sat in the car with the deputy's shoulder
jammed into his and watched the two others hurry up the
bricked walk; the door of the jail opened for them and
closed; then it opened again and he saw her. She wore a raincoat now; he saw her for an instant as the two men hurried
her out and the door closed again; it was not until the next
day that she showed him the dress now in shreds and the
scratches and bruises on the insides of her legs and on her
jaw and face and the cut in her lip. They thrust her into the
car, beside him. The officer was about to follow when the
second deputy shoved him roughly away. "Ride in front,"
the deputy said. "I'll ride back here." There were now four in
the back seat; Shumann sat rigid with the first deputy's shoulder jammed into his and Laverne's rigid flank and side
jammed against him so that it seemed to him that he could
feel through her rigidity the second deputy crowding and

dragging his flank against Laverne's other side. "All right,"
the officer said. "Let's get away from here while we can."—
"Where are we going?" Shumann asked. The officer did not
answer. He leaned out, looking back at the jail as the car
gathered speed, going fast now. "Go on," he said. "Them
boys may not can hold him and there's been too much
whore's hell here already." The car rushed on, out of the village; Shumann realised that they were going in the direction
of the field, the airport. The car swung in from the road; its
headlights fell upon the aeroplane standing as he had
jumped out of it, already running, in the afternoon; as the
car stopped the lights of a second one came into sight, coming fast down the road. The officer began to curse. "Durn
him. Durn them boys. I knew they couldn't——" He turned
to Shumann. "There's your airship. You and her get out of
here."—"What do you want us to do?" Shumann said.
"You're going to crank up that flying machine and get out of
this town. And you do it quick; I was afraid them boys
couldn't hold him."—"Tonight?" Shumann said. "I haven't
got any lights."—"Aint nothing going to run into you up
there, I guess," the officer said. "You get her into it and get
away from here and dont you never come back." Now the
second car slewed from the road, the lights swung full upon
them; it rushed up, slewing again, with men already jumping out of it before it had stopped. "Hurry!" the officer cried.
"We'll try to hold him."—"Get into the ship," Shumann told
her. At first he thought that the man was drunk. He watched
Laverne, holding the raincoat about her, run down the long
tunnel of the cars' lights and climb into the aeroplane and
vanish, then he turned and saw the man struggling while the
others held him. But he was not drunk, he was mad, he was

insane for the time; he struggled toward Shumann who saw in his face not rage, not even lust, but almost a counterpart of that terror and wild protest against bereavement and division which he had seen in Laverne's face while she clung to the strut and looked back at him. "I'll pay you!" the man screamed. "I'll pay her! I'll pay either of you! Name it! Let me fuck her once and you can cut me if you want!"—"Go on, I tell you!" the older officer panted at him. He ran too; for an instant the man ceased to struggle; perhaps for the instant he believed that Shumann had gone to fetch her back. Then he began to struggle and scream again, cursing now, screaming at Laverne, calling her whore and bitch and pervert in a tone wild with despair until the engine blotted it. But Shumann could still see him struggling with the men who held him, the group silhouetted by the lights of the two cars, while he sat and warmed the engine as long as he dared. But he had to take it off cold after all; he could hear the shouts now and against the headlights he saw the man running toward him, toward the aeroplane; he took it off from where it stood, with nothing to see ahead but the blue flames at the exhaust ports, into a night without moon; thirty minutes later, using a dimlyseen windmill to check his altitude and making a fast blind landing in an alfalfa field, he struck an object which he found the next morning, fifty feet from the overturned aeroplane, to be a cow.

It was now about nine-thirty. The reporter thought for a moment of walking on over to Grandlieu Street and its celluloid and confettirained uproar and down it to Saint Jules and so back to the paper that way, but he did not. When he moved it was to turn back into the dark cross street out of which the cab had emerged a half hour before. There was no

reason for him to do this anymore than there would have
been any reason to return by Grandlieu Street: it was as
though the grim Spectator himself had so ordained and
arranged that when the reporter entered the twin glass doors
and the elevator cage clashed behind him this time, stooping
to lift the facedown watch alone and look at it he would contemplate unwitting and unawares peace's ultimate morato-
rium in the exact second of the cycle's completion—the
inexplicable and fading fury of the past twenty-four hours cir-
cled back to itself and become whole and intact and objec-
tive and already vanishing slowly like the damp print of a
lifted glass on a bar. Because he was not thinking about time,
about any postulated angle of clockhands on a dial; he had
even less reason to do that than he had to choose either of
the two directions, since the one moment out of all the future which he could see where his body would need to coincide with time or dial would not occur for almost twelve
hours yet; he was not even to recognise at once the cycle's
neat completion toward which he walked steadily, not fast,
from block to block of the narrow cross street notched out of
the blunt and now slumbering backends of commerce while
at each intersection where he waited during the traffic-
dammed moment or while there reached him, as in the cab
previously, the faint rumor, the sound felt rather than heard,
of Grandlieu Street: the tonight's Nilebarge clatterfalque—
the furious faint butterflyspawn, substanceless oblivious and
doomed, against the choraldrop of the dawn's biding white
wings—and at last Saint Jules Avenue itself running broad
and suave between the austere palms springing full immobile and monstrous like burlesqued bunches of country
broomsedge set on scabby posts, and then the twin doors and

the elevator cage where the elevator man, glancing up at him from beneath shaggy pepper-and-salt brows that looked like his moustache had had twins suddenly, said with grim and vindictive unction, "Well, I see how this afternoon another of them tried to make the front page, only he never quite——"

"Is that so," the reporter said pleasantly, laying the watch back. "Two past ten, huh? That's a fine hour for a man not to have nothing to do until tomorrow but go to work, aint it?"

"That ought not to be much hardship on a man that dont only work except when he aint got nothing else to do," the elevator man said.

"Is that so too," the reporter said pleasantly. "You better close that door; I think I felt a——" It clashed behind him. "Two minutes past ten," he thought. "That leaves......." But that fled before he had begun to think it; he hung in a slow long backwash of peaceful and serene waiting, thinking *Now she will be. ...* Just above the button on the bellplate the faintly oxidised streak of last night's match still showed; the match now, without calculation, without sight to guide it, almost followed the mark. The washroom was the last door: a single opaque sheet of glass stencilled GENTLE-MEN in a frame without knob ("Maybe that's why only gentlemen," the reporter thought) inswinging into eternal creosote. He removed even his shirt to wash, fingering gingerly the left side of his face, leaning to the blunt wavering mirror the replica of his gingerly grimace as he moved his jaw back and forth as he contemplated the bluish autograph of violence upon his diplomacolored flesh like tattooing, thinking quietly, "Yair. Now she will be......." Now the cityroom (he scratched this match on the door itself) the barncavern, looming: the copydesk like a cluttered island, the other single desks beneath the single greenshaded bulbs had that quality of profound and lonely isolation of buoy-marked shoals in an untravelled and forgotten sea, his own among them. He had not seen it in twenty-four hours it is true, yet as he stood beside it he looked down at its cluttered surface—the edgenotching of countless vanished cigarettes, the halffilled sheet of yellow copy in the typewriter—with slow and quiet amaze as though not only at finding anything of his own on the desk but at finding the desk itself still in its old place, thinking how he could not possibly have got that drunk and got that sober in just that time. There was some-one else at Hagood's desk when he passed and so Hagood had not seen him yet; he had been at his desk for almost an hour while yellow sheet after yellow sheet passed steadily through the typewriter when the copyboy came.

"He wants you," the boy said.

"Thanks," the reporter said. In his shirt sleeves and with his tie loose again though still wearing his hat, he stopped at the desk and looked down at Hagood with pleasant and cour-teous interrogation. "You wanted me, chief?" he said.

"I thought you went home. It's eleven oclock. What are you doing?"

"Buggering up a Sunday feature for Smitty. He asked me to do it."

"Asked you to?"

"Yair. I had caught up. I was all through."

"What is it?"

"It's all right. It's about how the loves of Antony and Cleopatra had been prophesied all the time in Egyptian ar-chitecture only they never knew what it meant; maybe they had to wait on the Roman papers. But it's all right. Smitty's got some books and a couple or three cuts to run, and all you have to do is try to translate the books so that any guy with a dime can understand what it means, and when you dont know yourself you just put it down like the book says it and that makes it better still because even the censors dont know what it says they were doing." But Hagood was not listening.

"You mean you are not going home tonight?" The reporter looked down at Hagood, gravely and quietly. "They are still down yonder at your place, are they?" The reporter looked at him. "What are you going to do tonight?"

"I'm going home with Smitty. Sleep on his sofa."

"He's not even here," Hagood said.

"Yair. He's at home. I told him I would finish this for him first."

"All right," Hagood said. The reporter returned to his desk.

"And now it's eleven oclock," he thought. "And that leaves. . . . . . . *Yair. She will be.* . . . . . ." There were three or four others at the single desks, but by midnight they had snapped off their lights and gone; now there was only the group about the copydesk and now the whole building began to tremble to the remote travail of the presses; now about the copydesk the six or seven men, coatless and collarless, in their green eyeshades like a uniform, seemed to concentrate toward a subterranean crisis, like so many puny humans conducting the lyingin of a mastodon. At half past one Hagood himself departed; he looked across the room toward the desk where the reporter sat immobile now, his hands still on the keyboard and his lowered face shaded and so hidden by his hatbrim; it was at two oclock that one of the

proofreaders approached the desk and found that the reporter was not thinking but asleep, sitting bolt upright, his
bony wrists and his thin hands projecting from his frayed
clean tooshort cuffs and lying peaceful and inert on the typewriter before him.

"We're going over to Joe's," the proofreader said. "Want
to come?"

"I'm on the wagon," the reporter said. "I aint through
here, anyway."

"So I noticed," the other said. "Only you better finish it
in bed.—What do you mean, on the wagon? That you are
going to start buying your own? You can do that with us;
maybe Joe wont drop dead."

"No," the reporter said. "On the wagon."

"Since when, for Christ's sake?"

"I dont know. Some time this morning.—Yair, I got to
finish this. Dont you guys wait on me." So they went out,
putting on their coats, though almost at once two char-
women came in. But the reporter did not heed them. He removed the sheet from the typewriter and laid it on the stack
and evened them meticulously, his face peaceful. "Yair," he
thought. "It aint the money. It aint that.——Yair. And now
she will be......." The women did not pay him any mind
either as he went to Hagood's desk and turned on the light
above it. He chose the right drawer at once and took out the
pad of blank note forms and tore off the top one and put the
pad back into the drawer. He did not return to his own desk,
neither did he pause at the nearest one because one of
the women was busy there. So he snapped on the light above
the next one and sat down and racked the note form into the
typewriter and began to fill it in, carefully—the neat conve-

nient flimsy scrap of paper which by a few marks became transposed into an implement sharper than steel and more enduring than stone and by means of which the final and fatal step became anesthetised out of the realm not only of dread but of intelligence too, into that of delusion and mindless hope like the superscription on a loveletter: . . . . *February 16, 1935* . . . . *February 16, 1936 we* . . . . *The Ord-Atkinson Aircraft Corp., Blaisedell, Franciana*. . . . . . . ——He did not pause at all, his fingers did not falter; he wrote in the sum exactly as though he were writing two words of a column head: *Five Thousand Dollars* ($5000.00). . . . . . . ——Now he did pause, his fingers poised, thinking swiftly while the charwoman did something in the wastebasket beside the desk in front of him, producing a mute deliberate scratching like a huge rat: "There's one of them is against the law, only if I put in the other one it might look fishy." So he wrote again, striking the keys clean and firm, spelling out the *e-i-g-h-t* and flipping the note out; now he went to the copydesk itself, since he did not own a fountain pen, and turned on the light there and signed the note on the first signature line and blotted it and sat looking at it quietly for a moment, thinking, "Yair. In bed now. And now he will. . . . . . . Yair," he said aloud, quietly, "that looks o.k." He turned, speaking to either of the two women: "You all know what time it is?" One of them leaned her mop against a desk and began to draw from the front of her dress an apparently interminable length of shoestring, though at last the watch—a heavy old-fashioned gold one made for a man to carry—came up.

"Twenty-six minutes to three," she said.

"Thanks," the reporter said. "Dont neither of you smoke cigarettes, do you?"

"Here's one I found on the floor," the second one said. "It dont look like much. It's been walked on." Nevertheless some of the tobacco remained in it, though it burned fast; at each draw the reporter received a sensation precarious and lightly temporary, as though at a breath tobacco fire and all would evacuate the paper tube and stop only when it struck the back of his throat or the end of his lungs; three draws consumed it.

"Thanks," he said. "If you find any more, will you put them on that desk back there where the coat is? Thanks.—Twenty-two to three," he thought. "That dont even leave six hours."—*Yair*, he thought, then it blew out of his mind, vanished, again into the long peaceful slack nothope, notjoy: just waiting, thinking how he ought to eat, then he thought how the elevator would not be running now, so that should settle that. "Only I could get some cigarettes," he thought. "Jesus, I ought to eat something." There was no light now in the corridor, but there would be one in the washroom; he returned to his desk and took the folded paper from his coat and went out again; and now, leaning against the carbolised wall he opened the paper upon the same boxheadings, the identical from day to day—the bankers the farmers the strikers, the foolish the unlucky and the merely criminal—distinguishable from one day to another not by what they did but by the single brief typeline beneath the paper's registered name. He could stand easily so, without apparent need to shift his weight in rotation among the members which bore it; now with mere inertia and not gravity to contend with he had even less of bulk and mass to support than he had carried running up the stairs at eight oclock, so that he moved only when he said to himself, "It must be after three now." He folded the paper neatly and returned to the corridor, where one glance into the dark cityroom showed him that the women were done. "Yair. It's making toward four," he thought, thinking, wondering if it were actually dawn which he felt, or that anyway the dark globe on which people lived had passed the dead point at which the ill and the weary were supposed to be prone to die and now it was beginning to turn again, soon beginning to spin again out of the last laggard reluctance of darkness—the garblement which was the city: the scabby hoppoles which elevated the ragged palmcrests like the monstrous broomsage out of an old country thought, the spent stage of last night's clatterfalque Nilebarge supine now beneath today's white wings treadling, the hydrant-gouts gutterplaited with the trodden tinseldung of stars. "And at Alphonse's and Renaud's the waiters that can not only understand Mississippi Valley French but they can even fetch back from the kitchen what you were not so sure yourself you told them to," he thought, passing among the desks by feel now and rolling the paper into his coat for pillow before stretching out on the floor. "Yair," he thought, "in bed now, and he will come in and she will say *Did you get it?* and he will say *What? Get what? Oh, you mean the ship. Yair, we got it. That's what we went over there for.*"

It was not the sun that waked him, nor what would have been the sun save for the usual winter morning's overcast: he just waked, regardless of the fact that during the past forty-eight hours he had slept but little more than he had eaten, like so many people who, living always on the outside of the mechanical regimentation of hours, seem able at need to coincide with a given moment with a sort of unflagging instinctive facility. But the train would be ordered by mechanical postulation though, and there would be no watch or clock in the building yet; gaunt, worn (he had not even paused to wash his face) he ran down the stairs and along the street itself, still running, and turned in this side of the window and the immemorial grapefruit halves which apparently each morning at the same moment at which the street lamps went out would be set, age- and timeproved for intactness and imperviousness like the peasant vases exhumed from Greek and Roman ruins, between the paper poinsettias and the easel bearing the names of food printed upon interchangeable metal strips. In the cityroom they called it the dirty spoon: one of ten thousand narrow tunnels furnished with a counter, a row of buttockpolished backless stools, a coffeeurn and a Greek proprietor resembling a retired wrestler adjacent to ten thousand newspapers and dubbed by ten thousand variations about the land; the same thickbodied Greek in the same soiled drill jacket might have looked at him across the same glass coffin filled with bowls of cereal and oranges and plates of buns apparently exhumed along with the grapefruit in the window, only just this moment varnished. Then the reporter was able to see the clock on the rear wall; it was only fifteen past seven. "Well, for Christ's sake," he said.

"Coffee?" the Greek said.

"Yair," the reporter said. "I ought to eat too," he thought, looking down into the glasswalled and -topped gutter beneath his hands, not with any revulsion now, but with a kind of delicate distasteful abstemiousness like the old novel women. And not from impatience, hurry: just as last night he seemed to see his blind furious course circling implacably back to the point where he had lost control of it like a kind of spiritual groundloop, now he seemed to feel it straighten out at last, already lifting him steadily and as implacably and undeviatingly onward so that now he need make no effort to move with it; all he had to do now was to remember to carry along with him everything which he was likely to need because this time he was not coming back. "Gimme one of these," he said, tapping the glass with one hand while with the other he touched, felt, the folded slip of paper in his watchpocket. He ate the bun along with his coffee, tasting neither, feeling only the coffee's warmth; it was now twenty-five past seven. "I can walk," he thought. The overcast would burn away later. But it still lay overhead when he entered the station where Shumann rose from the bench. "Had some breakfast yet?" the reporter said.

"Yes," Shumann said. The reporter looked at the other with a kind of bright grave intensity.

"Come on," he said. "We can get on now." The lights still burned in the trainshed; the skylight was the same color of the sky outside. "It will be gone soon though," the reporter said. "Maybe by the time we get there; you will probably fly the ship back in the sun. Just think of that." But it was gone before that; it was gone when they ran clear of the city; the car (they had the entire end of it to themselves) ran almost at once in thin sunlight. "I told you you would fly back in the sunshine," the reporter said. "I guess we had better fix this up now, too." He took out the note; he watched with that grave bright intensity while Shumann read it and then seemed to muse upon it soberly.

"Five thousand," Shumann said. "That's. . . . . . ."

"High?" the reporter said. "Yair. I didn't want there to be

any hitch until we got into the air with it, got back to the airport with it. To look like a price that even Marchand wouldn't dare refuse to. . . . . . ." He watched Shumann, bright, quiet, grave.

"Yair," Shumann said. "I see." He reached into his coat. Then perhaps it was the fountain pen, though the reporter did not move yet and the brightness and intensity and gravity had not altered yet as he watched the deliberate, unhurried, slightly awkward movement of the pen across the blank signature line beneath the one where he had signed, watching the letters emerge: *Roger Shumann* But he did not move even yet; it was not until the pen without stopping dropped down to the third line and was writing again that he leaned and stopped it with his hand, looking at the half finished third name: *Dr Carl S*

"Wait," he said. "What's that?"

"It's my father's name."

"Would he let you sign it on this?"

"He'd have to, after it was done. Yes. He would help you out on it."

"Help me out on it?"

"I wouldn't be worth even five hundred unless I managed to finish that race first." A trainman passed, swinging from seatback to seatback, pausing above them for a moment.

"Blaisedell," he said. "Blaisedell."

"Wait," the reporter said. "Maybe I didn't understand. I aint a flyer; all I know is that hour's dual Matt gave me that time. I thought maybe what Matt meant was he didn't want to risk having the undercarriage busted or the propeller bent or maybe a wingtip——" He looked at Shumann, bright, grave, his hand still holding Shumann's wrist.

"I guess I can land it all right," Shumann said. But the reporter did not move, looking at Shumann.

"Then it will be all right? it'll just be landing it, like what Matt said about the time he landed it?"

"I guess so," Shumann said. The train began to slow; the oleander bushes, the mosshung liveoaks in which light threads of mistsnared gossamer glinted in the sun; the vineshrouded station flowed up, slowing; it would not quite pass.

"Because, Jesus, it's just the money prize; it's just one afternoon. And Matt will help you build your ship back and you will be all set with it for the next meet——" They looked at one another.

"I guess I can get it back down," Shumann said.

"Yair. But listen——"

"I can land it," Shumann said.

"All right," the reporter said. He released the other's wrist; the pen moved again, completing the signature steadily: *Dr Carl Shumann, by Roger Shumann* The reporter took the note, rising.

"All right," he said. "Let's go." They walked again; it was about a mile; presently the road ran beside the field beyond which they could see the buildings—the detached office, the shop, the hangar with a broad legend above the open doors: ORD-ATKINSON AIRCRAFT CORPORATION— all of pale brick, as neat as and apparently contemporaneous with Ord's new house. Sitting on the ground a little back from the road they watched two mechanics wheel out the red-and-white monoplane with which Ord had set his record and start it and warm it, and then they saw Ord himself come out of the office and get into the racer and taxi to the end of the field and turn and takeoff straight over their heads, already travelling a hundred feet ahead of his own sound. "It's forty miles over to Feinman from here," the reporter said. "He flies it in ten minutes. Come on. You let me do the talking. Jesus," he cried, in a kind of light amazed exultation, "I never told a lie in my life that anybody believed; maybe this is what I have been needing all the time!" When they reached the hangar the doors were now closed to a crack just large enough for a man to enter. Shumann entered, already looking about, until he found the aeroplane—a lowwing monoplane with a big nose and a tubular fuselage ending in a curiously flattened tailgroup which gave it the appearance of having been drawn lightly and steadily through a huge lightlyclosed gloved fist. "There it is," the reporter said.

"Yair," Shumann said. "I see.—Yes," he thought, looking quietly at the queer empennage, the blunt short cylindrical body; "I guess Ord wasn't so surprised, at that." Then he heard the reporter speaking to someone and he turned and saw a squat man with a shrewd Cajun face above a scrupulously clean coverall.

"This is Mr Shumann," the reporter said, saying in a tone of bright amazement: "You mean Matt never told you? We have bought that ship." Shumann did not wait. For a moment he watched Marchand, the note in both hands, looking at it with that baffled immobility behind which the mind flicks and darts like a terrier inside a fence.

"Yair," Shumann thought, without grimness, "he cant pass five thousand dollars anymore than I could. Not without warning, anyway." He went on to the aeroplane, though once or twice he looked back and saw Marchand and the reporter, the Cajun still emanating that stubborn and slowly crystallising bewilderment while the reporter talked, flapped, before him with an illusion of being held together only by the clothes he wore; once he even heard the reporter:

"Sure, you could telephone to Feinman and catch him. But for God's sake dont let anybody overhear how Matt stuck us for five thousand bucks for the damn crate. He promised he wouldn't tell." But there was no telephoning done apparently, because almost at once (or so it seemed to Shumann) the reporter and Marchand were beside him, the reporter quiet now, watching him now with that bright attention.

"Let's get it out where we can look at it," Shumann said. They rolled it out onto the apron, where it squatted again, seemed to. It had none of the waspwaisted trimness of the ones at the airport. It was blunt, a little thickbodied, almost sluggish looking; its lightness when moved by hand seemed curiously paradoxical. For a good minute the reporter and Marchand watched Shumann stand looking at it with thoughtful gravity. "All right," he said at last. "Let's wind her up." Now the reporter spoke, leaning lightly and slightly just off balance like a ragged penstaff dropped pointfirst into the composition apron:

"Listen. You said last night maybe it was the distribution of the weight; you said how maybe if we could shift the weight somehow while it was in the air that maybe you could find——" Later (almost as soon as Shumann was out of sight the reporter and Marchand were in Marchand's car on the road to the village, where the reporter hired a cab, scrambling into it even before he had asked the price and yelling out of his gaunt and glarefixed face, "Hell, no! Not New Valois! Feinman Airport!") he lived and relived the blind timeless period during which he lay on his stomach in the barrel, clutching the two bodymembers, with nothing to see but

Shumann's feet on the rudderpedals and the movement of the aileron balancerod and nothing to feel but terrific motion—not speed and not progress—just blind furious motion like a sealed force trying to explode the monococque barrel in which he lay from the waist down on his stomach, leaving him clinging to the bodymembers in space; he was still thinking, "Jesus, maybe we are going to die and all it is is a taste like sour hot salt in your mouth" even while looking out the car window at the speeding marsh and swamp through which they skirted the city, thinking with a fierce and triumphant conviction of immortality, "We flew it! We flew it!" Now the airport, the forty miles accomplished before he knew it, what with his skull still cloudy with the light tagends of velocity and speed like the drifting feathers from a shot bird so that he had never become conscious of the sheer inertia of dimension, space, distance through which he had had to travel. He was thrusting the five dollar bill at the driver before the car began to turn into the plaza and he was out of it before it had stopped, running toward the hangar, probably not even aware that the first race was in progress. Wildfaced, gaunt and sunkeneyed from lack of sleep and from strain, his clothes ballooning about him, he ran into the hangar and on to where Jiggs stood at the workbench with a new bottle of polish and a new tin of paste open before him, shining the boots, working now with tedious and intent concern at the scar on the instep of the right one. "Did he——" the reporter cried.

"Yair, he landed it, all right," Jiggs said. "He used all the field, though. Jesus, I thought for a while he was going to run out of airport before he even cut the gun; when he stopped you couldn't have dropped a match between the prop and the seawall. They are all upstairs now, holding the caucus."

"It'll qualify itself!" the reporter cried. "I told him that. I may not know airplanes but I know sewage board Jews!"

"Yair," Jiggs said. "Anyway, he wont have to make but two landings with it. And he's already made one of them."

"Two?" the reporter cried; now he glared at Jiggs with more than exultation: with ecstasy. "He's already made two! We made one before he left Ord's!"

"We?" Jiggs said. With the boot and the rag poised he blinked painfully at the reporter with the one good hot bright eye. "We?"

"Yair; him and me! He said how it was the weight, that maybe if we could just shift the weight somehow while it was in the air, and he said Are you afraid? and I said Hell yes. But not if you aint, because Matt gave me an hour once, or maybe if I had had more than an hour I wouldn't have been. So Marchand helped us take the seat out and we rigged another one so there would be room under it for me and I slid back into the fuselage because it aint got any crossbracing, it's mon—mon—"

"Monococque," Jiggs said. "Jesus Christ, do you mean——"

"Yair. And him and Marchand rigged the seat again and he showed me where to hold on and I could just see his heels and that was all; I couldn't tell; yair, after a while I knew we were flying but I couldn't tell forward nor backward or anything because, Jesus, I just had one hour with Matt and then he cut the gun and then I could hear him, he said quiet, Jesus, we might have been standing on the ground; he said 'Now slide back. Easy. But hold tight.' And then I was hanging just by my hands; I wasn't even touching the floor of it at all; Jesus, I was thinking 'Well, here it is then; it will be tough about that race this afternoon'; I didn't even know we were on the ground again until I found out it was him and Marchand lifting the seat out and Marchand saying 'Goddamn. Goddamn. Goddamn' and him looking at me and the bastard crate standing there quiet as one of them photographs on Grandlieu Street, and him looking at me and then he says, 'Would you go up again?' and I said 'Yes. You want to go now?' and he said, 'Let's get her on over to the field and qualify'."

"Sweet Jesus Christ," Jiggs said.

"Yair," the reporter cried. "It was just weight distribution: him and Marchand rigged up a truck inner tube full of sand on a pulley so he can——And put the seat back and even if they see the end of the cable they wouldn't——Because the only ship in it that can beat him is Ord and the purse aint but two thousand and Ord dont need it, he is only in it so New Valois folks can see him fly the Ninety-Two once and he aint going to beat that fifteen-thousand-dollar ship to death just to——"

"Here; here," Jiggs said. "You're going to blow all to pieces in a minute. Smoke a cigarette; aint you got some?" The reporter fumbled the cigarettes out at last, though it was Jiggs who took two from the pack and struck the match while the reporter stooped to it, trembling. The dazed spent wild look was still on his face but he was quieter now.

"So they were all out to meet him, were they?"

"Jesus, did they," Jiggs said. "And Ord out in front; he recognised the ship as soon as it come in sight; Jesus, I bet he recognised it before Roger even recognised the airport, and by the time he landed you would have thought he was Lindbergh. And him sitting there in the cockpit and looking at them and Ord hollering at him and then they all come back up the apron like Roger was a kidnapper or something and went into the administration building and a minute later the microphone begun to holler for the inspector, what's his—"

"Sales," the reporter said. "It's licensed; they cant stop him."

"Sales can ground it, though," Jiggs said.

"Yair." The reporter was already turning, moving. "But Sales aint nothing but a Federal officer; Feinman is a Jew and on the sewage board."

"What's that got to do with it?"

"What?" the reporter cried, glaring, gaunt, apparently having already rushed on and out of his precarious body so that only the shell glared back at Jiggs. "What? What's he holding this meet for? What did he—do you think maybe he built this airport just for a smooth place for airplanes to land on?" He went on, not running yet but fast; as he hurried up the apron the aeroplanes overtook and passed him and banked around the field pylon and faded on; he did not even look at them. Then suddenly he saw her, leading the little boy by the hand, emerge from the crowd about the gate to intercept him, wearing now a clean linen dress under the trenchcoat, and a hat, the brown hat of the first evening. He stopped. His hand went into his pocket and into his face came the expression bright, quiet, almost smiling as she walked fast up to him, staring at him with pale and urgent intensity.

"What is it?" she said. "What is this you have got him into?" He looked down at her with that expression not yearning nor despair but profound tragic and serene like in the eyes of bird dogs.

"It's all right," he said. "My signature is on the note too. It will hold. I am going in right now to testify; that's all that's holding them; that's all that Ord has to——" He drew out the nickel and gave it to the boy.

"What?" she said. "Note? Note? The ship, you idiot!"

"Oh." He smiled down at her. "The ship. We flew it, tested it over there. We made a field hop before we——"

"We?"

"Yes. I went with him. I laid on the floor in the tail, so we could find out where the weight ought to be to pass the burble. That's all it was. We have a sandbag rigged now on a cable so he can let it slide back. It's all right."

"All right?" she said. "Good God, what can you know about it? Did he say it was all right?"

"Yes. He said last night he could land it. I knew he could. And now he wont need to make but one more——" She stared at him, the eyes pale cold and urgent, at the face worn, dreamy, and peaceful in the soft bright sun; again the aeroplanes came in and snored on and away. Then he was interrupted; it was the amplifier; all the amplifiers up and down the apron began to call his name, telling the stands, the field, the land and lake and air, that he was wanted in the superintendent's office at once. "There it is," he said. "Yair. I knew that the note would be the only thing that Ord could. . . . . . . That was why I signed it too. And dont you worry; all I need to do is walk in and say Yes, that's my signature. And dont you worry. He can fly it. He can fly anything. I used to think that Matt Ord was the best pilot alive, but now I——" The amplifier began to repeat itself. It faced him; it seemed to stare straight at him while it roared his name deliberately as though he had to be summoned not out of the living world of population but evoked peremptory and repetitive out of the air itself; the one in the rotundra was just beginning again when he entered; the sound followed him through the door and across the anteroom, though beyond that it did not reach, not into the board room of yesterday where now Ord and Shumann alone occupied the hard chairs since they were ushered in a half hour ago and sat down and faced the men behind the table and Shumann saw Feinman for the first time, sitting not in the center but at one end of the table where the announcer had sat yesterday, his suit, double-breasted still, tan instead of gray beneath the bright splash of the carnation. He alone wore his hat; it appeared to be the smallest object about him; from beneath it his dark smooth face began at once to droop into folds of flesh which, con-stricted for the instant by his collar, swelled and rolled again beneath the tight creases of his coat. On the table one hand bearing a goldclamped ruby held a burning cigar. He did not even glance at Shumann and Ord; he was looking at Sales, the inspector—a square bald man with a blunt face which by ordinary would be quite pleasant, though not now—who was saying bluntly:

"Because I can ground it. I can forbid it to fly."

"You mean, you can forbid anybody to fly it, dont you?" Feinman said.

"Put it that way if you want to," Sales said.

"Let's say, put it that way for the record," another voice said—a young man, sleek, in horn rim glasses, sitting just back of Feinman. He was Feinman's secretary; he spoke now with a kind of silken insolence, like the pampered intelligent ha-teridden eunuchmountebank of an eastern despot: "Colonel Feinman is, even before a public servant, a lawyer."

"Yair; lawyer," Feinman said. "Maybe country lawyer to Washington. Let me get this straight. You're a government agent. All right. We have had our crops regimented and our fisheries regimented and even our money in the bank regimented. All right. I still dont see how they did it but they did, and so we are used to that. If he was trying to make his living out of the ground and Washington come in and regimented him, all right. We might not understand it any more than he did, but we would say all right. And if he was trying to make his living out of the river and the government come in and regimented him, we would say all right too. But do you mean to tell me that Washington can come in and regiment a man that's trying to make his living out of the air? Is there a crop reduction in the air too?" They—the others about the table (three of them were reporters)—laughed. They laughed with a kind of sudden and loud relief, as though they had been waiting all the time to find out just how they were supposed to listen and now they knew. Only Sales and Shumann and Ord did not laugh; then they noticed that the secretary was not laughing either and that he was already speaking, seeming to slide his silken voice into the laughter and stop it as abruptly as a cocaine needle in a nerve:

"Yes. Colonel Feinman is lawyer enough (perhaps Mr Sales will add, country enough) to ask even a government official to show cause. As the colonel understands it, this airplane bears a license which Mr Sales approved himself. Is that true, Mr Sales?" For a moment Sales did not answer. He just looked at the secretary grimly.

"Because I dont believe it is safe to fly," he said. "That's the cause."

"Ah," the secretary said. "For a moment I almost expected Mr Sales to tell us that it would not fly; that it had perhaps walked over here from Blaisedell. Then all we would need to say would be 'Good; we will not make it fly; we will just let it walk around the pylons during the race this afternoon'——" Now they did laugh, the three reporters scribbling furiously. But it was not for the secretary: it was for Feinman. The secretary seemed to know this; while he waited for it to subside his unsmiling insolent contempt touched them all face by face. Then he spoke to Sales again. "You admit that it is licensed, that you approved it yourself—meaning, I take it, that it is registered at Washington as being fit and capable of discharging the function of an airplane, which is to fly. Yet you later state that you will not permit it to fly because it is not capable of discharging the function for which you yourself admit having approved it—in simple language for us lawyers, that it cannot fly. Yet Mr Ord has just told us that he flew it in your presence. And Mr——" he glanced down; the pause was less than pause—"Shumann states that he flew it once at Blaisedell before witnesses, and we know that he flew it here because we saw him. We all know that Mr Ord is one of the best (we New Valoisians believe *the* best) pilots in the world, but dont you think it barely possible, barely I say, that the man who has flown it twice where Mr Ord has flown it but once. . . . . . . Wouldn't this almost lead one to think that Mr Ord has some other motive for not wanting this airplane to compete in this race——"

"Yair," Feinman said. He turned to look at Ord. "What's the matter? Aint this airport good enough for your ships? Or aint this race important enough for you? Or do you just think he might beat you? Aint you going to use the airplane you broke the record in? Then what are you afraid of?" Ord glared from face to face about the table, then at Feinman again.

"Why do you want this ship in there this afternoon? What is it? I'd lend him the money, if that's all it is."

"Why?" Feinman said. "Aint we promised these folks out there—" he made a jerking sweep with the cigar—"a series of races? Aint they paying their money in here to see them? And aint it the more airplanes they will have to look at the better they will think they got for the money? And why should he want to borrow money from you when he can maybe earn it at his job where he wont have to pay it back or even the interest? Now, let's settle this business." He turned to Sales. "The ship is licensed, aint it?" After a moment Sales said,

"Yes." Feinman turned to Ord.

"And it will fly, wont it?" Ord looked at him for a long moment too.

"Yes," he said. Now Feinman turned to Shumann.

"Is it dangerous to fly?" he said.

"They all are," Shumann said.

"Well, are you afraid to fly it?" Shumann looked at him. "Do you expect it to fall with you this afternoon?"

"If I did I wouldn't take it up," Shumann said. Suddenly Ord rose; he was looking at Sales.

"Mac," he said, "this aint getting anywhere. I will ground the ship myself." He turned to Shumann. "Listen, Roger——"

"On what grounds, Mr Ord?" the secretary said.

"Because it belongs to me. Is that grounds enough for you?"

"When an authorised agent of your corporation has accepted a legal monetary equivalent for it and surrendered the machine?"

"But they are not good for the note. I know that. I was a damn stickstraddler myself until I got a break. Why, damn it, one of the names on it is admitted to not be signed by the owner of it. And listen; yair; I dont even know whether Shumann did the actual signing; whoever signed it signed it before I saw it or even before Marchand saw it. See?" He glared at the secretary, who looked at him in turn with his veiled contemptuous glance.

"I see," the secretary said pleasantly. "I was waiting for you to bring that up. You seem to have forgotten that the note has a third signer." Ord stared at him for a minute.

"But he aint good for it either," he said.

"Possibly not, alone. But Mr Shumann tells us that his father is and that his father will honor this signature. So by your own token, the question seems to resolve to whether or not Mr Shumann did or did not sign his and his father's name to the note. And we seem to have a witness to that. It is not exactly legal, I grant you. But this other signer is known to some of us here; you know him yourself, you tell us, to be a person of unassailable veracity. We will have him in." Then it was that the amplifyers began to call the reporter's name; he entered; he came forward while they watched him. The secretary extended the note toward him. ("Jesus," the reporter thought, "they must have sent a ship over for Marchand.")

"Will you examine this?" the secretary said.

"I know it," the reporter said.

"Will you state whether or not you and Mr Shumann

signed it in each other's presence and in good faith?" The reporter looked about, at the faces behind the table, at Shumann sitting with his head bent a little and at Ord halfrisen, glaring at him. After a moment Shumann turned his head and looked quietly at him.

"Yes," the reporter said. "We signed it."

"There you are," Feinman said. He rose. "That's all. Shumann has possession; if Ord wants anymore to be stubborn about it we will just let him run to town and see if he can get back with a writ of replevin before time for the race."

"But he cant enter it!" Ord said. "It aint qualified." Feinman paused long enough to look at Ord for a second with impersonal inscrutability.

"Speaking for the citizens of Franciana who donated the ground and for the citizens of New Valois that built the airport the race is going to be run on, I will waive qualification."

"You cant waive the A.A.A.," Ord said. "You cant make it official if he wins the whole damn meet."

"Then he will not need to rush back to town to pawn a silver cup," Feinman said. He went out; the others rose from the table and followed. After a moment Ord turned quietly to Shumann.

"Come on," he said. "We'd better check her over."

The reporter did not see them again. He followed them through the rotundra, through the amplifyer's voice and through the throng at the gates, or so he thought because his policecard had passed him before he remembered that they would have had to go around to reach the apron. But he could see the aeroplane with a crowd standing around it, and then the woman had forgot too that Shumann and Ord would have to go around and through the hangar; she emerged again from the crowd beneath the bandstand. "So they did it," she said. "They let him."

"Yes. It was all right. Like I told you."

"They did it," she said, staring at him yet speaking as though in amazed soliloquy. "Yes. You fixed it."

"Yes. I knew that's all it would be. I wasn't worried. And dont you——" But she was gone; she didn't move for a moment; there was nothing of distraction especially; he just seemed to hang substanceless in the long peaceful backwash of waiting, saying quietly out of the dreamy smiling, "Yair. Ord talking about how he would be disqualified for the cup, the prize, like that would stop him, like that was what. . . ." not even aware that it was only the shell of her speaking quietly back to him, asking him if he would mind the boy.

"Since you seem to be caught up for the time."

"Yair," he said. "Of course." Then she was gone, the white dress and the trenchcoat lost in the crowd—the ones with ribbon badges and the ones in dungarees—which streamed suddenly down the apron toward the darkhorse, the sensation. As he stood so, holding the little boy by one damp sticky hand, the Frenchman Despleins passed again down the runway which parallelled the stands, on one wheel; the reporter watched him takeoff and half roll, climbing upside down: now he heard the voice; he had not heard it since it called his own name despite the fact that it had never ceased, perhaps because of the fact:

"——oh oh oh mister, dont, dont! Oh, mister! Please get up high enough so your parachute can try to open! Now, now; now, now——Oh, Mac! Oh, Mr Sales! Make him stop!" The reporter looked down at the boy.

"I bet you a dime you haven't spent that nickel," he said.

"Naw," the boy said. "I aint had a chance to. She wouldn't let me."

"Well, my goodness!" the reporter said. "I owe you twenty cents then, dont I? Come——" He paused, turning; it was the photographer, the man whom he had called Jug, laden again with the enigmatic and faintly macabre utensils of his calling so that he resembled vaguely a trained dog belonging to a country doctor.

"Where in hell you been?" the photographer said. "Hagood told me to find you at ten oclock."

"Here I am," the reporter said. "We're just going inside to spend twenty cents. Want to come?" Now the Frenchman came up the runway about twenty feet high and on his back, his head and face beneath the cockpitrim motionless and alert like that of a roach or a rat immobile behind a crack in a wainscoat, his neat short beard unstirred by any wind as though cast in one piece of bronze.

"Yair," the photographer said; perhaps it was the bilious aspect of an inverted world seen through a hooded lens or emerging in grimacing and attitudinal miniature from stinking trays in a celibate and stygian cell lighted by a red lamp: "and have that guy come down on his whiskers and me not here to get it?"

"All right," the reporter said. "Stay and get it." He turned to go on.

"Yair; but Hagood told me——" the photographer said. The reporter turned back.

"All right," he said. "But hurry up."

"Hurry up what?"

"Snap me. You can show it to Hagood when you go in."

He and the boy went on; he did not walk back into the voice, he had never walked out of it:

"——an in-ver-ted spin, folks; he's going into it still upside down—oh oh oh oh——" The reporter stooped suddenly and lifted the boy to his shoulder.

"We can make better time," he said. "We will want to get back in a few minutes." They passed through the gate, among the gaped and upturned faces which choked the gangway. "That's it," he thought quietly, with that faint quiet grimace almost like smiling; "they aint human. It aint adultery; you cant anymore imagine two of them making love than you can two of them aeroplanes back in the corner of the hangar, coupled." With one hand he supported the boy on his shoulder, feeling through the harsh khaki the young brief living flesh. "Yair; cut him and it's cylinder oil; dissect him and it aint bones: it's little rockerarms and connecting rods——" The restaurant was crowded; they did not wait to eat the icecream there on a plate; with one cone in his hand and one in the boy's and the two chocolate bars in his pocket they were working back through the crowded gangway when the bomb went and then the voice:

"—fourth event: unlimited free-for-all, Vaughn Trophy race, prize two thousand dollars. You will not only have a chance to see Matt Ord in his famous Ninety-Two Ord-Atkinson Special in which he set a new land plane speed record, but as a surprise entry through the courtesy of the American Aeronautical Association and the Feinman Airport Commission, Roger Shumann who yesterday nosed over in a forced landing, in a special rebuilt job that Matt Ord rebuilt himself. Two horses from the same stable, folks, and two pilots both of whom are so good that it is a pleasure to give the citizens of New Valois and Franciana the chance to see them pitted against each other——" He and the boy watched the takeoff, then they went on; presently he found her—the brown hat and the coat—and he came up and stood a little behind her steadying the boy on his shoulder and carrying the second melting cone in his other hand as the four aeroplanes came in on the first lap—the red-and-white monoplane in front and two more side by side and some distance back, so that at first he did not even see Shumann. Then he saw him, higher than the others and well outside, though the voice now was not from the amplifyer but from a mechanic:

"Jesus, look at Shumann! It must be fast: he's flying twice as far as the rest of them—or maybe Ord aint trying. . . . . . . Why in hell dont he bring it on in?" Then the voice was drowned in the roar, the snarl, as the aeroplanes turned the field pylon and, followed by the turning heads along the apron as if the faces were geared to the sound, diminished singly out and over the lake again, Shumann still quite wide, making a turn that was almost a skid yet holding his position. They converged toward the second pylon, the lake one; in slightly irregular order and tiny now with distance and with Shumann still cautiously high and outside they wafted lightly upward and around the pylon. Now the reporter could hear the mechanic again: "He's coming in now, watch him. Jesus, he's second—he's diving in—Jesus, he's going to be right behind Ord on this pylon; maybe he was just feeling it out—" The noise was faint now and disseminated; the drowsy afternoon was domed with it and the four machines seemed to hover like dragonflies silently in vacuum, in various distancesoftened shades of pastel against the ineffable blue, with now a quality trivial, random, almost like notes of music—a harp, say—as the sun glinted and lost them. The reporter leaned down to the woman who was not yet aware of his presence, crying,

"Watch him! Oh, can he fly! Can he fly! And Ord aint going to beat the Ninety-Two to——Second money Thursday, and if Ord aint going to——Oh, watch him! Watch him!" She turned: the jaw, the pale eyes, the voice which he did not even listen to:

"Yes. The money will be fine." Then he even stopped looking at her, staring down the runway as the four aeroplanes, now in two distinct pairs, came in toward the field, increasing fast. The mechanic was talking again:

"He's in! Jesus, he's going to try Ord here! And look at Ord giving him room——" The two in front began to bank at the same time, side by side, the droning roar drawing down and in as though sucked down out of the sky by them in place of being produced by them. The reporter's mouth was still open; he knew that by the needling of nerves in his sore jaw; later he was to remember seeing the icecream cone crush in his fist and begin to ooze between his fingers as he let the little boy slide to the ground and took his hand, though not now; now the two aeroplanes, side by side and Shumann outside and now above, banked into the pylon as though bolted together, when the reporter suddenly saw something like a light scattering of burnt paper or feathers floating in the air above the pylontip. He was watching this, his mouth still open, when a voice somewhere said, "Ahhhhhhh!" and he saw Shumann now shooting almost straight upward and then a whole wastebasketful of the light trash blew out of the aeroplane; they said later about the apron that he used the last of his control before the fuselage broke to zoom out of the path of the two aeroplanes behind while he looked down at the closepeopled land and the empty lake, and made a choice before the tailgroup came completely free. But most of them were busy saying how his wife took it, how she did not scream nor faint (she was standing quite near the microphone, near enough for it to have caught the scream) but instead she just stood there and watched the fuselage break in two and said, "Oh damn you, Roger! Oh damn you! damn you!" and turned and snatched the little boy's hand and ran toward the seawall, the little boy dangling vainly on his short legs between her and the reporter who, holding the little boy's other hand, ran at his loose lightlyclattering gallop like a scarecrow in a gale, after the bright plain shape of love. Perhaps it was the added weight because she turned, still running, and gave him a single pale cold terrible look, crying,

"God damn you to hell! Get away from me!"

Lovesong of J. A. Prufrock

On the shell beach between the boulevard and the seaplane slip one of the electric company's trucks stood while its
crew set up a searchlight at the water's edge. When the photographer called Jug saw the reporter he was standing beside
the empty truck, in the backwash which it created between
the faces beyond the policeline, and the men—police and
newspapermen and airport officials and the others, the ones
without authority or object who manage to pass policelines
at all scenes of public violence—gathered along the beach.
The photographer approached at a flagging trot, the camera
banging against his flank. "Christ Almighty," he said. "I got
that, all right. Only Jesus, I near vomited into the box while
I was changing plates." Beyond the crowd at the wateredge
and just beyond the outer markers of the seaplane basin a police launch was scattering the fleet of small boats which, like
most of the people on the beach itself, had appeared as
though by magic from nowhere like crows, to make room for
the dredgeboat to anchor over the spot where the aeroplane

was supposed to have sunk. The seaplane slip, dredged out, was protected from the sluggish encroachment of the lake's muddy bottom by a sunken mole composed of various refuse from the city itself—shards of condemned paving and masses of fallen walls and even discarded automobile bodies—any and all the refuse of man's twentieth century clotting into communities large enough to pay a mayor's salary—dumped into the lake. Either directly above or just outside of this mass the aeroplane was believed, from the accounts of three oystermen in a dory who were about two hundred yards away, to have struck the water. The three versions varied as to the exact spot, despite the fact that both wings had reappeared on the surface almost immediately and were towed ashore, but then one of the oystermen (from the field, the apron, Shumann could be seen struggling to open the cockpit hatch as though to jump, as though with the intention of trying to open his parachute despite his lack of height)—one of the oystermen claimed that the body had fallen free of the machine, having either extricated itself or been flung out. But the three agreed that the body and the machine were both either upon or beside the mole from whose vicinity the police launch was now harrying the small boats. It was after sunset. Upon the mirrorsmooth water even the little foul skiffs—the weathered and stinking dories and dinghys of oyster- and shrimpmen—had a depthless and fairy-light quality as they scattered like butterflies or moths before a mechanical reaper, just ahead of the trim low martial-colored police launch, onto which at the moment the photographer saw being transferred from one of the skiffs two people whom he recognised as being the dead pilot's wife and child; among them the dredge looked like something antediluvian crawled for the first time into light, roused but not alarmed by the object or creature out of the world of light and air which had plunged without warning into the watery fastness where it had been asleep. "Jesus," the photographer said. "Why wasn't I standing right here: Hagood would have had to raise me then. Jesus God," he said in a hoarse tone of hushed and unbelieving amazement, "how's it now for being a poor bastard that never even learned to rollerskate?" The reporter looked at him, for the first time. The reporter's face was perfectly calm; he looked down at the photographer, turning carefully as though he were made of glass and knew it, blinking a little, and spoke in a peaceful dreamy voice such as might be heard where a child is sick—not sick for a day or even two days, but for so long that even wasting anxiety has become mere surface habit:

"She told me to go away. I mean, to go clean away, like to another town."

"She did?" the photographer said. "To what town?"

"You dont understand," the reporter said, in that peaceful baffled voice. "Let me explain to you."

"Yair; sure," the photographer said. "I still feel like vomiting too. But I got to get on in with these plates. And I bet you aint even phoned in. Have you?"

"What?" the reporter said. "Yes. I phoned in. But listen. She didn't understand. She told me——"

"Come on, now," the other said. "You will have to call in with the buildup on it. Jesus, I tell you I feel bad too. Here, smoke a cigarette. Yair. I could vomit too. But what the hell? He aint our brother. Come on, now." He took the cigarettes from the reporter's coat and took two from the pack and struck a match. The reporter roused somewhat; he took the burning match himself and held it to the two cigarettes. But then at once the photographer seemed to watch him sink back into that state of peaceful physical anesthesia as though the reporter actually were sinking slowly away from him into clear and limpid water out of which the calm, slightly distorted face looked and the eyes blinked at the photographer with that myopic earnestness while the voice repeated patiently,

"But you dont understand. Let me explain it to——"

"Yair; sure," the other said. "You can explain it to Hagood while we are getting a drink." The reporter moved obediently. But before they had gone very far the photographer realised that they had reassumed their customary mutual physical complementing when working together: the reporter striding on in front and the photographer trotting to keep up. "That's the good thing about being him," the photographer thought. "He dont have to move very far to go nuts in the first place and so he dont have so far to come back."

"Yair," the reporter said. "Let's move. We got to eat, and the rest of them have got to read. And if they ever abolish fornication and blood, where in hell will we all be?—Yair. You get on in with what you got; if they get it up right away it will be too dark to get anything. I'll stay out here and cover it. You can tell Hagood."

"Yair; sure," the photographer said, trotting, the camera bouncing against his flank. "We'll have a shot and we'll feel better. For Christ's sake, we never made him go up in it." Before they reached the rotundra the sunset had faded; even while they walked up the apron the boundary lights came on, and now the flat swordlike sweep of the beacon swung in across the lake and vanished for an instant in a long *flick!* as the turning eye faced them full, and then reappeared again as it swung now over the land to complete its arc. The field, the apron, was empty, but the rotundra was full of people and with a cavernous murmuring sound which seemed to linger not about the mouths which uttered it but to float somewhere about the high serene shadowy dome overhead; as they entered a newsboy screamed at them, flapping the paper, the headline: **PILOT KILLED. SHUMANN CRASHES INTO LAKE. SECOND FATALITY OF AIRMEET.** as it too flicked away. The bar was crowded too, warm with lights and with human bodies. The photographer led the way now, shouldering into the rail, making room for the reporter beside him. "Rye, huh?" he said, then to the bartender, loudly: "Two ryes."

"Yair; rye," the reporter said. Then he thought quietly, "I cant. I cannot." He felt no revulsion from his insides; it was as though his throat and the organs of swallowing had experienced some irrevocable alteration of purpose from which he would suffer no inconvenience whatever but which would forever more mark the exchange of an old psychic as well as physical state for a new one, like the surrendering of a maidenhead. He felt profoundly and peacefully empty inside, as though he had vomited and very emptiness had supplied into his mouth or somewhere about his palate like a lubricant a faint thin taste of salt which was really pleasant: the taste not of despair but of Nothing. "I'll go and call in now," he said.

"Wait," the photographer said. "Here comes your drink."

"Hold it for me," the reporter said. "It wont take but a minute." There was a booth in the corner, the same from which he had called Hagood yesterday. As he dropped the coin in he closed the door behind him. The automatic dome light came on; he opened the door until the light went off again; he spoke not loud, his voice murmuring back from the close walls as he recapitulated at need with succinct and patient care as though reading into the telephone in a foreign tongue: "—yes, f-u-s-e-l-a-g-e. The body of the airplane, broke off at the tail. . . . . . . No, he couldn't have landed it. The pilots here said he used up what control he had left getting out of the way of the others and to head toward the lake instead of the grandst. . . . . . . No, they say not. He wasn't high enough for the chute to have opened even if he had got out of the ship. . . . . . . yair, dredgeboat was just getting into position when I. . . . . . .they say probably right against the mole; it may have struck the rocks and slid down. . . . . . . Yair, if he should be close enough to all that muck the dredgeboat cant. . . . . . .yair, probably a diver tomorrow, unless sometime during the night. And by that time the crabs and gars will have. . . . . . .yair, I'll stay out here and flash you at midnight." When he came out of the booth, back into the light, he began to blink again like he might have a little sand in his eyes, trying to recall exactly what eyemoisture tasted like, wondering if perhaps the thin moist salt in his mouth might not somehow have got misplaced from where it belonged. The photographer still held his place at the bar and the drink was waiting, though this time he only looked down at the photographer, blinking, almost smiling. "You go on and drink it," he said. "I forgot I went on the wagon yesterday." When they went out to the cab, it was dark; the photographer, ducking, the camera jouncing on its strap, scuttled into the cab, turning a face likewise amazed and spent.

"It's cold out here," he said. "Jesus, I'm going to lock the

damn door and turn on both them red lamps and fill me a
good big tray to smell and I'm going to just sit there and get
warm. I'll tell Hagood you are on the job." The face vanished, the cab went on, curbing away toward the boulevard
where beyond and apparently just behind the ranked palms
which lined it the glare of the city was visible even from here
upon the overcast. People were still moiling back and forth
across the plaza and in and out of the rotundra, and the
nightly overcast had already moved in from the lake; against
it the measured and regular swordsweep of the beacon was
quite distinct, and there was some wind in it too; a long
breath of it at the moment came down over the building and
across the plaza and the palms along the boulevard began to
clash and hiss with a dry wild sound. The reporter began to
inhale the dark chill wind; it seemed to him that he could
taste the lake, water, and he began to pant, drawing the air in
by lungsfull and expelling it and snatching another lungfull
of it as if he were locked inside a burning room and were
hunting handfull by handfull through a mass of cotton batting for the doorkey, ducking his head and hurrying past the
lighted entrance and the myriad eyes his face which for the
time had frozen like a piece of unoiled machinery freezes,
into a twisted grimace which filled his sore jaw with what felt
like icy needles so that Ord had to call him twice before he
turned and saw the other getting out of his roadster, still in
the suede jacket and the hind-part-before cap in which he
flew.

   "I was looking for you," Ord said, taking something from
his pocket—the narrow strip of paper folded again as it had
lain in the reporter's fob pocket this morning before he gave
it to Marchand. "Wait; dont tear it," Ord said. "Hold it a

minute." The reporter held it while Ord struck the match. "Go on," Ord said. "Look at it." With his other hand he opened the note out, holding the match so that the reporter could see it, identify it, waiting while the reporter stood with the note in his hand long enough to have examined it anyway. "That's it, aint it?" Ord said.

"Yes," the reporter said.

"All right. Stick it to the match. I want you to do it yourself. . . . . . . Damn it, drop it! Do you want to. . . . . . ." As it floated down the flame seemed to turn back and upward, to climb up the falling scrap and on into space, vanishing; the charred carbon leaf drifted on without weight or sound and Ord ground his foot on it. "You bastard," he said. "You bastard."

"God, yes," the reporter said, as quietly. "I'll make out another one tomorrow. You will just have to take me alone——"

"Like hell. What are they going to do now?"

"I dont know," the reporter said. Then at once he began to speak in that tone of peaceful and bemused incomprehensibility. "You see, she didn't understand. She told me to go away. I mean, away. Let me ex——" But he stopped, thinking quietly, "Wait. I mustn't start that. I might not be able to stop it next time." He said: "They dont know yet, of course, until after the dredge. . . . . . . I'll be here. I'll see to them."

"Bring her on over home if you want to. But you better go yourself and take a couple of drinks. You dont look so good either."

"Yair," the reporter said. "Only I quit yesterday. I got mixed up and went on the wagon."

"Yes?" Ord said. "Well, I'm going home. You better get in touch with her right away. Get her away from here. Just put her in a car and come on over home. If it's where they say it is, it will take a diver to get him out." He returned to the roadster; the reporter had already turned on too, back toward the entrance before he was aware of it, stopping again; he could not do it—the lights and the faces, not even for the warmth of lights and human suspirations, thinking, "Jesus, if I was to go in there I would drown." He could go around the opposite hangar and reach the apron and be on his way back to the seaplane slip. But when he moved it was toward the first hangar, the one in which it seemed to him that he had spent enough of breathing's incomprehensible and unpredictable frenzy and travail to have been born and raised there, walking away from the lights and sound and faces, walking in solitude where despair and regret could sweep down over the building and across the plaza and on into the harsh thin hissing of the palms and so at least he could breathe it, at least endure. It was as though some sixth sense, some economy out of profound inattention guided him, on through the blank door and the tool room and into the hangar itself where in the hard light of the overhead clusters the motionless aeroplanes squatted in fierce and depthless relief among one another's monstrous shadows, and on to where Jiggs sat on the tongue of a dolly, the shined boots rigid and fiercely highlighted on his outthrust feet, gnawing painfully at a sandwich with one side of his face, his head turned parallel to the earth like a dog eats while the one good eye rolled, painful and bloodshot, up at the reporter.

"What is it you want me to do?" Jiggs said. The reporter blinked down at him with quiet and myopic intensity.

"You see, she didn't understand," he said. "She told me to go away. To let her alone. And so I cant——"

"Yair," Jiggs said. He drew the boots under him and prepared to get up, but he stopped and sat so for a moment, his
head bent and the sandwich in one hand, looking at what
the reporter did not know, because at once the single eye was
looking at him again. "Will you look behind that junk over
in the corner there and get my bag?" Jiggs said. The reporter
found the canvas bag hidden carefully beneath a rubbish-
heap of empty oil cans and boxes and such; when he returned with it Jiggs was already holding one foot out. "Would
you mind giving it a pull?" The reporter took hold of the
boot. "Pull it easy."

"Have they made your feet sore?" the reporter said.

"No. Pull it easy." The boots came off easier than they did
two nights ago; the reporter watched Jiggs take from the sack a
shirt not soiled but filthy, and wipe the boots carefully, with an
air thoughtful, intent, bemused, upper sole and all, and wrap
them in the shirt and put them into the sack and, again in the
tennis shoes and the makeshift leggings, hide the sack once
more in the corner, the reporter following him to the corner
and then back as if it were now the reporter who was the dog.

"You see," he said (even as he spoke it seemed to him to
be not himself speaking but something inside him which insisted on preempting his tongue) — "you see, I keep on trying
to explain to somebody that she didn't understand. Only she
understands exactly, dont she? He's out there in the lake and
I cant think of anything plainer than that. Can you?" The
main doors were locked now; they had to return through the
tool room as the reporter had entered. As they emerged
the beacon's beam swept overhead again with its illusion of
powerful and slow acceleration. "So they gave you all a bed
this time," he said.

"Yair," Jiggs said. "The kid went to sleep on the police boat. Jack brought him in and they let them have a bed this time. She didn't come in. She aint going to leave now, anyway. I'll try if you want to, though."

"Yes," the reporter said. "I guess you are right. I didn't mean to try to make——I just wanted to. . . . . . ." He began to think *now. now.* NOW. and it came: the long nebulous swordstroke sweeping steadily up from beyond the other hangar until almost overhead and then accelerating with that illusion of terrific strength and speed which should have left a sound, a swish, behind it but did not. "You see, I dont know about these things. I keep on thinking about fixing it up so that a woman, another woman——"

"All right," Jiggs said. "I'll try."

"Just so she can see you and call you if she needs— wants. . . . . . .if. . . . . . . She wont even need to know I am——but if she should. . . . . . ."

"Yair. I'll fix it if I can." They went on around the other hangar. Now they could see half of the beacon's entire arc; the reporter could watch it now as it swung across the lake, watching the skeletonlattice of the empty bleachers come into relief against it, and the parapet of staffs from which the purple-and-gold pennons, black now, streamed rigid in the rising wind from the lake as the beam picked them up one by one and discarded them in swift and accelerating succession as it swept in and overhead and on, and they could see the looped bunting too tossing and laboring and even here and there blown out of the careful loops of three days ago and whipping in forlorn and ceaseless shreds as though, sentient itself, it had anticipated the midnight bells from town which would signal the beginning of Lent. And now, beyond the black rampart of the seawall the searchlight beside whose truck the photographer had found the reporter was burn-ing—a fierce white downwardglaring beam brighter though smaller than the beacon—and they saw presently another one on the tower of the dredgeboat itself. In fact it was as though when they reached the seawall they would look down into a pit filled not by one steady source of light but by a luminous diffusion as though from the airparticles, beyond which the shoreline curved twinkling faintly away into dark-ness. But it was not until they reached the wall that they saw that the light came not from the searchlight on the shore nor the one on the dredgeboat nor the one on the slowly cruising police launch engaged still in harrying away the little skiffs from some of which puny flashlights winked but in most of which burned the weak turgid flame of kerosene, but from a line of automobiles drawn up along the boulevard. Extend-ing for almost a mile along the shore and facing the water, their concerted refulgence, broken at short intervals by the buttons and shields of policemen and now by the sidearms and putties of a national guard company, glared down upon the disturbed and ceaseless dark water which seemed to surge and fall and surge and fall as though in travail of amazement and outrage. There was a skiff just landing from the dredgeboat; while the reporter waited for Jiggs to return the dark steady chill wind pushed hard against him, through his thin clothes; it seemed to have passed through the lights, the faint human sounds and movement, without gaining anything of warmth or light; after a while he believed that he could discern the faint hissing plaint of the ground and pow-

dered oystershells on which he stood even above the deep
steady humming of the searchlight not far away. The men
from the skiff came up and passed him, Jiggs following. "It's
like they said," Jiggs said. "It's right up against the rocks. I
asked the guy if they had hooked anything yet and he said
hooked, hell; they had hooked something the first throw with
one hook and aint even got the hook loose yet. But the other
hook came up with a piece of that damn monococque ply-
wood, and he said there was oil on it." He looked at the reporter. "So that will be from the belly."

"Yes," the reporter said.

"So it's bottomupwards. The guy says they think out
there that it is fouled on some of them old automobiles and
junk they throwed in to build it with.—Yair," he said,
though the reporter had not spoken, but had only looked at
him: "I asked that too. She's up yonder at that lunchwagon
getting——" The reporter turned; like the photographer
Jiggs now had to trot to keep up, scrabbling up the shelving
beach toward the ranked automobiles until he bumped into
the reporter who had paused in the headlights' glare with
his head lowered and one arm raised before his face. "Over
this way," Jiggs said, "I can see." He took the reporter's arm
and guided him on to the gap in the cars where the steps led
up from the beach and through the gap to where, across the
boulevard, they could see the heads and shoulders against
the broad low dingy window. Jiggs could hear the reporter
breathing, panting, though the climb up from the beach
had not been that hard. When the reporter's fumbling hand
touched his own it felt like ice.

"She hasn't got any money," the reporter said. "Hurry.
Hurry." Jiggs went on. Then the reporter could still see them

(for the instant he made one as he pushed through them and went around the end of the lunchwagon to the smaller window)—the faces pressed to the glass and looking in at her where she sat on one of the backless stools at the counter between a policeman and one of the mechanics whom the reporter had seen about the hangar. The trenchcoat was open and there was a long smear either of oil or mud across the upper part of her white dress and she was eating, a sandwich, wolfing it and talking to the two men; he watched her drop the fragments back into the plate and wipe her hand across her mouth and lift the thick mug of coffee and drink, wolfing the coffee too, the coffee running down her chin from the toofast swallowing like the food had done. At last Jiggs finally found him, still standing there though now the counter was vacant and the faces had gone away too, followed back to the beach.

"Even the proprietor wanted to washout the check, but I got there in time," Jiggs said. "She was glad to get it, too; you were right, she never had any money with her. Yair. She's like a man about not bumming from just any guy. Always was. So it's o.k." But he was still looking at the reporter with an expression which a more observing person than the reporter could not have read now in the tough face to which the blue and swollen eye and lip lent no quality evoking compassion or warmth but on the contrary merely increased a little the face's brutality. When he spoke again it was not in a rambling way exactly but with a certain curious alertness as of imminent and irrevocable dispersion; the reporter thought of a man trying to herd a half dozen blind sheep through a passage a little wider than he could span with his extended arms. Jiggs now had one hand in his pocket but the reporter did not notice it. "So she's going to have to be out here all night, in case they begin to—And the kid's already asleep; yair, no need to wake him up, and maybe tomorrow we will all know better where we—Yair, a night or two to sleep on it makes a lot of difference about anything, no matter how bad you think you h—I mean. . . . . . ." He stopped. ("He aint only not held the sheep, he aint even holding out his arms anymore," the reporter thought) The hand came out of his pocket, opening; the doorkey glinted faintly on the grained palm. "She told me to give it back to you when I saw you," Jiggs said. "You come on and eat something yourself, now."

"Yes," the reporter said. "It will be a good chance to, wont it. Besides, we will be in out of the cold for a little while."

"Sure," Jiggs said. "Come on." It was warm inside the lunchwagon; the reporter stopped shaking even before the food came. He ate a good deal of it, then he realised that he was going to eat all of it, without taste or enjoyment especially but with a growing conviction of imminent satisfaction like when a tooth cavity that has not been either pleasant or unpleasant is about to be filled without pain. The faces were gone from the window now, following her doubtless back to the beach, or as near to it as the police and soldiers would let them, where they now gazed no doubt at the police boat or whatever other boat she had reembarked in; nevertheless he and Jiggs still sat in it, breathed and chewed it along with the stale hot air and the hot rancid food—the breathing, the exhalation, the variations of the remark which the photographer had made; the ten thousand different smug and gratulant behind sighted forms of *I might be a bum and a bastard but I am not out there in that lake.* But he did not see

her again. During the next three hours until midnight he did
not leave the beach, while the ranked cars glared steadily
downward and the searchlights hummed and the police
launch cruised in slow circles while the little boats moved
outward before its bows and inward again behind its stern
like so many minnows in the presence of a kind of harmless
and vegetarian whale, and steadily, with clocklike and deliberate precision, the long sicklebar of the beacon swept inward from the lake, to vanish at the instant when the yellow
eye came broadside on and apparently halting there with
only a slow and terrific centrifugal movement within the eye
itself until with that gigantic and soundless *flick!* the beam
shot incredibly outward across the dark sky. But he did not
see her, though presently one of the little skiffs came in and
beached to take on another bootleg cargo of twenty-five-cent
passengers and Jiggs got out. "They are still fast to it," he said.
"They thought they had it started once but something happened down there and when they hauled up all they had was
the cable; they were even short the hook. They say now it
must have hit on one of those big blocks of concrete and
broke it loose and they both went down together only the
ship got there first. They're going to send the diver down at
daylight to see what to do. Only they dont want to use dynamite because even if it starts him back up it will bust the
mole all to pieces. But they'll know tomorrow. — Didn't you
want to call the paper at midnight or something?" There was
a paystation in the lunchwagon, on the wall. Since there was
no booth he had to talk into the telephone with his other ear
plugged with his hand against the noise and again spending
most of the time answering questions; when he turned away
he saw that Jiggs was asleep on the backless stool, his arms

folded on the counter and his forehead resting on them. It
was quite warm inside, what with the constant frying of meat
and with the human bodies with which the room was filled
now long after its usual closing hour; the window facing the
lake was fogged over so that the lighted scene beyond was
one diffused glow such as might be shining behind falling
snow; looking at it the reporter began to shake again, slowly
and steadily inside the suit to which there was apparently no
waistcoat, while there grew within him the first active sensation or impulse which he could remember since he watched
Shumann begin to bank into the field pylon for the last
time—a profound reluctance to go out which acted not on
his will but on his very muscles. He went to the counter;
presently the proprietor saw him and took up one of the thick
cups.

"Coffee?"

"No," the reporter said. "I want a coat. Overcoat. Have
you got one you could lend me or rent me? I'm a reporter,"
he added. "I got to stick around down there at the beach
until they get through."

"I aint got a coat," the proprietor said. "But I got a piece
of tarpaulin I keep my car under. You can use that if you will
bring it back."

"All right," the reporter said. He did not disturb Jiggs;
when he emerged into the cold and the dark this time he resembled a soiled and carelessly setup tent. The tarpaulin was
stiff and heavy to hold and presently heavy to carry too, but
inside it he ceased to shake. It was well after midnight now
and he had expected to find that the cars drawn up along the
boulevard to face the lake would have thinned somewhat,
but they had not. Individually they might have changed, but

the ranked line was still intact—a silhouetted row of oval rearwindows framing the motionless heads whose eyes, along with the headlights, stared with immobile and unmurmuring patience down upon the scene in which they were not even aware that nothing was happening—that the dredge squatted inactive now, attached as though by one steel umbilical cord not to one disaster but to the prime oblivious mother of all living and derelict too. Steady and unflagging the long single spoke of the beacon swept its arc across the lake and vanished into the full broadside of the yellow eye and, already outshooting, swept on again, leaving that slow terrific vacuum in mind or sense which should have been filled with the flick and the swish which never came. The sightseeing skiff had ceased to ply, perhaps having milked the business or perhaps having been stopped by authority; the next boat to land came direct from the dredge, one of the passengers the mechanic who had sat beside the woman in the lunchwagon. This time the reporter did his own asking.

"No," the other said. "She went back to the field about an hour ago, when they found out they would have to wait for the diver. I'm going to turn in, myself. I guess you can knock off now yourself, cant you?"

"Yes," the reporter said. "I can knock off now too." At first he thought that perhaps he was going in, walking in the dry light treacherous shellpowder, holding the harsh stiff tarpaulin with both hands to ease the dead weight of it on his neck and shoulders; it was the weight, the cold rasp of it on his fingers and palms. "I'll have to take it back first, like I promised," he thought. "If I dont now, I wont do it at all." The ramp of the boulevard rose here, so that the carlights passed over his head and he walked now in comparative darkness to where the seawall made its right angle with the boulevard. The wind did not reach here and since he could sit on the edge of the tarpaulin and fold it about him knees and all and so soon his body heated it inside like a tent. Now he did not have to watch the beacon sweep in from across the lake in its full arc but only when the beam materialised slicing across the pieshaped quarter of sky framed by the right angle of wall and ramp. It was the warmth; all of a sudden he had been telling Shumann for some time that she did not understand. And he knew that that was not right; all the while that he was telling Shumann he was also telling himself that that was not right; his cramped chin came up from the bony peaks of his knees; his feet were cold too or were probably cold because at first he did not feel them at all until they filled suddenly with the cold needles; now (the searchlight on the shore was black and only the one on the dredge stared as before downward into the water) the police boat layto and there was not one of the small boats in sight at all and he saw that most of the cars were gone too from the ramp overhead even while he was thinking that it could not possibly have been that long. But it had; the steady clocklike sweep flick! sweep. sweep flick! sweep of the beacon had accomplished something apparently, it had checked something off; as he looked upward the dark seawall overhead came into abrupt sharp relief and then simultaneous with the recognition of the glow as floodlights he heard the displacing of air and then saw the navigation lights of the transport as it slid, quite low, across the black angle and onto the field. "That means it's after four oclock," he thought. "That means it's tomorrow." It was not dawn yet though; before that he was trying to draw himself back as though by the arm while he was saying again to Shumann, "You see, it looks like I have just got to try to explain to somebody that she——" and jerked himself upward (he had not even leaned his head down to his knees this time and so had nowhere to jerk back to), the needles not needles now but actual ice and his mouth open as though it were not large enough to accommodate the air which his lungs required or the lungs not large enough to accommodate the air which his body had to have, and the long arm of the beacon sweeping athwart his gaze with a motion peremptory ruthless and unhurried and already fading and it some time even yet before he realised that it was not the beacon fading but the brightening sky. The sun had risen before the diver went down and came up, and most of the cars were back by then too, ranked into the ubiquitous blue-and-drab rampart. The reporter had returned the tarpaulin; relieved of its stiff and chafing weight he now shook steadily in the pink chill of the first morning of the entire four days to be ushered in by no overcast. But he did not see her again at all. There was a somewhat larger crowd than there had been the evening before (It was Sunday, and there were now two police launches and the number of skiffs and dories had trebled as though the first lot had spawned somewhere during the night) yet he had daylight to assist him now. But he did not see her. He saw Jiggs from a distance several times, but he did not see her; he did not even know that she had been to the beach again until after the diver came up and reported and he (the reporter) was climbing back toward the boulevard and the telephone and the parachute jumper called to him. The jumper came down the beach, not from the water but from the direction of the field, jerking the injured leg from which he had burst the dressing and the fresh scab in making his jump yesterday savagely after him, as though in raging contempt of the leg itself.

"I was looking for you," he said. From his pocket he took a neatlyfolded sheaf of bills. "Roger said he owed you twenty-two dollars. Is that right?"

"Yes," the reporter said. The jumper held the money clipped between two fingers and folded over under his thumb.

"You got time to attend to some business for us or are you going to be busy?" he said.

"Busy?" the reporter said.

"Yes. Busy. If you are, say so so I can find somebody else to do it."

"Yes," the reporter said. "I'll do it."

"You sure? If not, say so. It wont be much trouble; anybody can do it. I just thought of you because you seem to have already got yourself pretty well mixed up with us, and you will be here."

"Yes," the reporter said. "I'll do it."

"All right, then. We're going to get away today. No use hanging around here. Those bastards out there—" he jerked his head toward the lake, the clump of boats on the rosy water "—aint going to get him out from under all that muck with just a handfull of ropes. So we're going. What I want to do is leave some money with you in case they do fuck around out there and finally get him up."

"Yes," the reporter said. "I see." The jumper stared at him with that bleak tense quiet.

"Dont think I like to ask this anymore than you like to

hear it. But maybe you never sent for us to come here, and maybe we never asked you to move in on us; you'll have to admit that. Anyway, it's all done now; I cant help it anymore than you can." The jumper's other hand came to the money; the reporter saw how the bills had already been separated carefully into two parts and that the part which the jumper extended toward him was clipped neatly with two paper clips beneath a strip of paper bearing a neatly printed address, a name which the reporter read at a glance because he had seen it before when he watched Shumann write it on the note. "Here's seventy-five bucks, and that's the address. I dont know what it will cost to ship him. But if it is enough to ship him and still pay you your twenty-two bucks, do it. And if it aint enough to pay you your twenty-two and still ship him, ship him and write me and I will send you the difference." This time the slip of paper came, folded, from his pocket. "This is mine. I kept them separate so you wouldn't get them mixed. Do you understand? Send him to the first address, the one with the money. And if there aint enough left to pay you your twenty-two, write to me at the second one and I will send it to you. It may take some time for the letter to catch up with me, but I will get it sooner or later and I will send you the money. Understand?"

"Yes," the reporter said.

"All right. I asked you if you would attend to it and you said you would. But I didn't say anything about promise. Did I?"

"I promise," the reporter said.

"I dont want you to promise that. What I want you to promise is another thing. Something else. Dont think I want to ask it; I told you that; I dont want to ask it anymore than you want to hear it. What I want you to promise is, dont send him collect."

"I promise," the reporter said.

"All right. Call it a gamble on your twenty-two dollars, if you want to. But not collect. The seventy-five may not be enough. But all we got now is my nineteen-fifty from yesterday and the prize money from Thursday. That was a hundred and four. So I cant spare more than seventy-five. You'll have to chance it. If the seventy-five wont ship him ho—to that address I gave you, you can do either of two things. You can pay the difference yourself and write me and I will send you the difference and your twenty-two. Or if you dont want to take a chance on me, use the seventy-five to bury him here; there must be some way you can do it so they can find him later if they want to. But dont send him collect. I am not asking you to promise to put out any money of your own to send him back; I am just asking you to promise not to leave it so they will have to pay him out of the freight or the express office. Will you?"

"Yes," the reporter said. "I promise."

"All right," the jumper said. He put the money into the reporter's hand. "Thanks. I guess we will leave today. So I guess I will tell you goodbye." He looked at the reporter, bleak, his face spent with sleeplessness too, standing with the injured leg propped stiffly in the shelldust. "She took a couple of big drinks and she is asleep now." He looked at the reporter with that bleak speculation which seemed to be almost clairvoyant. "Dont take it too hard. You never made him try to fly that crate anymore than you could have kept him from it. No man will hold that against you, and what she might hold against you wont hurt you because you wont ever see her again, see?"

"Yes," the reporter said. "That's true."

"Yair. So sometime when she is feeling better about it I will tell her how you attended to this and she will be obliged to you, and for the rest of it too. Only take a tip from me and stick to the kind of people you are used to after this."

"Yes," the reporter said.

"Yair." The jumper moved, shifting stiffly the injured leg to turn, then he paused again, looking back. "You got my address; it may take some time for the letter to catch up with me. But you will get your money. Well——" He extended his hand; it was hard, not clammy, just absolutely without warmth. "Thanks for attending to this and for trying to help us out. Be good to yourself." Then he was gone, limping savagely away. The reporter did not watch him; after a while it was one of the soldiers who called him and showed him the gap.

"Better put that stuff into your pocket, doc," the soldier said. "Some of these guys will be cutting your wrist off." The cab, the taxi, ran with the sun, yet a ray of it fell through the back window and glinted on a chromium fitting on the collapsible seat and though after a while the reporter gave up trying to move the seat and finally thought of laying his hat over the lightpoint, he still continued to try to blink away that sensation of light fine sand inside his lids. It didn't matter whether he watched the backwardstreaming wall of moss and liveoaks above the dark waterglints or whether he tried to keep vision, sight, inside the cab. As soon as he closed them he would find himself, out of some attenuation of weariness, sleeplessness, confusing both the living and the dead without concern now, with profound conviction of the complete unimportance of either or of the confusion itself, trying with that mindless and unflagging optimism to explain to someone that she did not understand and now without bothering to decide or care whether or not and why or not he was asleep. The cab did not have to go as far up as Grandlieu Street and so he did not see a clock, though by the position of the balcony's shadow across the door beneath it he guessed it to be about nine. In the corridor he quit blinking, and on the stairs too; but no sooner had he entered the room with the sun coming into the windows and falling across the bright savage bars of the blanket on the cot (even the other blankets on the walls, which the sun did not reach, seemed to have confiscated light into their harsh red-white-and-black lightnings and which they released slowly into the room as other blankets might have soaked up and then emitted the smell of horses) he began to blink again, with that intent my-opic bemusement. He seemed to await the office of something outside himself before he moved and closed the jalousies before the windows. It was better then because for a while he could not see at all; he just stood there in some ultimate distillation of the savage bright neartropical day, not knowing now whether he was still blinking or not, in an implacable infiltration which not even walls could stop, from the circumambient breathing of fish and coffee and sugar and fruit and hemp and swampland dyked away from the stream because of which they came to exist, so that the very commercebearing units of their breath and life came and went not beside or among them but above them like straying skyscrapers putting in from and out to the sea. There was

even less light beyond the curtain, though it was not completely dark. "How could it be," he thought, standing quietly
with his coat in one hand and the other already slipping the
knot of his tie, thinking how no place where a man has lived
for almost two years or even two weeks or even two days is
completely dark to him without he has got so fat in the senses
that he is already dead walking and breathing and all places
are dark to him even in sunlight; not completely dark but
just enough so that now the room's last long instant of illim-
itable unforgetting seemed to draw in quietly in a long immobility of fleeing, with a quality poised and imminent but
which could not be called waiting and which contained
nothing in particular of farewell, but just paused inbreathing
and without impatience and incurious, for him to make the
move. His hand was already on the light, the switch.

He had just finished shaving when Jiggs began to call his
name from the alley. He took from the bed in passing the
fresh shirt which he had laid out, and went to the window
and opened the jalousie. "It's on the latch," he said. "Come
on in." He was buttoning the shirt when Jiggs mounted the
stairs, carrying the canvas sack, wearing the tennis shoes and
the bootlegs.

"Well, I guess you have heard the news," Jiggs said.

"Yes. I saw Holmes before I came to town. So I guess
you'll all be moving now."

"Yair," Jiggs said. "I'm going with Art Jackson. He's been
after me a good while. He's got the chutes, see, and I have
done some exhibition jumping and so it wont take me long
to pick up free jumping, delayed. . . . . . . Then we can split
the whole twenty-five bucks between ourselves. But Jesus, it
wont be like racing. Maybe I'll go back to racing after a

while, after I have. . . . . . ." He stood motionless in the center of the room, holding the dragging canvas bag, the battered brutal face lowered and sober and painfully bemused. Then the reporter discovered what he was looking at. "Jesus," Jiggs said, "I tried again to put them on this morning and I couldn't even seem to open the bag and take them out." That was about ten oclock because almost immediately the negress Leonora came in, in the coat and hat and carrying the neat basket beneath its neat cloth so fresh that the ironed creases were still visible. But the reporter only allowed her to put the basket down.

"A bottle of wood alcohol and a can of that stuff you take grease out of clothes with," he told her, giving her the bill; then to Jiggs: "What do you want to fix that scratch with?"

"I got something for that," Jiggs said. "I brought that with me." He took it from the bag—a coca cola bottle stoppered with paper and containing wingdope. The negress left the basket and went out and returned with the two bottles, and made a pot of coffee and set it with cups and sugar on the table and looked again about the untouched, unused rooms, and took up the basket and stood for a while and watched what they were doing with prim and grim inscrutability before departing for good. And the reporter too, sitting on the couch and blowing quietly into his cup to cool it, watched Jiggs squatting before the two gleaming boots, in the tight soiled clothes and the tennis shoes now upturned behind him, and he thought how never before had he ever heard of rubber soles wearing through. "Because what the hell do I need with a pair of new boots for Christ's sake, when probably this time next month I wont even have on anything to stuff into the tops of them?" Jiggs said. That was toward eleven. By noon, still holding the cold stale cup between his hands, the reporter had watched Jiggs remove the polish from the boots, first with the alcohol, watching the cold dark flowing of the liquid move, already fading, up the length of each boot like the shadow of a cloud travelling along a road, and then by scraping them with the back of a knifeblade, so that at last the boots had returned to the mere shape of what they were like the blank gunstocks manufactured for sale to firearms amateurs. He watched Jiggs, sitting on the couch now and with the soiled shirt for padding and the inverted boot clamped between his knees, with sandpaper remove delicately from the sole all trace of contact with the earth; and last of all, intent, his blunt grained hands moving with minute and incredible lightness and care, with the wingdope begin to fill in the heelmark on the right boot's instep so that presently it was invisible to the casual glance of anyone who did not know that it had been there. "Jesus," Jiggs said, "if I only hadn't walked in them. Just hadn't creased them at the ankle. But maybe after I get them rubbed smooth again——" But when the cathedral clock struck one they had not accomplished that. Rubbing only smoothed them and left them without life; the reporter suggested floorwax and went out and got it, and it had to be removed.

"Wait," he said, looking at Jiggs—the gaunt, the worn, the face worn with fatigue and lack of sleep and filled with a spent unflagging expression of quiet endurance like a hypnotised person. "Listen. That magazine with the pictures of what you wish you could get your white American servants to wear so you could think they were English butlers, and what if you wore yourself maybe the horse would think he was in England too unless the fox happened to run under a bill-

board or something. . . . . . . About how a fox's tail is the
only. . . . . . ." He stared at Jiggs, who stared back at him with
blinking and oneeyed attention. "Wait. No. It's the horse's
bone. Not the fox; the horse's shin bone. That's what we
need."

"A horse's shinbone?"

"For the boots. That's what you use."

"All right. But where——"

"I know where. We can pick it up on the way out to see
Hagood. We can rent a car." They had to walk up to Grandlieu Street to rent the car.

"Want me to drive?" Jiggs said.

"Can you?"

"Sure."

"Then I guess you will have to," the reporter said. "I
cant." It was a bright soft sunny day, quite warm, the air filled,
breathing, with a faint suspiration which made the reporter
think of organs and bells—of mortification and peace and
shadowy kneeling—though he heard neither. The streets
were crowded though the throngs were quiet, not only with
ordinary Sunday decorum but with a certain slow tranquillity
as though the very brick and stone had just recovered from
fever. Now and then, in the lees of walls and gutters as they
left downtown behind them the reporter saw little drifts of the
spent confetti but soiled and stained now until it resembled
more dingy sawdust or even dead leaves. Once or twice he
saw tattered loops of the purple-and-gold bunting and once at
a corner a little boy darted almost beneath the wheels with a
tattered streamer of it whipping behind him. Then the city
dissolved into swamp and marsh again; presently the road ran
into a broad expanse of saltmarsh broken by the dazzling sun-

blanched dyke of a canal; presently a rutted lane turned off
into the saltgrass. "Here we are," the reporter said. The car
turned into the lane and they began to pass the debris, the
silent imperishable monument tranquil in the bright sun—
the old carbodies without engines or wheels, the old engines
and wheels without bodies; the rusted scraps and sections of
iron machinery and standpipes and culverts rising halfburied
out of the blanched sand and shelldust which was so white itself that for a time Jiggs saw no bones at all. "Can you tell a
horse from a cow?" the reporter said.

"I dont know," Jiggs said. "I aint very certain whether I
can even tell a shinbone or not."

"We'll get some of everything and try them all," the reporter said. So they did; moving about, stooping (the reporter
was blinking again now between the fierce quiet glare of the
pigmentless sand and the ineffable and cloudless blue) they
gathered up about thirty pounds of bones. They had two
complete forelegs both of which were horses' though they
did not know it, and a set of shoulderblades from a mule and
Jiggs came up with a full set of ribs which he insisted belonged to a colt but which were actually those of a big dog,
and the reporter had one object which turned out not to be
bone at all but the forearm from a piece of statuary. "We
ought to have something in here that will do," he said.

"Yair," Jiggs said. "Now which way?" They did not need
to return through the city. They skirted it, leaving the saltmarsh behind and now, crossing no actual boundary or de-
marcation and challenged by no sentry, they entered a
region where even the sunlight seemed different, where it fil-
tered among the ordered liveoaks and fell suavely upon
parked expanses and vistas beyond which the homes of the

rich oblivious and secure presided above clipped lawns and terraces, with a quality of having itself been passed by appointment through a walled gate by a watchman. Presently they ran along a picketline of palmtrunks beyond which a clipped fairway stretched, broken only by sedate groups of apparently armed men and boys all moving in one direction like a kind of decorouslyembattled skirmish advance.

"It aint four yet," the reporter said. "We can wait for him right here, at number fifteen." So after a time Hagood, preparing to drive with his foursome, his ball teed and addressed, looked up and saw them standing quietly just inside the club's grounds, the car waiting in the road behind them, watching him—the indefatigable and now ubiquitous cadaver and the other, the vicious halfmetamorphosis between thug and horse—the tough hard blunt face to which the blue swollen eye lent no quality of pity or suffering, made it look not at all like a victim or one deserving compassion, but merely like a pirate. Hagood stepped down from the tee.

"A message from the office," he said quietly. "You fellows drive and play on; I'll catch you." He approached Jiggs and the reporter. "How much do you want this time?" he said.

"Whatever you will let me have," the reporter said.

"So," Hagood said quietly. "It's that bad this time, is it?" The reporter said nothing; they watched Hagood take his wallet from his hip pocket and open it. "This is the last, this time, I suppose?" he said.

"Yes," the reporter said. "They're leaving tonight." From the wallet Hagood took a thin sheaf of check blanks.

"So you wont suggest a sum yourself," Hagood said. "You are using psychology on me."

"Whatever you can. Will. I know I have borrowed more

from you than I have paid back. But this time maybe I can. . . . . . ." He drew something from his coat now and extended it—a postcard, a colored lithograph; Hagood read the legend: *Hotel Vista del Mar, Santa Monica, California,* the plump arrow drawn by a hotel pen and pointing to a window.

"What?" Hagood said.

"Read it," the reporter said. "It's from mamma. Where they are spending their honeymoon, her and Mr Hurtz. She said how she has told him about me and he seems to like me all right and that maybe when my birthday comes on the first of April. . . . . . ."

"Ah," Hagood said. "That will be very nice, wont it?" He took a short fountain pen from his shirt and glanced about; now the second man, the cartoon comedy centaur who had been watching him quietly and steadily with the one bright hot eye, spoke for the first time.

"Write on my back if you want to, mister," he said, turning and stooping, presenting a broad skintight expanse of soiled shirt, apparently as hard as a section of concrete, to Hagood.

"And get the hell kicked out of me and serve me right," Hagood thought viciously. He spread the blank on Jiggs' back and wrote the check and waved it dry and folded it and handed it to the reporter.

"Do you want me to sign anyth——" the reporter began.

"No. But will you let me ask a favor of you?"

"Yes, chief. Of course."

"Go to town and look in the book and find where Doctor Legendre lives and go out there. Dont telephone; go out there; tell him I sent you, tell him I said to give you some pills that will put you to sleep for about twenty-four hours, and go home and take them. Will you?"

"Yes, chief," the reporter said. "Tomorrow when you fix the note for me to sign you can pin the postcard to it. It wont be legal, but it will be——"

"Yes," Hagood said. "Go on, now. Please go on."

"Yes, chief," the reporter said. They went on. When they reached home it was almost five oclock. They unloaded the bones and now they both worked, each with a boot, fast. It seemed to be slow work, nevertheless the boots were taking on a patina deeper and less brilliant than wax or polish.

"Jesus," Jiggs said. "If I just hadn't creased the ankles, and if I just had kept the box and paper when I unwrapped them. . . . . . ." Because he had forgot that it was Sunday. He knew it; he and the reporter had known it was Sunday all day but they had both forgotten it; they did not remember it until, at half past five, Jiggs halted the car before the window into which he had looked four days ago—the window from which now both boots and photographs were missing. They looked at the locked door quietly for a good while. "So we didn't need to hurry after all," he said. "Well, maybe I couldn't have fooled them, anyway. Maybe I'd a had to went to the pawnshop just the same anyway.—We might as well take the car back."

"Let's go to the paper and cash the check first," the reporter said. He had not yet looked at it; while Jiggs waited in the car he went in and returned. "It was for a hundred," he said. "He's a good guy. He's been white to me, Jesus." He got into the car.

"Now where?" Jiggs said.

"Now we got to decide how. We might as well take the car back while we are deciding." The lights were on now; when they emerged from the garage, walking, they moved in

red-green-and-white glare and flicker, crossing the outfall
from the theatre entrances and the eating places, passing
athwart the hour's rich resurgence of fish and coffee. "You
cant give it to her yourself," the reporter said. "They would
know you never had that much."

"Yair," Jiggs said. "All I could risk would have been that
twenty bucks. But I'll have room for some of it, though. If I
get as much as ten from Uncle Isaac I will want to pinch myself."

"And if we slipped it to the kid, it would be the. . . . . . .
Wait," he said; he stopped and looked at Jiggs. "I got it. Yair.
Come on." Now he was almost running, weaving on through
the slow Sunday evening throng, Jiggs following. They tried
five drugstores before they found it—a blue-and-yellow toy
hanging by a piece of cord before a rotary ventilator in similitude of flight. It had not been for sale; Jiggs and the reporter
fetched the stepladder from the rear of the store in order to
take it down. "You said the train leaves at eight," the reporter
said. "We got to hurry some." It was half past six now as they
left Grandlieu Street; when they reached the corner where
Shumann and Jiggs had bought the sandwich two nights
ago, they parted.

"I can see the balls from here," Jiggs said. "Aint any need
of you going with me; I guess I wont have any trouble carrying what they will give me for them. You get the sandwiches
and leave the door unlocked for me." He went on, the news-
paperwrapped boots under his arm; even now as each foot
flicked backward with that motion like a horse's hock, the reporter believed that he could see the coinshaped patch of
blackened flesh in each pale sole: so that when he entered
the corridor and set the door ajar and mounted the stairs and

turned on the light, he did not open the sandwiches at once. He put them and the toy aeroplane on the table and went beyond the curtain. When he emerged he carried in one hand the gallon jug (it contained now about three pints) and in the other a pair of shoes which looked as much like him as his hair or hands looked. He was sitting on the cot, smoking, when Jiggs entered, carrying now a biggish bundle, a bundle bigger even though shorter than the boots had been. "He gave me five bucks for them," Jiggs said. "I give twenty-two and a half and wear them twice and he gives me five. Yair. He throws it away." He laid the bundle on the couch. "So I decided that wasn't even worth the trouble of handing to her. So I just got some presents for all of them." He opened the parcel. It contained a box or chest of candy about the size of a suitcase and resembling a miniature bale of cotton and lettered heavily by some pyrographic process: *Souvenir of New Valois. Come back again* and three magazines—Boy's Life, The Ladies' Home Journal, and one of the pulp magazines of war stories in the air. Jiggs' blunt grained hands riffled them and evened the edges again, his brutal battered face was curiously serene. "It will give them something to do on the train, see? Now let me get my pliers and we will fix that ship." Then he saw the jug on the table as he turned. But he did not go to it; he just stopped, looking at it, and the reporter saw the good eye rush sudden and inarticulate and hot. But he did not move. It was the reporter who went and poured the first drink and gave it to him, and then the second one. "You need one too," Jiggs said.

"Yes," the reporter said. "I will in a minute." But he didn't for a while, though he took one of the sandwiches when Jiggs opened them and then watched Jiggs, his jaw bulged by a huge bite, stoop and take from the canvas sack the cigarbox and from the box produced a pair of pliers; not beginning yet to eat his own sandwich the reporter watched Jiggs raise the metal clamps which held the toy aeroplane's tin body together and open it. The reporter produced the money—the seventy-five which the jumper had given him and the hundred from Hagood—and they wedged it into the toy and Jiggs clamped it to again.

"Yair, he'll find it, all right," Jiggs said. "Every toy he gets he plays with it a couple of days and then he takes it apart. To fix it, he says. But Jesus, he came by that natural; Roger's old man is a doctor, see. A little country town where it's mostly Swede farmers and the old man gets up at any hour of the night and rides twenty or thirty miles in a sleigh and borns the babies and cuts off arms and legs and a lot of them even pay him; sometimes it aint but a couple or three years before they will bring him in a ham or a bedspread or something on the installment. So the old man wanted Roger to be a doctor too, see, and he was hammering that at Roger all the time Roger was a kid and watching Roger's grades in school and all: so that Roger would have to doctor up his report cards for the old man but the old man never found it out; he would see Roger start off for school every morning (they lived in a kind of big place, half farm, a little ways out of town that never nobody tried to farm much Roger said, but his old man kept it because it was where his old man, his father's old man, had settled when he come into the country) over in town and he never found it out until one day he found out how Roger hadn't even been inside the school in six months because he hadn't never been off the place any further than out of sight down the road where he could turn and come back through the woods to an old mill his grandfather had built and Roger had built him a motorcycle in it out of scraps saved up from mowing machines and clocks and such, and it run, see. That's what saved him. When his old man saw that it would run he let Roger go then and quit worrying him to be a doctor; he bought Roger the first ship, the Hisso Standard, with the money he had been saving up to send Roger to the medical school, but when he saw that the motorcycle would run, I guess he knew he was whipped. And then one night Roger had to make a landing without any lights and he run over a cow and cracked it up and the old man paid for having it rebuilt; Roger told me once the old man must have borrowed the jack to do it with on the farm and that he aimed to pay his old man back the first thing as soon as he could but I guess it's o.k. because a farm without a mortgage on it would probably be against the law or something. Or maybe the old man didn't have to mortgage the farm but he just told Roger that so Roger would pick out a vacant field next time." The cathedral clock had struck seven shortly after Jiggs came in with his bundle; it must be about half past seven now. Jiggs squatted now, holding one of the shoes in his hand. "Jesus," he said. "I sure wont say I dont need them. But what about you?"

"I couldn't wear but one pair of them, no matter how many I had," the reporter said. "You better go ahead and try them on."

"They'll fit, all right. There are two garments that will fit anybody: a handkerchief when your nose is running and a pair of shoes when your feet are on the ground."

"Yes," the reporter said. "That was the same ship that he and Laverne——"

"Yair. Jesus, they were a pair. She was glad to see him when he come into town that day in it. One day she told me something about it. She was a orphan, see; her older sister that was married sent for her to come live with them when her folks died. The sister was about twenty years older than Laverne and the sister's husband was about six or eight years younger than the sister and Laverne was about fourteen or fifteen; she hadn't had much fun at home with a couple of old people like her father and mother, and she never had much with her sister neither, being that much younger; yair, I dont guess the sister had a whole lot of fun either with the kind of guy the husband seemed to be. So when the husband started teaching Laverne how to slip out and meet him and they would drive to some town forty or fifty miles away when the husband was supposed to be at work or something and he would buy her a glass of soda water or maybe stop at a dive where the husband was sure nobody he knowed would see them and dance, I guess she thought that was all the fun there was in the world and that since he would tell her it was all right to twotime the sister that way, that it was all right for her to do the rest of it he wanted. Because he was the big guy, see, the one that paid for what she wore and what she ate. Or maybe she didn't think it was all right so much as she just thought that that was the way it was—that you was either married and wore down with housework to where your husband was just the guy that twotimed you and you knew it and all you could do about it was nag at him while he was awake and go through his clothes while he was asleep to see if you found any hairpins or letters or rubbers in his pockets, and then cry and moan about him to your younger sister while he was gone; or you were the one that somebody else's husband

was easing out with and that all the choice you had was the
dirty dishes to wash against the nickel sodas and a half an
hour of dancing to a backalley orchestra in a dive where nobody give his right name and then being wallowed around
on the back seat of a car and then go home and slip in and
lie to your sister and when it got too close, having the guy
jump on you too to save his own face and then make it up by
buying you two sodas next time. Or maybe at fifteen she just
never saw any way of doing better because for a while she
never even knowed that the guy was holding her down himself, see, that he was hiding her out at the cheap dives not so
they would not be recognised but so he would not have any
competition from anybody but guys like himself; no young
guys for her to see or to see her. Only the competition come;
somehow she found out there was sodas that cost more than
even a dime and that all the music never had to be played in
a back room with the shades down. Or maybe it was just
him, because one night she had used him for a stalking horse
and he hunted her down and the guy she was with this time
finally had to beat him up and so he went back home and
told the sister on her——" The reporter rose, quickly. Jiggs
watched him go to the table and pour into the glass, splash-
ing the liquor onto the table. "That's right," Jiggs said. "Take
a good one." The reporter lifted the glass, gulping, his throat
filled with swallowing and the liquor cascading down his
chin; Jiggs sprang up quickly too but the other passed him,
running toward the window and onto the balcony where
Jiggs, following, caught him by the arms as he lunged outward as the liquor, hardly warmed, burst from his mouth.
The cathedral clock struck the half hour; the sound followed

them back into the room and seemed to die away too, like the light, into the harsh bright savage zigzags of color on the blankethung walls. "Let me get you some water," Jiggs said. "You sit down now, and I will——"

"I'm all right now," the reporter said. "You put on your shoes. That was half past seven then."

"Yair. But you better——"

"No. Sit down; I'll pull your leggings for you."

"You sure you feel like it?"

"Yes. I'm all right now." They sat facing one another on the floor again as they had sat the first night, while the reporter took hold of the rivetted strap of the right bootleg. Then he began to laugh. "You see, it got all mixed up," he said, laughing, not loud yet. "It started out to be a tragedy. A good orthodox Italian tragedy. You know: one Florentine falls in love with another Florentine's wife and he spends three acts fixing it up to put the bee on the second Florentine and so just as the curtain falls on the third act the Florentine and the wife crawl down the fire escape and you know that the second Florentine's brother wont catch them until daylight and they will be asleep in the monk's bed in the monastery? But it went wrong. When he come climbing up to the window to tell her the horses was ready, she refused to speak to him. It turned into a comedy, see?" He looked at Jiggs, laughing, not laughing louder yet but just faster.

"Here, fellow!" Jiggs said. "Here now! Quit it!"

"Yes," the reporter said. "It's not that funny. I'm trying to quit it. I'm trying to. But I cant quit. See? See how I cant quit?" he said, still holding to the strap, his face twisted with laughing, which as Jiggs looked, burst suddenly with drops of moisture running down the cadaverous grimace which for an instant Jiggs thought was sweat until he saw the reporter's eyes.

It was after half past seven; they would have to hurry now. But they found a cab at once and they got the green light at once at Grandlieu Street even before the cab began to slow, shooting athwart the glare of neon, the pulse and glitter of electrics which bathed the idle slow Sunday pavementthrong as it drifted from window to window beyond which the immaculate, the unbelievable wax men and women gazed back at them with expressions inscrutable and delphic. Then the palms in Saint Jules Avenue began to swim and flee past—the scabby picket posts, the sage dusters out of the old Southern country thought; the lighted clock in the station façade said six minutes to eight.

"They are probably already on the train," Jiggs said.

"Yes," the reporter said. "They'll let you through the gate, though."

"Yair," Jiggs said, taking up the toy aeroplane and the package which he had rewrapped. "Dont you want to come inside?"

"I'll just wait here," the reporter said. He watched Jiggs enter the waitingroom and vanish. He could hear the announcer calling another train; moving toward the doors he could see passengers begin to rise and take up bags and bundles and move toward the numbered gates, though quite a few still remained for other trains. "But not long," the reporter thought. "Because they can go home now"; thinking of all the names of places which railroads go to, fanning out from the River's mouth to all of America; of the cold February names:

Minnesota and Dakota and Michigan, the high iceclad river-reaches and the long dependable snow; "yair, home now, knowing that they have got almost a whole year before they will have to get drunk and celebrate the fact that they will have more than eleven months before they will have to wear masks and get drunk and blow horns again." Now the clock said two minutes to eight; they had probably got off the car to talk to Jiggs, perhaps standing now on the platform, smoking maybe; he could cross the waitingroom and doubtless even see them, standing beside the hissing train while the other passengers and the redcaps hurried past; she would carry the bundle and the magazines and the little boy would have the aeroplane already, probably performing wingovers or vertical turns by hand. "Maybe I will go and look," he thought, waiting to see if he were until suddenly he realised that now, opposite from when he had stood in the bedroom before turning on the light, it was himself who was the nebulous and quiet ragtag and bobend of touching and breath and experience without visible scars, the waiting incurious unbreathing and without impatience, and another save him this time to make the move. There was a second hand on the clock too—a thin spidery splash; he watched it now as it moved too fast to follow save between the intervals of motion when it became instantaneously immobile as though drawn across the clock's face by a pen and a ruler—9. 8. 7. 6. 5. 4. 3. 2. and done; it was now the twenty-first hour, and that was all. No sound, as though it had not been a steam train which quitted the station two seconds ago but rather the shadow of one on a magic lantern screen until the child's vagrant and restless hand came and removed the slide.

"Well," Jiggs said, "I guess you'll be wanting to get home and catch some shuteye."

"Yair," the reporter said, "we might as well be moving." They got into the cab, though this time Jiggs lifted the canvas sack from the floor and sat with it on his lap.

"Yair," Jiggs said. "He'll find it. He already dropped it a couple of times trying to make it spin on the platform. — You told him to stop at Main Street, didn't you?"

"I'll take you on to the hotel," the reporter said.

"No, I'll get out at Main. Jesus, it's a good thing I dont live here; I never would get back home unless somebody took me; I couldn't even remember the name of the street I lived on even if I could pronounce it to ask where it was."

"Grandlieu," the reporter said. "I will take you——" The cab slowed into the corner and stopped; Jiggs gathered up the canvas bag and opened the door.

"This'll be fine. It aint but eight-fifteen; I aint to meet Art until nine. I'll just walk up the street a ways and get a little air."

"I wish you'd let me——Or if you'd like to come on back home and——"

"No; you get on home and go to bed; we have kept you up enough, I guess." He leaned into the cab, the cap raked above his hard blue face and the violent plumcolored eye; suddenly the light changed to green and the bell clanged and shrilled. Jiggs stuck out his hand; for an instant the hot hard limp rough palm sweated against the reporter's as if the reporter had touched a piece of machinery belting. "Much obliged. And thanks for the drinks. I'll be seeing you." The cab moved; Jiggs banged the door; his face fled backward past the window; the green and red and white electrics waned and pulsed and flicked away too as through the rear window the reporter watched Jiggs swing the now limp dirty sack over his shoulder and turn on into the crowd. The reporter leaned forward and tapped on the glass.

"Out to the airport," he said.

"Airport?" the driver said. "I thought the other fellow said you wanted to go to Noyades street."

"No; airport," the reporter said. The driver looked forward again; he seemed to settle himself, to shape his limbs for comfort for the long haul even while the one-way arrows of the old constricted city flicked past. But presently the old quarter gave way to outraveling and shabby purlieus, mostly lightless now, and the cab went faster; presently the street straightened and became the ribbonstraight road running across the terraqueous plain and the cab was going quite fast, and now the illusion began, the sense of being suspended in a small airtight glass box clinging by two puny fingers of light in the silent and rushing immensity of space. By looking back he could still see the city, the glare of it, no further away; if he were moving, regardless at what terrific speed and in what loneliness, so was it, parallelling him. He was not escaping it; symbolic and encompassing, it outlay all gasolinespanned distances and all clock- or sunstipulated destinations. It would be there—the eternal smell of the coffee the sugar the hemp sweating slow iron plates above the forked deliberate brown water and lost lost lost all ultimate blue of latitude and horizon; the hot rain gutterfull plaiting the eaten heads of shrimp; the ten thousand inescapable mornings wherein ten thousand airplants swinging stippleprop the soft scrofulous soaring of sweating brick and ten thousand pairs of splayed brown hired Leonorafeet tigerbarred by jaloused armistice with the invincible sun: the thin black coffee, the myriad fish stewed in a myriad oil—tomorrow and tomorrow and tomorrow; not only not to hope, not even to wait: just to endure.

The Scavengers

At midnight—one of the group of newspapermen on the beach claimed to have watched the mate of the dredge-boat and the sergeant of the police launch holding flashlights on their watches for fifteen minutes—the dredge upped anchor and stood offshore and steamed away while the police launch, faster, had taken its white bone beyond the seawall almost before the dredge had got enough offing to turn. Then the five newspapermen—four in overcoats with upturned collars—turned too and mounted the beach toward where the ranked glaring cars were beginning to disperse while the policemen—there were not so many of them now—tried to forestall the inevitable jam. There was no wind tonight, neither was there any overcast. The necklace of lights along the lakeshore curved away faint and clear, with that illusion of tremulous wavering which distance and clarity gave them, like bright not-quite-settled roosting birds, as did the boundary lights along the seawall; and now the steady and measured rake of the beacon seemed not to travel so much as to murmur like a moving forefoot of wind across water, among the thick faint stars. They mounted the beach to where a policeman, hands on hips, stood as though silhouetted not against the crisscrossing of headlights but against the blatting and honking uproar as well, as though contemplating without any emotion whatever the consummation of that which he had been waiting on for twenty hours now. "Aint you talking to us too, sergeant?" the first newspaperman said. The policeman looked back over his shoulder, squinting down at the group from under his raked cap.

"Who are you?" he said.

"We are the press," the other said in a smirking affected voice.

"Get on, get on," a second said behind him. "Let's get indoors somewhere." The policeman had already turned back to the cars, the racing engines, the honking and blatting.

"Come, come, sergeant," the first said. "Come come come come. Aint you going to send us back to town too?" The policeman did not even look back. "Well, wont you at least call my wife and tell her you wont make me come home, since you wear the dark blue of honor integrity and purity——" The policeman spoke without turning his head.

"Do you want to finish this wake out here or do you really want to finish it in the wagon?"

"Ex-actly. You have got the idea at last. Boys, he's even com——"

"Get on, get on," the second said. "Let him buy a paper and read it." They went on, the reporter (he was the one without an overcoat) last, threading their way between the blatting and honking, the whining and clashing of gears, the glare of backbouncing and crossing headlight beams and reached the boulevard and crossed it toward the lunchstand. The first led the way in, his hatbrim crumpled on one side and his overcoat caught one button awry and a bottleneck protruding from one pocket. The proprietor looked up at them with no especial pleasure; he was about to close up.

"That fellow out there kept me up all last night and I am about wore out," he said.

"You would think we were from the District Attorney's office and trying to padlock him instead of a press delegation trying to persuade him to stay open and accept our pittances," the first said. "You are going to miss the big show at daylight, let alone all the country trade that never heard about it until the noon train got in with the papers."

"How about coming to the back room and letting me lock the door and turn out the lights up here, then?" the proprietor said.

"Sure," they told him. So he locked up and turned off the lights and led them to the back, to the kitchen—a stove, a zinc table encrusted with weekend after weekend of slain meat and fish—and supplied them with glasses and bottles of coca cola and a deck of cards and beercases to sit on and a barrelhead for table, and prepared to retire.

"If anybody knocks, just sit quiet," he said. "And you can beat on that wall there when they get ready to begin; I'll wake up."

"Sure," they told him. He went out. The first opened the bottle and began to pour into the five glasses. The reporter stopped him.

"None for me. I'm not drinking."

"What?" the first said. He set the bottle carefully down

and took out his handkerchief and went through the pan-
tomime of removing his glasses and polishing them and re-
placing them and staring at the reporter, though before he
had finished the fourth took up the bottle and finished pouring the drinks. "You what?" the first said. "Did I hear my ears,
or was it just blind hope I heard?"

"Yes," the reporter said; his face wore that faint, spent,
aching expression which a man might wear toward the end
of a private babyshow. "I've quit for a while."

"Thank God for that," the first breathed, then he turned
and began to scream at the one who now held the bottle,
with that burlesque outrage and despair of the spontaneous
amateur buffoon. But he ceased at once and then the four of
them (again the reporter declined) sat about the barrel and
began to deal blackjack. The reporter did not join them. He
drew his beercase aside, whereupon the first, the habitual
opportunist who must depend upon all unrehearsed blundering and recalcitrant circumstance to be his stooge, noticed at once that he had set his beercase beside the now cold
stove. "If you aint going to take the drink yourself maybe you
better give the stove one," he said.

"I'll begin to warm up in a minute," the reporter said.
They played; the fourth had the deal; their voices came quiet
and brisk and impersonal above the faint slapping of the
cards.

"That's what I call a guy putting himself away for keeps,"
he said.

"What do you suppose he was thinking about while he
was sitting up there waiting for that water to smack him?" the
first said.

"Nothing," the second said shortly. "If he had been a

man that thought, he would not have been up there in the first place."

"Meaning he would have had a good job on a newspaper, huh?" the first said.

"Yes," the second said. "That's what I mean." The reporter rose quietly. He lit a cigarette, his back turned a little to them, and dropped the match carefully into the cold stove and sat down again. None of the others appeared to have noticed him.

"While you are supposing," the fourth said, "what do you suppose his wife was thinking about?"

"That's easy," the first said. "She was thinking, 'Thank God I carry a spare'." They did not laugh; the reporter heard no sound of laughter, sitting quiet and immobile on his beer-case while the cigarette smoke lifted in the unwinded stale air and broke about his face, streaming on, and the voices spoke back and forth with a sort of brisk dead slap-slap-slap like that of the cards.

"Do you suppose it's a fact that they were both laying her?" the third said.

"That's not news," the first said. "But how about the fact that Shumann knew it too? Some of these mechanics that have known them for some time say they dont even know who the kid belongs to."

"Maybe both," the fourth said. "A dual personality: the flying Jekyll and Hyde brother, who flies the ship and makes the parachute jump all at once."

"Unless he cant ever tell which one of him it is that's getting the insertion into the ship," the third said.

"Well, that will be all right too," the first said. "Just so it's one of them and actually inserted, the ship wont care which one it is." The reporter did not move, only his hand, the arm bending at the elbow which rested upon his knee, rose with the cigarette to his mouth and became motionless again while he drew in the smoke with an outward aspect of intense bemused concentration, trembling quietly and steadily and apparently not only untroubled by it but not even aware of it, like a man who has had palsy for years and years; the voices might have indeed been the sound of the cards or perhaps leaves blowing past him.

"You bastards," the second said. "You dirtymouthed bastards. Why dont you let the guy rest? Let them all rest. They were trying to do what they had to do, with what they had to do it with, the same as all of us only maybe a little better than us. At least without squealing and bellyaching."

"Sure," the first said. "You get the point exactly. What they could do, with what they had to do it with: that's just what we were talking about when you called us dirtyminded bastards."

"Yes," the third said. "Grady's right. Let him rest; that's what she seems to have done herself. But what the hell: probably nowhere to send him, even if she had him out of there. So it would be the same whether she stayed any longer or not, besides the cost. Where do you suppose they are going?"

"Where do people like that go?" the second said. "Where do mules and vaudeville acts go? You see a wagon broken down in the ditch or you see one of those trick bicycles with one wheel and the seat fourteen feet from the earth in a pawnshop. But do you wonder whatever became of whatever it was that used to make them move?"

"Do you mean you think she cleared out just to keep from having to pay out some jack to bury him if they get him up?" the fourth said.

"Why not?" the second said. "People like that dont have money to spend on corpses because they dont use money. It dont take money especially to live; it's only when you die that you or somebody has got to have something put away in the sock. A man can eat and sleep and keep the purity squad off of him for six months on what the undertaker will make you believe you cant possibly be planted for a cent less and preserve your selfrespect. So what would they have to bury him with even if they had him to bury?"

"You talk like he didn't kill himself taking a chance to win two thousand dollars," the third said.

"That's correct. Oh, he would have taken the money, all right. But that wasn't why he was flying that ship up there. He would have entered it if he hadn't had anything but a bicycle, just so it would have got off the ground. But it aint for money. It's because they have got to do it, like some women have got to be whores. They cant help themselves. Ord knew that the ship was dangerous, and Shumann must have known it as well as Ord did—dont you remember how for the first lap he stayed so far away he didn't even look like he was in the same race, until he forgot and came in and tried to catch Ord? If it had just been the money, do you think he could have thought about money hard enough to have decided to risk his life to get it in a machine that he knew was unsafe, and then have forgot about the money for a whole lap of the race while he hung back there not half as close to the pylons as the judges were, just riding around? Dont kid yourself."

"And dont kid yourself," the first said. "It was the money. Those guys like money as well as you and me. What would he have done with it? Hell, what would any other three people do with two thousand bucks? She would have bought herself a batch of new clothes and they would have moved to the hotel from wherever it was they were staying, and they would have taken a couple of days and blowed it out good. That's what they would have done. But they didn't get it and so you are right, by God: what she did was the sensible thing: when a game blows up in your face you dont sit down on the pocketbook that used to make a bump on your ass and cry about it, you get out and hustle up another roll and go on and find another game that maybe you can beat. Yes. They want money, all right. But it aint to sweat just to have something in the sock when the snow flies, or to be buried with either. So I dont know anymore than you guys do but if somebody told me that Shumann had some folks somewhere and then they told me the name of the town she bought hers and the kid's tickets to, I would tell you where Shumann used to live. And then I would bet a quarter maybe that the next time you see them, the kid wont be there. Because why? Because that's what I would do if I were her. And so would you guys."

"No," the second said.

"You mean you wouldn't or she wouldn't?" the first said. The reporter sat motionless, the cigarette's windless upstream breaking upon his face. "Yes," the first said. "Before, they might not have known whose the kid was, but it was Shumann's name he went under and so in comparison to the whole mess they must have lived in, who had actually fathered the kid didn't matter. But now Shumann's gone; you asked a while ago what she was thinking about while he was sitting up there waiting for that water to hit him. I'll tell you what she and the other guy were both thinking about: that

now that Shumann was gone, they would never get rid of
him. Maybe they took it night about: I dont know. But now
they couldn't even get him out of the room; even turning off
the light wont do any good, and all the time they would be
awake and moving there he will be, watching them right out
of the mixedup name, Jack Shumann, that the kid has. It
used to be the guy had one competitor; now he will have to
compete with every breath the kid draws and be cuckolded
by every ghost that walks and refuses to give his name. So if
you will tell me that Shumann has some folks in a certain
town, I will tell you where she and the kid——" The reporter
did not move. He sat quite still while the voice ceased on that
note of abrupt transition, hearing out of the altered silence
the voices talking at him and the eyes talking at him while he
held himself rigid, watching the calculated hand flick the
ash carefully from the cigarette. "You hung around them a
lot," the first said. "Did you ever hear any of them mention
any kin that Shumann or she had?" The reporter did not
move; he let the voice repeat the question; he even raised the
cigarette again and flicked the ash off, or what would have
been ash if he had not flicked it only a second ago. Then he
started; he sat up, looking at them with an expression of startled interrogation.

"What?" he said. "What was that? I wasn't listening."

"Did you ever hear any mention of Shumann having any
kinfolks, mother and father and such?" the first said. The reporter's face did not alter.

"No," he said. "I dont believe I did. I believe his mechanic told me that he was an orphan."

It was two oclock then but the cab went fast, so it was just
past two-thirty when the cab reached the Terrebonne and

the reporter entered and leaned his gaunt desperate face across the desk while he spoke to the clerk. "Dont you call yourselves the headquarters of the American Aeronautical Association?" he said. "You mean you didn't keep any registration of contestants and such? that the committee just let them scatter to hell and gone over New Valois without——"

"Who is it you want to find?" the clerk said.

"Art Jackson. A stunt flyer."

"I'll see if there is any record. The meet was over yesterday." The clerk left the window. The reporter leaned in it, not panting, just completely motionless until the clerk returned.

"There is an Arthur Jackson registered as staying at the Bienville Hotel yesterday. But whether or not he is——" But the reporter was gone, not running, but fast, back toward the entrance; a porter with a longhandled brush sweeping the floor jerked it back just before the reporter was about to walk through the brushhandle like it was a spiderweb. The taxi driver did not know exactly where the Bienville was, but at last they found it—a side street, a sign reading mostly Turkish Bath, then a narrow entrance, a corridor dimly lighted and containing a few chairs and a few palms and more spittoons than either and a desk beside which a negro in no uniform slept—a place ambiguous, redolent of hard Saturday nights, whose customers seldom had any baggage and beyond the turnings of whose dim and threadbare corridors there seemed to whisk forever bright tawdry kimonos in a kind of hopeful nostalgic convocation of all the bought female flesh which ever breathed and perished. The negro waked; there was no elevator; the reporter was directed to the room from his description of Jiggs and knocked beneath the ghost of two numbers attached to the door's surface by the ghost of four tacks until the door opened and Jiggs blinked at him with the good eye and the injured one, wearing now only the shirt. The reporter held in his hand the slip of paper which had been clipped to the money the jumper gave him. He did not blink, himself: he just stared at Jiggs with that desperate urgency.

"The tickets," he said. "Where——"

"Oh," Jiggs said. "Myron, Ohio. Yair, that's it on the paper. Roger's old man. They're going to leave the kid there. I thought you knew. You said you saw Jack at the——Here, doc! What is it?" He opened the door wider and put out his hand, but the reporter had already caught the doorjamb. "You come on in and set down a——"

"Myron, Ohio," the reporter said. His face wore again that faint wrung quiet grimace as with the other hand he continued to try to put Jiggs' hand aside even after Jiggs was no longer offering to touch him. He began to apologise to Jiggs for having disturbed him, talking through that thin wash over his wasted gaunt face which would have been called smiling for lack of anything better.

"It's all right, doc," Jiggs said, watching him, blinking still with a sort of brutal concern. "Jesus, aint you been to bed yet? Here; you better come in here; me and Art can make room——"

"Yes, I'll be getting on." He pushed himself carefully back from the door as though he were balancing himself before turning the door loose, feeling Jiggs watching him. "I just happened to drop in. To say goodbye." He looked at Jiggs with that thin fixed grimace while Jiggs blinked at him.

"Goodbye, doc. Only you better——"

"And good luck to you. Or do you say happy landings to a parachute jumper?"

"Jesus," Jiggs said. "I hope so."

"Then happy landings too."

"Yair. Thanks. The same to you, doc." The reporter turned away. Jiggs watched him go down the corridor, walking with that curious light stiff care, and turn the corner and vanish. The light was even dimmer on the stairs than it had been in the corridor, though the brass strips which bound the rubber tread to each step glinted bright and still in the center where the heels had kept it polished. The negro was already asleep again in the chair beside the desk; he did not stir as the reporter passed him and went on and got into the cab, stumbling a little on the step.

"Back to the airport," he said. "You needn't hurry. We got until daylight." He was back on the beach before daylight, though it was dawn before the other four saw him again, before they came out of the dark lunchstand and passed again through another barricade of parked cars though not so many this time since it was now Monday, and descended to the beach. They saw him then. The smooth water was a pale rose color from the waxing east, so that the reporter in silhouette against it resembled a tatting Christmas gift made by a little girl and supposed to represent a sleeping crane.

"Good Lord," the third said. "You suppose he has been down here by himself all the time?" But they did not have much time to wonder about it; they were barely on time themselves; they heard the aeroplane taking off before they reached the beach and then they watched it circling; it came over into what they thought was position and the sound of the engine died for a time and then began again and the aeroplane went on, though nothing else happened. They saw nothing fall from it at all, they just saw three gulls converge suddenly from nowhere and begin to slant and tilt and scream above a spot on the water some distance away, making a sound like rusty shutters in a wind. "So that's that," the third said. "Let's go to town." Again the fourth one spoke the reporter's name.

"Are we going to wait for him?" he said. They looked back, but the reporter was gone.

"He must have got a ride with somebody," the third said. "Come on. Let's go."

When the reporter got out of the car at the Saint Jules Avenue corner the clock beyond the restaurant's window said eight oclock. He did not look at the clock; he was looking at nothing for the time, shaking slowly and steadily. It was going to be another bright vivid day; the sunlight, the streets and walls themselves emanated that brisk up-and-doing sobriety of Monday morning. But he was not looking at that either; he was not looking at anything; when he began to see it was as if the letters were beginning to emerge from the back of his skull—the broad page under a rusting horseshoe, the quality of grateful astonishment which Monday headlines have like when you learn that the uncle whom you believed to have perished two years ago in a poorhouse fire died yesterday in Tucson, Arizona and left you five hundred dollars: **AVIATOR'S BODY RESIGNED TO LAKE GRAVE.** Then he quit seeing it. He had not moved; his pupils would still have repeated the page in inverted miniature, but he was not seeing it at all, shaking quietly and steadily in the bright warm sun until he turned and looked into the window with an expression of quiet and bemused despair—the notflies or were-

flies, the two grapefruit halves, the printed names of food like
the printed stations in a train schedule and set on an easel
like a family portrait—and experienced that profound and
unshakable not only reluctance but actual absolute refusal
of his entire organism. "All right," he said. "If I wont eat, then
I am going to take a drink. If I wont go in here then I am
going to Joe's." It was not far: just down an alley and through
a barred door—one of the places where for fifteen years the
United States had tried to keep them from selling whiskey
and where for one year now it had been trying to make them
sell it. The porter let him in and poured him a drink in the
empty bar while starting the cork in the bottle itself. "Yair,"
the reporter said. "I was on the wagon for an entire day.
Would you believe that?"

"Not about you," the porter said.

"Neither would I. It surprised me. It surprised the hell
out of me until I found out it was two other guys. See?" He
laughed too; it wasn't loud; it still didn't seem loud even after
the porter was holding him up, calling him by name too,
mister too, like Leonora, saying,

"Come on, now; try to quit now."

"All right," the reporter said. "I've quit now. If you ever
saw any man quitter than me right now I will buy you an airplane."

"O.K.," the porter said. "Only make it a taxi cab and you
go on home."

"Home? I just come from home. I'm going to work now.
I'm o.k. now. Give me another shot and just point me toward
the door and I will be all right. All right, see? Then I learned
by mistake that it was two other guys——" But he stopped
himself, this time; he held himself fine while the porter

poured the other drink and brought it to him; he had himself
in hand fine now; he did not feel at all now: just the liquor
flowing slow down him, fiery, dead, and cold; soon he would
even quit shaking, soon he did quit; walking now with the
bright unsoiled morning falling upon him he did not have
anything to shake with. "So I feel better," he said. Then he
began to say it fast: "Oh God, I feel better! I feel better! I feel!
I feel!" until he quit that too and said quietly, looking at the
familiar wall, the familiar twin door through which he was
about to pass, with tragic and passive clairvoyance: "Something is going to happen to me. I have got myself stretched
out too far and too thin and something is going to bust." He
mounted the quiet stairs; in the empty corridor he drank
from the bottle, though this time it was merely cold and felt
like water. But when he entered the deserted city room he remembered that he could have drunk here just as well, and so
he did. "I see so little of it," he said. "I dont know the family's
habits yet." But it was empty, or comparatively so, because he
kept on making that vertical reverse without any rudder or
flippers and looking down on the closepeopled land and the
empty lake and deciding, and the dredgeboat hanging over
him for twenty hours and then having to lie there too and
look up at the wreath dissolving faintly rocking and stared at
by gulls away, and trying to explain that he did not know. "I
didn't think that!" he cried. "I just thought they were all
going. I dont know where, but I thought that all three of
them, that maybe the hundred and seventy-five would be
enough until Holmes could. . . . . . .and that then he would
be big enough and I would be there; I would maybe see her
first and she would not look different even though he was out
there around the pylon and so I wouldn't be either even if it

was forty-two instead of twenty-eight and he would come on in off the pylons and we would go up and she maybe holding my arm and him looking at us over the cockpit and she would say, 'This is the one back in New Valois that time. That used to buy you the icecream'." Then he had to hurry, saying, "Wait. Stop now. Stop" until he did stop, tall, humped a little, moving his mouth faintly as if he were tasting, blinking fast now and now stretching his eyelids to their full extent like a man trying to keep himself awake while driving a car; again it tasted, felt, like so much dead icy water, that cold and heavy and lifeless in his stomach; when he moved he could both hear and feel it sluggish and dead within him as he removed his coat and hung it on the chairback and sat down and racked a sheet of yellow paper into the machine. He could not feel his fingers on the keys either: he just watched the letters materialise out of thin air, black sharp and fast, along the creeping yellow.

During the night the little boy slept on the seat facing the woman and the parachute jumper, the toy aeroplane clutched to his chest; when daylight came the train was running in snow. They changed trains in snow too, and when in midafternoon the trainman called the town and looking out the window the woman read the name on the little station, it was snowing hard. They got out and crossed the platform, among the milkcans and the fowlcrates, and entered the waitingroom where a porter was putting coal into the stove. "Can we get a cab here?" the jumper asked him.

"There's one outside now," the porter said. "I'll call him."

"Thanks," the jumper said. The jumper looked at the

woman; she was buttoning the trenchcoat. "I'll wait here," he said.

"Yes," she said. "All right. I dont know how——"

"I'll wait. No use standing around anywhere else."

"Aint he coming with us?" the little boy said. He looked at the jumper, the toy aeroplane under his arm now, though he still spoke to the woman. "Dont he want to see Roger's old man too?"

"No," the woman said. "You tell him goodbye now."

"Goodbye?" the boy said. He looked from one to the other. "Aint we coming back?" He looked from one to the other. "I'll stay here with him until you get back. I'll see Roger's old man some other time."

"No," the woman said. "Now." The boy looked from one to the other. Suddenly the jumper said,

"So long, kid. I'll be seeing you."

"You're going to wait? You aint going off?"

"No. I'll wait. You and Laverne go on." The porter came in.

"He's waiting for you folks," he said.

"The cab's waiting," the woman said. "Tell Jack so long."

"O.K.," the boy said. "You wait here for us. Soon as we get back we'll eat."

"Yair; sure," the jumper said. Suddenly he set the bag down and stooped and picked the boy up.

"No," the woman said; "you wait here out of the——" But the jumper went on, carrying the little boy, swinging his stiff leg along. The woman followed him, into the snow again. The cab was a small touring car with a lettered sign on the windshield and a blanket over the hood and driven by a man with a scraggly grayish moustache. The driver opened the door; the jumper swung the boy in and stepped back and helped the woman in and leaned again into the door; now his face wore an expression which anyone who had seen very much of the reporter lately would have recognised—that faint grimace (in this instance savage too) which would have been called smiling for lack of anything better.

"So long, old fellow," he said. "Be good now."

"O.K.," the boy said. "You be looking around for somewhere to eat before we get back."

"O.K.," the jumper said.

"All right, mister," the woman said. "Let's go." The car moved, swinging away from the station; the woman was still leaning forward. "Do you know where Doctor Carl Shumann lives?" she said. For an instant the driver did not move. The car still swung on, gaining speed, and there was little possible moving for the driver to do. Yet during that moment he seemed to have become caught in that sort of instantaneous immobility like when a sudden light surprises a man or an animal out of darkness. Then it was gone.

"Doctor Shumann? Sure. You want to go there?"

"Yes," the woman said. It was not far; the town was not large; it seemed to the woman that almost at once the car had stopped and looking out through the falling snow she saw a kind of cenotaph, penurious and without majesty or dignity, of forlorn and victorious desolation—a bungalow, a tight flimsy mass of stoops and porte-cochères and flat gables and bays not five years old and built in that colored mud-and-chickenwire tradition which California moving picture films have scattered across North America as if the celluloid carried germs, not five years old yet wearing already an air of dilapidation and rot; a quality furious and recent as if immediate disintegration had been included in the architect's blueprints and inherent in the wood and plaster and sand of its mushroom growth. Then she found the driver looking at her.

"This is it," he said. "Or maybe you were thinking about his old place? or are you acquainted with him that well?"

"No," the woman said. "This is it." He made no move to open the door; he just sat halfturned, watching her struggling with the doorhandle.

"He used to have a big old place out in the country until he lost it a few years back. His son took up av-aytion and he mortgaged the place to buy his son a flying machine and then his son wrecked the machine and so the doctor had to borrow some more money on the place to fix the machine up. I guess the boy aimed to pay it back but he just never got around to it maybe. So he lost the old place and built this one. Probly this one suits him just as well, though; womenfolks usually like to live close to town——" But she had got the door open now and she and the boy got out.

"Do you mind waiting?" she said. "I dont know how long I'll be. I'll pay you for the time."

"Sure," he said. "That's my business. What you do with the car while you are hiring it is yours, not mine." He watched them enter the gate and go on up the narrow concrete walk in the snow. "So that's her," he thought. "Only she dont look a whole lot like a widow. But then I hear tell she never acted a whole lot like a wife." He had a robe, another horseblanket, in the seat beside him. He bundled himself into it, which was just as well because dark had come and the snow drifted and whirled, funneled now by the downglare of a streetlamp nearby before the door opened and he recognised against the light the silhouette of the trenchcoat and then that of Doctor Shumann as they came out and the door shut behind them. He threw the robe off and started the engine. But after a while he cut the switch and drew the robe about him again though it was too dark and the snow was falling too fast for him to see the two people standing on the stoop before the entrance of the house.

"You are going to leave him like this?" Dr Shumann said. "You are going to leave him asleep and go away?"

"Can you think of any better way?" she said.

"No. That's true." He was speaking loudly, too loudly. "Let us understand one another. You leave him here of your own free will; we are to make a home for him until we die: that is understood."

"Yes. I agreed to that inside," she said patiently.

"No; but let us understand. I. . . . . ." He talked in that curious loud wild rushing manner, as though she were still moving away and were at some distance now: "We are old; you cannot understand that, that you will or can ever reach a time when you can bear so much and no more; that nothing else is worth the bearing; that you not only cannot, you will not; that nothing is worth anything but peace, peace, peace, even with bereavement and grief—nothing! nothing! But we have reached that stage. When you came here with Roger that day before the boy was born, you and I talked and I talked different to you. I was different then; I meant it when you told me you did not know whether or not Roger was the father of your unborn child and that you would never know, and I told you, do you remember? I said 'Then make Roger his father from now on.' And you told me the truth, that you would not promise, that you were born bad and could not help it or did

not think you were going to try to help it; and I told you nobody is born anything, bad or good God help us, anymore
than anybody can do anything save what they must: do you remember? I meant that then. But I was younger then. And now
I am not young. And now I cant—I cannot——I——"

"I know. If I leave him with you, I must not try to see him
again until you and she are dead."

"Yes. I must; I cannot help it. I just want peace now. I
dont want equity or justice, I dont want happiness; I just want
peace. We wont live very much longer, and then. . . . ."

She laughed, short, mirthless, not moving. "And then he
will have forgotten me."

"That's your risk. Because, remember," he cried; "remember! I dont ask this. I did not ask you to leave him, to
bring him to us. You can go up now and wake him and take
him with you. But if you do not, if you leave him with us and
turn your back on this house and go away——Think well. If
you like, take him with you tonight, to the hotel or wherever
and think about it and make up your mind and bring him
back tomorrow or come yourself and tell me what you have
decided."

"I have decided now," she said.

"That you leave him here of your own free will. That we
give him the home and care and affection which is his right
both as a helpless child and as our gra—grand——and that in
return for this, you are to make no attempt to see him or
communicate with him as long as we live. That is your un-
derstanding, your agreement? Think well."

"Yes," she said. "I have to do it."

"But you do not. You can take him with you now; all this
tonight can be as if it had never happened. You are his

mother; I still believe that any mother is better—better than.
. . . . . . How do you have to?"

"Because I dont know whether I can buy him enough
food to eat and enough clothes to keep him warm and medicine if he is sick," she said. "Do you understand that?"

"I understand that this—your——this other man does
not earn as much in his line as Roger did in his. But you tell
me that Roger did not always earn enough for the four of
you: nevertheless you never thought while Roger was alive of
leaving the boy with us. And now, with one less mouth to
feed, you try to tell me that you——"

"I'll tell you, if you will listen a minute," she said. "I'm
going to have another child." Now he did not speak at all; his
unfinished sentence seemed to hang between them. They
stood face to face but they could not see one another: just the
two vague shapes with the snow falling between them and
upon them, though since her back was to the streetlamp she
could see him the better of the two. After a while he said quietly,

"I see. Yes. And you know that this other child is——is
not——"

"Not Roger's. Yes. Roger and I were——But no matter. I
know, this time. Roger and I both know. So we will need
money and that's what Roger was trying to do in that meet.
The ship he won a prize with the first day was too slow, obsolete. But that was all we could get and he outflew them,
beat them on the pylons, by turning the pylons closer than
the others dared for that little money. Then Saturday he had
a chance to fly a ship that was dangerous, but he had a
chance to win two thousand dollars in the race. That would
have fixed us up. But the ship came to pieces in the air.

Maybe I could have stopped him. I dont know. But maybe I could have. But I didn't. I didn't try, anyhow. So now we didn't get that money, and we left most of the first day's prize to send his body here when they get it out of the lake."

"Ah," Dr Shumann said. "I see. Yes. So you are giving us the chance to—the opportunity to. . . . . ." Suddenly he cried: "If I just knew that he is Roger's! If I just knew! Cant you tell me? Cant you give me some sign, some little sign? Any little sign?" She didn't move. The light came through the snow, across her shoulder, and she could see him a lit-tle—a small thin man with untidy thin irongray hair and the snow whispering in it, standing with his face turned aside and his hand not before it exactly but held palmout between his face and hers. After a while she said,

"Maybe you would rather take a little time to think about it. To decide." She could not see his face now: only the lifted hand; she seemed to be speaking to the hand: "Suppose I wait at the hotel until tomorrow, so——" The hand moved, a faint motion from the wrist as though it were trying to push her voice away. But she repeated, once more, as though for a record: "You mean you dont want me to wait?" But only the hand moved again, replied; she turned quietly and went down the steps, feeling for each step beneath the snow, and went on down the walk, vanishing into the drowsing pan-tomime of the snow, not fast. She did not look back. Dr Shu-mann did not watch her. He heard the engine of the car start, but he was already turning, entering the house, fum-bling at the door for a moment before he found the knob and entered, his hair and shoulders (he was in his shirtsleeves) powdered with snow. He went on down the hall; his wife, sit-ting beside the bed in the darkened room where the boy was asleep, heard him blunder against something in the hall and then saw him come into the door, framed so against the lighted hall, holding to the doorframe, the light glinting in the melting snow in his untidy hair.

"If we just had a sign," he said. He entered, stumbling again. She rose and approached him but he pushed her aside, entering. "Let me be," he said.

"Shhhhhh," she said. "Dont wake him. You come on and eat your supper."

"Let me alone," he said, pushing with his hand at the empty air now since she stood back now, watching him approach the bed, fumbling at the footboard. But his voice was quiet enough. "Go out," he said. "Leave me be. Go away and leave me be."

"You come on and eat your supper and lay down."

"Go on. I'm all right, I tell you." She obeyed; he stood holding to the bed's footboard and heard her feet move slowly up the hall and cease. Then he moved, fumbling until he found the lightcord, the bulb, and turned it on. The little boy stirred, turning his face from the light. The garment in which he slept was a man's shirt, an oldfashioned garment with a onceglazed bosom, soft now from many washings, pinned about his throat with a gold brooch and with the sleeves cut recently off at his wrists. On the pillow beside him the toy aeroplane rested. Suddenly Dr Shumann stooped and took the boy by the shoulder and began to shake him. The toy aeroplane slid from the pillow; with his other hand Dr Shumann flipped it to the floor, still shaking the little boy. "Roger," he said, "wake up. Wake up, Roger." The boy waked; without moving he blinked up at the man's face bending over him.

"Laverne," he said. "Jack. Where's Laverne? Where'm I at?"

"Laverne's gone," Dr Shumann said, still shaking the boy as though he had forgot to tell his muscles to desist. "You're at home, but Laverne is gone. Gone, I tell you. Are you going to cry? Hey?" The boy blinked up at him, then he turned and put out his hand toward the pillow beside him.

"Where's my new job?" he said. "Where's my ship?"

"Your ship, hey?" Dr Shumann said. "Your ship, hey?" He stooped and caught up the toy and held it up, his face twisted into a grimace of gnomelike rage, and whirled and hurled the toy at the wall and, while the boy watched him, ran to it and began to stamp upon it with blind maniac fury. The little boy made one sharp sound: then, silent, raised on one elbow, his eyes a little wide as though with curious interest alone, he watched the shabby wildhaired old man jumping up and down upon the shapeless trivial mass of blue-and-yellow tin in maniacal ludicrosity. Then the little boy saw him pause, stoop, take up the ruined toy and apparently begin to try to tear it to pieces with his hands. His wife, sitting beside the livingroom stove, heard his feet too through the flimsy walls, feeling the floor shake too, then she heard him approaching up the hall, fast now. She was small too—a faded woman with faded eyes and a quiet faded face sitting in the stuffy room containing a worn divan and fumed oak chairs and a fumed oak revolving bookcase racked neatly with battered medical books from whose bindings the gilt embossed titles had long since vanished, and a table littered with medical magazines and on which lay at the moment a thick cap with earmuffs, a pair of mittens and a small scuffed black bag. She did not move: she was sitting there watching the door when Dr Shumann came in, holding one hand out before him; she did not stir even then: she just looked quietly at the mass of money. "It was in that airplane!" he said. "He even had to hide his money from her!"

"No," the wife said. "She hid it from him."

"No!" he shouted. "He hid it from her. For the boy. Do you think a woman would ever hide money and or anything else and then forget where she put it? And where would she get a hundred and seventy-five dollars, anyway?"

"Yes," the wife said, the faded eyes filled with immeasurable and implacable unforgiving; "where would she get a hundred and seventy-five dollars that she would have to hide from both of them in a child's toy?" He looked at her for a long moment.

"Ah," he said. He said it quietly: "Oh. Yes. I see." Then he cried, "But no matter! It dont matter now!" He stooped and swung open the door of the stove and shut it again; she did not move, not even when, glancing past him as he stooped, she saw in the door and looking in at them, the little boy in the man's shirt and carrying the battered mass of the toy in one hand and the clothes which he had worn wadded in the other, against his chest and his cap already on. Dr Shumann had not seen him yet; he rose from the stove; it was the draft of course, from the opening and closing of the door, but it did seem as though it were the money itself passing in flame and fire up the pipe with a deep faint roar into nothing as Dr Shumann stood again, looking down at her. "It's our boy," he said; then he shouted: "It's our boy, I tell you!" Then he collapsed; he seemed to let go all at once though not hard because of his spareness, onto his knees beside the chair, his head in her lap, crying.

When the city room began to fill that evening a copyboy
noticed the overturned wastebasket beside the reporter's desk
and the astonishing amount of savagely defaced and torn
copy which littered the adjacent floor. The copyboy was a
bright lad, about to graduate from highschool; he had not
only ambitions but dreams too. He gathered up all the
sheets, whole and in fragments, from the floor and emptied
the wastebasket and, sitting at the reporter's desk he began to
sort them, discarding and fitting and resorting at the last to
paste; and then, his eyes big with excitement and exultation
and then downright triumph, he regarded what he had salvaged and restored to order and coherence—the sentences
and paragraphs which he believed to be not only news but
the beginning of literature:

> On Thursday Roger Shumann flew a race against four
> competitors, and won. On Saturday he flew against but
> one competitor. But that competitor was Death, and
> Roger Shumann lost. And so today a lone aeroplane
> flew out over the lake on the wings of dawn and circled
> the spot where Roger Shumann got the Last Check-
> ered Flag, and vanished back into the dawn from
> whence it came.

> Thus two friends told him farewell. Two friends, yet
> two competitors too, whom he had met in fair contest
> and conquered in the lonely sky from which he fell,
> dropping a simple wreath to mark his Last Pylon

It stopped there, but the copyboy did not. "O Jesus," he whispered. "Maybe Hagood will let me finish it!" already moving

toward the desk where Hagood now sat though the copyboy had not seen him enter. Hagood had just sat down; the copyboy, his mouth already open, paused behind Hagood. Then he became more complete vassal to surprise than ever, for lying on Hagood's desk and weighted neatly down by an empty whiskey bottle was another sheet of copy which Hagood and the copyboy read together:

At midnight last night the search for the body of Roger Shumann, racing pilot who plunged into the lake Saturday p.m. was finally abandoned by a threeplace biplane of about eighty horsepower which managed to fly out over the water and return without falling to pieces and dropping a wreath of flowers into the water approximately three quarters of a mile away from where Shumann's body is generally supposed to be since they were precision pilots and so did not miss the entire lake. Mrs Shumann departed with her husband and children for Ohio, where it is understood that their six year old son will spend an indefinite time with some of his grandparents and where any and all finders of Roger Shumann are kindly requested to forward any and all of same.

and beneath this, savagely in pencil: *I guess this is what you want you bastard and now I am going down to Amboise st. and get drunk a while and if you dont know where Amboise st. is ask your son to tell you and if you dont know what drunk is come down there and look at me and when you come bring some jack because I am on a credit*

EDITORS' NOTE

This volume reproduces the text of *Pylon* that has been established by Noel Polk. It is based on William Faulkner's own typescript, which has been emended to account for his revisions in proof, his indisputable typing errors, and certain other mistakes and inconsistencies that clearly demand correction. Faulkner typed and proofread this document himself, and it also bears alterations of varying degrees of seriousness by his editors.

Faulkner began *Pylon* in October 1934, writing so rapidly that he sent chapters to his publisher in November and December, as he typed them. However, his publisher made a great many changes in Faulkner's text—shortening sentences, adjusting paragraphs, and similar alterations—often without querying the author. In his galley proofs, Faulkner restored much of his original writing but also on occasion rewrote around the editorial changes or simply retained the changes. The Polk text tries to distinguish between those changes made by Faulkner as a response to his text as he saw it in type for the first time and those caused by editorial intervention, although it is not always easy to do so.

Extant documents relevant to the editing of *Pylon* are the typescript setting copy at the University of Virginia's Alderman Library and the corrected galleys at the Humanities Research Center of the University of Texas. The holograph manuscript, at the University of Mississippi, is incomplete.

American English continues to fluctuate; for example, a word may be spelled more than one way, even in the same work. Commas are sometimes used expressively to suggest the movements of the voice, and capitals are sometimes meant to give significances to a word beyond those it might have in its uncapitalized form. Since standardization would remove such effects, this volume preserves the spelling, punctuation, capitalization, and wording of the text as established by Noel Polk, which strives to be as faithful to Faulkner's usage as surviving evidence permits.

The following notes were prepared by Joseph Blotner and are reprinted with permission from *Novels 1930–1935*, one volume of the edition of Faulkner's collected works published by The Library of America, 1985. Numbers refer to page and line of the present volume (the line count includes chapter headings). For further information on *Pylon*, consult the appropriate portions of Joseph Blotner, *Faulkner: A Biography* (New York: Random House, 1974); Cleanth Brooks, *William Faulkner: Toward Yoknapatawpha and Beyond* (New Haven: Yale University Press, 1978); and Michael Millgate, *The Achievement of William Faulkner* (New York: Random House, 1965).

9.26–10.7 FEINMAN . . . DOLLARS] On February 9, 1934, New Orleans' Shushan Airport, constructed on land reclaimed from Lake Pontchartrain, was officially dedicated. It was named after Colonel A. L. Shushan, president of the Levee Board. Beginning on February 14, several days of aerial competition and exhibitions followed. The events of the air meet, postponed because of bad weather, coincided with the Mardi Gras festivities. In December 1934, Faulkner wrote his publisher about his use of New Orleans and Shushan Airport and added, "But there all actual resemblance stops . . . the incidents in Pylon are all fiction and Feinman is fiction so far as I know, the only more or less deliberate copying of fact, or the nearest to it, is the character 'Matt Ord,' who is Jimmy Weddell."

21.13   Jules Despleins] One of the Shushan competitors was Michael de Troyat, billed as the "European acrobatic champion."

24.26–27   Vas . . . Sharlie?] The frequent refrain of a radio comedian of the 1930s who called himself the Baron Munchausen.

25.9–10   modest . . . lapel] Faulkner occasionally wore on his lapel a small pair of silver wings bearing the initials QB, which stood for Quiet Birdmen, an organization of pilots formed after World War I for charitable purposes, later a purely social group.

32.25–26   dot-dot-dash-dot] The Morse code signal for F identifies Feinman Airport.

43.15–19   FIRST . . . Plane] The night Faulkner and Omlie arrived at Shushan Airport, Capt. W. Merle Nelson died in the crash of his "Comet plane."

48.11   "Laughing . . . Poik!"] Here reporting a race result, the newsboy employs one variety of New Orleans dialect, one of several in the novel.

50.20   (i n r i)] This abbreviation stands for *Iesus Nazarenus*,

Rex Iudaeorum, which Pilate ordered placed above Jesus' head on the cross. (John 19:19)

52.29   tomorrow and tomorrow] From the passage in Shakespeare's *Macbeth,* V, v, 19–28; also used for the titles of the fourth and fifth chapters and the title of *The Sound and the Fury.*

66.1   *the Vieux Carré*] The old square, the site of the original city of New Orleans, later called the French Quarter, the hundred-odd square blocks stretching from Canal Street on the south to Esplanade on the north, and from North Rampart Street to the Mississippi River.

66.6–7   spent . . . clatterfalque;] The debris left after the passage in the Mardi Gras parade of one of the ornate floats built by particular social groups ("Krewes") according to a dominant theme. Cf. ll. 77–78 of *The Waste Land,* by T. S. Eliot, and the passage from which these lines are derived in Shakespeare's *Antony and Cleopatra,* II, ii, 196–97.

70.1   "Toulouse,"] Street in the French Quarter. The following fictional streets are apparently derived from real ones in New Orleans: Grandlieu St. from Canal St., St. Jules Ave. from St. Charles Ave., Barricade St. from Rampart St., and perhaps Lanier Ave. from Claiborne Ave. Alphonse's Restaurant is probably based on Antoine's, and Renaud's upon Arnaud's.

101.18   miked] Used a micrometer to measure the valves in the airplane engine to ensure that they are within the proper tolerance for efficient operation.

104.10–11   there . . . eat] Cf. "i sing of olaf glad and big," by E. E. Cummings.

182.7–8 *The . . . Franciana*] This corporation is probably modeled on that of Jimmy Weddell and Harry T. Williams, The Weddell–Williams Air Corporation at Patterson, Louisiana, on which the Blaisedell of the novel is based.

197.3 We . . . regimented.] Feinman is referring to regulatory agencies of the Roosevelt administration such as the A.A.A., the Agricultural Adjustment Administration.

208.1 *Lovesong of J. A. Prufrock*] From the poem by T. S. Eliot.

*"For range of effect, philosophical weight, originality of
style, variety of characterization, humor, and tragic
intensity, Faulkner's works are without equal in
our time and country."* —Robert Penn Warren

ABSALOM, ABSALOM!

One of Faulkner's finest achievements, *Absalom, Absalom!* is the
story of Thomas Sutpen and the ruthless, single-minded pursuit of
his grand design—to forge a dynasty in Jefferson, Mississippi, in
1830—which is ultimately destroyed (along with Sutpen himself)
by his two sons.

Fiction/Literature

AS I LAY DYING

As I Lay Dying is Faulkner's harrowing account of the Bundren
family's odyssey across the Mississippi countryside to bury Addie,
their wife and mother. Told in turns by each of the family members—including Addie herself—the novel ranges in mood from
dark comedy to the deepest pathos.

Fiction/Literature

A FABLE

Winner of the Pulitzer Prize and the National Book Award, this
allegorical novel about World War I is set in the trenches of
France and deals with a mutiny in a French regiment.

Fiction/Literature

BIG WOODS

The best of Faulkner's hunting stories are woven together brilliantly in *Big Woods*. First published in 1955, the volume includes Faulkner's most famous story, "The Bear," together with "The Old People," "A Bear Hunt," and "Race at Morning." Each of the stories is introduced by a prelude, and the final one is followed by an epilogue, which serve as almost musical bridges between them. Together, these pieces create a seamless whole, a work that displays the full eloquence, emotional breadth, and moral complexity of Faulkner's vision.

Short Stories/Literature

COLLECTED STORIES

"A Rose For Emily," "Two Soldiers," "Victory," "The Brooch," "Beyond"—these are among the forty-two stories that make up this magisterial collection by the writer who stands at the pinnacle of modern American fiction. Compressing an epic expanse of vision into narratives as hard and wounding as bullets, William Faulkner's stories evoke the intimate textures of place, the deep strata of history and legend, and all the fear, brutality, and tenderness of which human beings are capable. These tales are populated by such characters as the Faulkner archetypes Flem Snopes and Quentin Compson ("A Justice") as well as by ordinary men and women who emerge in these pages so sharply and indelibly that they dwarf the protagonists of most novels.

Short Stories/Literature

FLAGS IN THE DUST

Flags in the Dust is the complete text of Faulkner's third novel. Written when he was twenty-nine, it appeared, with his reluctant consent, in a much cut version as *Sartoris*. "In either version, *Sartoris* or *Flags in the Dust* is an outstanding work. . . . The shorter work, in effect, 'tidies up' Faulkner's erratic prose. But Faulkner was about as impossible to tidy up, to civilize, as was Huck Finn—and *Flags in the Dust*, consequently, is a better book than *Sartoris*" (Philip Corwin, *National Observer*).

Fiction/Literature

Composed of seven interrelated stories (including the acclaimed "The Bear"), set in Faulkner's mythic Yoknapatawpha County, *Go Down, Moses* reveals the complex, changing relationships between blacks and whites, and between man and nature, weaving a cohesive work rich in implication and insight.

Fiction/Literature

THE HAMLET

The Hamlet, the first novel of Faulkner's Snopes trilogy, is both an ironic take on classical tragedy and a mordant commentary on the grand pretensions of the antebellum South and the depths of its decay in the aftermath of war and Reconstruction. It tells of the advent and the rise of the Snopes family in Frenchman's Bend, a small town built on the ruins of a once-stately plantation. Flem Snopes—wily, energetic, a man of shady origins—quickly comes to dominate the town and its people with his cunning and guile.

Fiction/Literature

THE TOWN

This is the second volume of Faulkner's trilogy about the Snopes family, his symbol for the grasping, destructive element in the post-bellum South. The story of Flem Snopes' ruthless struggle to take over the town of Jefferson, Mississippi, the book is rich in typically Faulknerian episodes of humor and profundity.

Fiction/Literature

THE MANSION

The Mansion completes Faulkner's great trilogy of the Snopes family in the mythical county of Yoknapatawpha, Mississippi. Beginning with the murder of Jack Houston, it traces the downfall of this indomitable post-bellum family who managed to seize control of the town of Jefferson within a generation.

Fiction/Literature

INTRUDER IN THE DUST

At once an engrossing murder mystery and an unflinching portrait of racial injustice, *Intruder in the Dust* is the story of Lucas Beauchamp, a black man wrongly arrested for the murder of a white man. Confronted by the threat of lynching, Lucas sets out to prove his innocence, aided by a white lawyer and his young nephew.

Fiction/Literature

LIGHT IN AUGUST

A novel about perseverance in the face of mortality, *Light in August* tells the tales of guileless, dauntless Lena Grove, in search of the father of her unborn child; Reverend Gail Hightower, who is plagued by visions of Confederate horsemen; and Joe Christmas, an enigmatic drifter consumed by his mixed ancestry.

Fiction/Literature

THE REIVERS

One of Faulkner's comic masterpieces and winner of a Pulitzer Prize, *The Reivers* is a picaresque tale that tells of three unlikely car thieves from rural Mississippi and their wild misadventures in the fast life of Memphis—from horse smuggling to bawdy houses.

Fiction/Literature

SANCTUARY

A powerful novel examining the nature of evil, *Sanctuary* is the dark, at times brutal, story of the kidnapping of Mississippi debutante Temple Drake, who introduces her own form of venality in the Memphis underworld where she is being held.

Fiction/Literature

One of the greatest novels of the twentieth century, *The Sound and the Fury* is the tragedy of the Compson family, featuring some of the most memorable characters in American literature: beautiful, rebellious Caddy; the man-child Benjy; haunted, neurotic Quentin; Jason, the brutal cynic; and Dilsey, their black servant.

Fiction/Literature

ALSO AVAILABLE:

Requiem for a Nun

Three Famous Short Novels

The Unvanquished

Uncollected Stories of William Faulkner

The Wild Palms

VINTAGE INTERNATIONAL
Available wherever books are sold.
www.randomhouse.com